PLUMAGE

OTHER BOOKS BY
NANCY SPRINGER

Fair Peril

Larque on the Wing

Metal Angel

PLUMAGE

NANCY SPRINGER

WILLIAM MORROW

An Imprint of HarperCollins*Publishers*

12 – 00

This is a work of fiction. The characters, incidents, and
dialogues are products of the author's imagination and are not to
be construed as real. Any resemblance to actual events or
persons, living or dead, is entirely coincidental.

HarperCollins books may be purchased for educational,
business, or sales promotional use. For information please write:
Special Markets Department, HarperCollins Publishers Inc.,
10 East 53rd Street, New York, NY 10022.

FIRST EDITION

Designed by Debbie Glasserman

Printed on acid-free paper

Library of Congress Cataloging-in-Publication Data has been applied for.

ISBN 0-380-80120-5

00 01 02 03 04 RRD 10 9 8 7 6 5 4 3 2 1

PLUMAGE

 **O N E**

Sassy Hummel knew she should get over it, but how? Twenty-seven years of her life she'd given to that man. Twenty-eight years if you counted the courtship. Twenty-eight years and seven months if you added up the odds and ends. Or maybe eight months. Twenty-eight years and seven or maybe eight months of dependably smiling, mediating between him and his clients or the kids or his parents, listening to him brag/bluster/bleat, calming him down, building him up, fetching the hammer and holding the light, cleaning up after him, making him go to the dentist/doctor/ in-laws, trying to figure out what he wanted for supper, getting lost because he wouldn't ask for directions, faking orgasm because he couldn't find her clitoris either—twenty-too-many years of coupons rebates Monday Night Football phone messages grocery lists Mount Saint Laundry

and off he went.

With another woman.

Younger. Had not yet started to look like her own mother. Skinnier.

Bitty little ass. Chickie-yellow wispie-poo hair.

Damn him. Damn everything.

Thinking about it, Sassy pushed the carpet sweeper as if she were pumping iron and tried not to contemplate what it was going to be like to spend the rest of her life alone and poor. Alone, because she knew what she was: a dowdy middle-aged housewife; who could possibly want her or love her? And poor, because take him for all he's worth her friends kept saying but it turned out he wasn't worth that much and now there were lawyers to pay.

Twenty-eight years. Twenty-nine, if you added the year of hard angry grieving she'd put in since Frederick had left, worse than if he had died. Now the divorce was final, congratulations! friends said. Time for fun.

Yeah, right.

Sassy slammed the carpet sweeper against the baseboard hard enough to jar her molars, trying not to think about Frederick anymore. It was bad enough to think about herself. Bad enough to think about what she was doing, which was immaculatizing the Sylvan Tower Hotel's already immaculate green-and-burgundy mezzanine carpet.

Bad enough to think about what she *was*, wearing a truly loathsome green poplin shirtwaist uniform dress and a frilled white apron.

A maid.

Twenty-eight years in a development house fulfilling every apple-pie requirement of the wife mythos, and the only job she could get was currying carpets and scrubbing potties at the Tower.

A hotel maid.

Not for the first time in her life, Sassy grew aware of the irony inherent in her own name. Calling her Sassy was like calling a midget Hercules. Damn, what a doormat she had been.

Still was.

"Damn" did not provide sufficient vent for her feelings, but it was the strongest expletive she permitted herself. Having been raised by a mother who scrubbed out her mouth with Lava Soap for taking the name of the Lord in vain, she could not help being a bit inhibited. She was not a shouter, for instance. When Frederick had gone away, she had not thrown any crockery into his earnest face, she had not screamed at him, and because it would have been childish, she had not said any of the things she now thought night and day. Puerile things, most of them. Juvenile. Being dumped puts a person in a childish mood. Tired of damning everything, "Poop," Sassy whispered the way she used to when she was ten, scowling at the carpet, giving the sweeper a truly vehement shove—and she felt something lightweight but ominous land on the top of her head.

She stopped sweeping and began to lift a hand to her head but stopped herself. She looked around.

From where she stood, on the third wedding-cake layer of the lobby, Sassy gazed up at the plumy tops of subtropical trees, their seventy-foot height no more impressive than petunias in the context of the Tower atrium soaring eighty-five glassy-sparkle fairy-tale stories above. The Sylvan Tower Hotel claimed, with some justification, to be the world's most spectacular luxury hotel, with a six-story lacework lobby blooming with kiosks and specialty shops, boutiques, bodegas, discotheques, ethnic eateries, bistros, cafés, promenades and terraces and fountains and gardens full of braided quince and gazebos and fishpools—koi-starred waterholes out of which arose, like technogods arising from the primordial brine, the twelve neon-limned glass elevators which rocketed up the central supporting tower, the arbor vitae of the place, to eighty-five catwalks leading to eighty-five vine-edged balconies and several thousand guest rooms—too many of which Sassy was tired of cleaning. She understood that the maids up top, where the locked floors and the suites surrounded a rotating haute-cuisine restaurant, wore different uniforms and were responsible for only a few luxurious rooms.

Maybe that should be her ambition in life now. To be a maid up top.

"Poop," Sassy muttered again.

Exertion and emotion had humidified her face, fogging her glasses. Sassy took them off, wiped them on her apron and put them on again. Squinting against the glare of too much decorator lighting as she flexed her tired shoulders, all she could see above her was darkly silhouetted tree fronds—she didn't know what the hothouse trees were called, but they looked like ficus on steroids. Something that felt faintly wet had disturbed her meek cap of mouse-colored hair; what was it? Once again she lifted a hand, but stopped the gesture in midair, because in the crown of one of the trees she saw a flitter of movement, like a leaf stirring—but there was no breeze in the atrium, or at least there shouldn't be, and some gloomy gut instinct told her what had happened.

No.

Yes.

Maybe.

Oh, for gosh sake—

"Racquel," she called to a tall woman loitering in the doorway of a nearby boutique, "could you come here a minute, please?"

"Sure thing, honey." Racquel roused, erected, and ambled toward Sassy, as lithe as a black rawhide whip even on four-inch heels.

Sassy knew Racquel only slightly, not having worked at the hotel for long. She knew that Racquel was the proprietor of

PLUMAGE, the boutique in the doorway of which she had been loafing. Other than that, Sassy knew of Racquel only what she saw: a handsome ebony woman of statuesque, even monumental height, lavishly dressed, and crowned unto an even greater altitude with a new metallic-luster hair sculpture each week.

"Could you see," Sassy appealed, gesturing with her hovering hand, "is there something on my head?"

Racquel could easily see. In heels, Racquel stood a good foot-and-a-half taller than Sassy.

"Good Lord," said Racquel in her rich contralto voice, studying the top of Sassy's flat straggle of hair, "it looks like bird poop."

"But—" Sassy's sense of the proper order of things in life had been much disturbed of late, and she didn't like it. She struggled with this latest violation. "But are there supposed to be birds in here?"

"Not that I know of." Despite perfectly correct diction, Racquel's low-pitched drawl still spoke of someplace south of Florida, making Sassy think of sugar and deep-throated velvety blossoms. "But I'm telling you, honey, it's bird poop."

Sassy contemplated this appraisal of her situation for a moment. Sassy felt her well-trained self-control tightening like steel bands around a narrow barrel. Her shoulders closed a warning grip on her neck, her butt clenched as if she might be spanked—but inexorably the emotion in her flat chest arose and rose, swelling like a tsunami, until she had no choice but to let it burst forth in a wail of existential angst. "Good grief," Sassy cried, "my mother gets Alzheimer's, my husband runs off with a chippie, I lose my house, they sell my miserable jewelry at auction, I have to take this scutty job, and now you're telling me a *bird pooped on me*?"

"Really? Sweeeet!" Gracefully Racquel bent at the knees to look into Sassy's face, studying her with newly piqued interest.

Sassy stamped her foot, clunky in its orthopedically correct white nursie shoe. "Would you get it *off* me?"

"Sure, honey. Just a minute, just let me get a Kleenex or something." Long-legged, potent, sleek in iridescent silk, with a length of chiffon floating from her neck, Racquel strode off toward her shop.

Waiting for her to come back, glowering at the smooth taffy-colored trunks of ficus-on-steroids trees, at sunlit glass casting rainbows on too much carpet, at designer-clad couples eating tiramisu at fountainside, Sassy pondered imponderables: Why? Why this, why now? *Why me?*

What damn bird?

Through her unhappy thoughts she heard something whirring, a dry, airy sound. Before she could quite focus, something, a blur of barbaric lime-green and lemon-yellow, shot down from above her, out of tree plumes and glassy skylight. Sassy heard a squawk of demonic glee as her already-violated hair stirred in its own personal whirlwind and the incubus thumped down upon the left rim of her glasses, throwing her world even more off-balance than it already was. In front of her left eye, smack against the forcibly tilted lens, separated from her tender cornea only by glass and a scant half inch of air, there appeared a yellow manifestation that she could not begin to interpret. She could only gawk, cross-eyed, at—what? She saw bilateral symmetry out of which her mind tried to organize a face, but the thing had too many eyes, six of them, a big pair of black ones and a little pair of kudzu-berry blue ones and those other ones off to the sides—and what was the hard brownish steeple where a nose should have been?

Then the steeple moved, knocking against her lens as if the yellow demon wanted in.

Sassy's overstressed self-control snapped entirely. She screamed.

She had not previously known that she was capable of such a scream, an exquisite supra-soprano paean of terror, a soaring, feral, thrilling bright yellow scream. Glass should have broken. Several hotel guests turned their bored, orthodontically correct heads to stare at her.

With the same powerful whir, the demon vanished from in front of Sassy's left eye. Undone by the sudden change of vectors, her glasses fell off, and she let out another wail, because she couldn't see and she was afraid to move to try to find them.

"A parakeet!" said Racquel's voice close behind her.

Sassy jumped, her hands grabbing at air. "What?" she bleated.

"A parakeet! How bogus can you get? A freakin' parakeet, hanging on your glasses with its tail up in the air." Racquel's voice moved in front of Sassy, and Sassy felt Racquel slipping her glasses back onto her head, but she still couldn't see anything but a blur; her eyes had filled with annoying, childish tears.

"I guess we know now what pooped on your head," Racquel said.

"It *scared* me." Sassy heard her voice starting to come apart, and hated herself. Saying a thing like that. Sounding like a three-year-old.

She felt Racquel dabbing gently at the top of her head. "It was just a dinky little parakeet," Racquel said, her contralto voice a bit too soothing, like that of a Victorian nanny crooning, *There, there.*

Sassy yelled, "I didn't know what it was! You try looking at a parakeet upside down all of a sudden and see if you can figure out what it is!"

"Shhhh!" But Racquel began to shake with silent laughter; her gentle hands shook atop Sassy's head. She gave up on the bird poop. "There. It's mostly gone." Her voice quivered with suppressed laughter. "What's left doesn't show much. Blends right in with the gray."

"Oh, *wonderful.* Thank you *so* much."

Racquel pressed several Kleenex into Sassy's hands—the supreme humiliation, from Sassy's point of view; she had hoped that Racquel wouldn't notice that she needed them. "Have a nice day," said Racquel with a chuckle as she strode away.

Abandoning her carpet sweeper, Sassy bolted for the nearest rest room.

She nearly fled into the men's by mistake, but caught herself in time and blundered into the ladies', which, mercifully, was unoccupied. After she washed her face with cold water and dried it with a paper towel and blew her nose and got herself together somewhat, she dared to face a mirror to see how she looked. Specifically, her hair; how bad was it? Bird poop blending right in with the gray, indeed.

The problem of poop on Sassy's mind, however, was quickly superseded by another. In the mirror, her reflection was not there.

Not. There.

Instead—

In the mirror, seemingly perched on air in the vicinity of what should have been Sassy's heart, a little blue parakeet looked back at her.

Sassy blinked.

Closed her eyes a moment.

Took a deep breath, opened her eyes again and looked.

Stared.

She was still not there.

And the parakeet still was.

There. In the mirror. Its head up. Staring back at her with eyes like tiny tourmalines set in silver.

Sassy glanced down at herself. She was still there. That was her potbellied body under green shirtwaist and stupid ruffled apron. Those were her hands, shaking. She lifted them to her head, felt her own solid skull, her own face, her own eyes, reassuringly gelatinous under rubbery eyelids; all the essential parts still seemed to be in place. Through her fingers she looked at the mirror again.

Parakeet.

It should have been a pretty little parakeet. Cobalt-blue, with a cute creamy white face. But Sassy did not find it pretty. She flinched and clenched her fingers together, hiding behind them.

"Give me a break," she whispered. Sassy was not a religious person, especially not lately, but her posture was undeniably that of prayer. "Give me a break," she whispered again, "please." Slowly she lowered her hands from her eyes.

It was still there. Little blue parakeet. Looking straight back at her.

Sassy didn't reason anything out—that the cant of the parakeet's head was the mirror image of hers, the stare of the beady eyes, the same as hers—she couldn't think; her mind was farting way too hard for thought. But ineluctably she knew: that bird was her reflection now. Her self.

. . .

Perched in sweetleaf, hidden in greenfree that matched his own green coverts, Kleet shivered in awe. He trembled, all his feathers prickling. Even his feet quivered on the twig they clutched, even his beak quivered—for he had just encountered Deity face-to-face.

Almost by mistake, prompted by some strange urging from beyond the hard air, he had annointed her plumage. Her limbs had lifted to him, her bare pale twigs had extended to him. He had flown to her; he had skreeked her and she had skreeked him back. It was the shellbreak day of his young life.

Only Deity knew what marvels would now ensue.

Sassy called in sick to work for the next three days and shut herself in her apartment, crying, contemplating her own sanity or lack thereof, looking in mirrors and trying not to look in mirrors because when she did, the parakeet that stared back at her remained as omnipresent and blue as ever. Sometimes it hunched its shoulders and stretched its wings. Sometimes it peered at her slantwise. Sometimes it bent into a U to preen its tail feathers, and once it scratched its own head, standing on one foot with the other foot stuck behind its wing, clownish. It wasn't always the same, but like a budgie in a cage, it was always there.

One time it gaped its beak at her in an infantile sort of toothless grin, which charmed her not at all. "Just go away," she told it, but it didn't.

Sassy tried to think of sensible solutions to her dilemma, but none came to mind.

The fourth day she had to go back to work, because after three days she would need a doctor's excuse, just like in junior high school, and hers was not the sort of problem one took to one's family physician. Also, she needed the hours. Her paycheck was going to be even more pathetic than usual this week.

"I won't look," she muttered, brushing her teeth over the bathroom sink with her eyes closed against the bathroom mirror. But instinct made her look in the mirror as she reached for her hairbrush, and she almost burst out crying. She stamped her bare foot on the linoleum instead.

"Ow!" she yelled at the bird in the mirror, because now her foot hurt. "You stupid budgie, what the—" But Sassy never said hell. "*What* do you want? I can't even see myself to comb my hair!"

It didn't really matter. Her hair, baby-fine and as flaccid as spaghetti, was useless for anything except to be scrunched under a ratty old scarf on the way to work.

The winter air breezed right through the scarf. Since when were these things supposed to protect your ears? Mama had always trained her to wear one to guard against earache, but then, look at Mama. Look at Sassy, her mama's image. Here came the mezzanine maid in her ugly babushka.

Sassy was supposed to enter the Sylvan Tower by a discreet back entrance, but she didn't. The parking garage was filled, she had to find a spot on the street, which meant that she had to put her lunch money into the meter, and the February morning was as cold as Frederick's heart, and damn everything. She scuttled in through the lofty doors to the main lobby and made her way through its labyrinth of gift shops and jewelers and haute couturiers and cafés and fountainside dining to the elevators, to go down to the swimming-pool level and the catacombs where she reported to work.

The Sylvan Tower Hotel was rife with mirrors. The hallways were mirrored, the bottoms of balconies were mirrored, the undersides of escalators were mirrored, every surface the decorators didn't know what else to do with was mirrored, including the elevator shaft, which was walled with gold-tone mirrors outlined in neon. Standing in front of one, waiting, Sassy braced herself and looked. Her parakeet was there, standing on air, as usual. Next to it, with its scaly black three-toed feet almost on the floor, stood a bored-looking six-foot brownish crane.

Sassy yelped.

"Something wrong, ma'am?" asked the businessman standing next to her.

"Uh, no. No, not at all." Babbling, Sassy glanced from the businessman to the crane, the crane to the businessman. Both were tall. There the resemblance ended. Yet—she knew it was him.

"You sure you're okay, ma'am? You look gray."

"Um, no, no, I'm fine." Blessedly, at that moment the elevator arrived. In an inflamed frame of mind, Sassy rode it down and reported to work.

By afternoon, when she cleaned the mezzanine, she had calmed down. After all, if she was going to be looking at a parakeet in the mirror for the rest of her life, what did it matter if she saw other people as birds too? Vacuuming, she observed with interest the beveled-glass mirrors beautifying the wall as hotel guests strode by. A fashionable woman minced past, and in the mirror a sparrow fluttered along beside her; how could that be? A teenage boy darted by with a gull skimming along in the mirror; that seemed more apt. A man stood talking to his wife, and there was a green-headed duck soundlessly quacking. The wife was a brown-mottled sort of quail or prairie chicken or something; Sassy wasn't sure. The next woman was easy, a crow, but then came a whole series of birds Sassy didn't know: a black-and-white pinto one, something that whizzed past trailing an immensely long tail, something large that stalked by on stiltlike legs, something red and blue that bobbed as it flew, a bird that (like its human) had an enormous mouth flanked by whiskers, and a bird striped like a convict, cowering on the mirrored floor.

Whew. After a while, feeling dizzy from trying to remember them all, Sassy stopped watching.

Nobody else was a parakeet. Or even a parrot, for that matter.

Sassy vacuumed her way past the boutique in which Racquel loomed behind the counter sweet-talking customers and bossing her employees. It occurred to Sassy that she owed Racquel an apology. She had been quite snippy to Racquel the other day when Racquel was only trying to help her.

It occurred to her, also, to wonder what sort of bird Racquel was.

Hey. This new affliction of hers could conceivably become fun. Finished vacuuming, Sassy snapped off the Hoover with panache and trotted across a quarter acre of pristine carpet to unplug it.

As she turned, a green-and-yellow blur whirred toward her.

"Hey!" Sassy flung up her hands, flailing. "Go away!" She windmilled, defending her glasses, batting wildly at the air and the parakeet. For an instant her fingers encountered the fluttery dryness of feathers, and she nearly screamed. Only her lifelong inhibitions kept her from shrieking.

They did not keep her from feeling a moment of triumph, however, as the parakeet zoomed away toward the treetops. Good. It could just go pick on somebody else.

Sassy got through the rest of her day in a lighter mood, and took the elevator up to the mezzanine after work, to see Racquel.

PLUMAGE Boutique specialized in featherwear for fancy

and frivolous occasions. A feathered cape worthy of an Aztec priest shimmered in the display window, plumed hats perched on racks, glorious and scary feathered masks stared down from the walls. There were feathered earrings and barbaric feathered necklaces, feather boas to go over slinky quilled evening gowns, feather-trimmed jackets, feather fans. Peacock, pheasant, egret, ostrich, marabou, jungle cock, nameless exotics and fabulous fakes. A small disclaimer posted on the door stated: "PLUMAGE stocks only the finest garments and accessories made from naturally shed feathers from free-range domesticated birds. No-kill. No endangered species." Hang-tags on garments declared the feathers used on them to be fade-resistant and hypo-allergenic, but did not say whether the feathers came from a happy hand-fed emu named Judy or from a nameless white turkey later to be rendered into croquettes.

"Yo, there!" Racquel called as Sassy walked in. Sitting behind the cash register, Racquel wore a regal ice-green faille dress with an ornate high collar, a ruff that, even though made of feathers, was more reminiscent of Queen Elizabeth I than of a grouse. Her hair was lacquered into a metallic-gold crest tastefully tufted with a few platinum-colored plumes. Blessedly, Racquel sat nowhere near any mirror, which allowed Sassy to focus on the task at hand.

"Um, hi." Sassy lagged toward her, feeling shy about this; Sassy had never been socially apt. "Listen, I'm sorry I was so huffy—"

"Hey, you were upset. You're entitled to be upset when you get pooped on. S'okay."

Obviously the tall woman meant it. Sassy knew with relief that she could quit apologizing—but now she felt an awkward friendliness, a need to hang around. "Um, nice place you got here." Aaak, what a dumb, standard thing to say.

"Thank you." Racquel sounded bored.

Sassy flushed and peered through her thick glasses at the dainty feathered toe rings and ankle bracelets under the countertop. Quail feathers. Sassy took in their translucence, their scalloped overlappings, their subtle fox-colored mottlings. Pretty. Had feathers always been so pretty? She turned to look at a downy dove capelet hanging from a rack, then wandered farther into PLUMAGE to gaze at feathers upon feathers, barred, speckled, laced, streaked, ticked, stippled, frizzled, iridescent, faux, bleached, dyed. So many feathers they gave off a pleasant, dry, spicy scent. Sassy breathed deeply of feathers, breathed in the infinitude of plumage, facing the blindly staring feral feathered masks on the back wall—

"You like feathers," said Racquel from right behind her.

Startled, Sassy turned. Racquel stood in front of a mirror, and in the mirror stood a large raven-black bird with brightly colored wattles—saffron, scarlet, cobalt blue—and a huge swelling hooked bill.

"You're a toucan or something," Sassy blurted. Then like a child she clapped her hand over her own mouth, feeling her face go hot.

But far from being offended, Racquel laughed with delight. No longer bored, "You're a funny little bird yourself," Racquel said.

That was what Frederick had called her. A bird. At first, when she was young, a skinny-legged chickie, he had meant it kindly. Or at least lustfully. Back when they were first married. Later, as she got older and gravity took hold, he had said it far less kindly. She was turning into a bird, he said disgustedly. Like her mother.

That was why he had left her.

Or, some days she thought that was why. Other days she

thought that it was because he didn't have the character to handle midlife, which was equally true. Or because he had been seduced, which might also be true. Or because he had watched too many James Bond movies. Or because he was confusing her with *his* mother, who had napped with him until he was twelve. Or, on her worst days, Sassy thought maybe it was because she didn't watch TV with him, wanting to read instead, or because of something else she had done or not done, that was why he didn't love her; why should he? Other days she thought she would never be able to stop thinking because she would never know the true answer. She thought, and thought, and thought about it, and all her thoughts made sense at the time, and all were useless.

Sassy became aware that Racquel was eyeing her with interest and something more—warmth? Concern? Racquel asked, "What's your name?"

Sassy told her.

"You don't seem real sassy."

"It's short for Sassafras."

"*Sassafras?*"

"Don't ask me what my mother was thinking."

"What's your *mother's* name?"

"Magnolia."

"Oh. Was she a Southern belle?"

"More of a Southern frump."

Racquel laughed again, even more diverted. "Let's go get you a cappuccino or something."

"No, that's okay, I—"

"Come on. After being pooped on, don't you deserve a cappuccino?"

Undeniably true. Sassy followed Racquel meekly.

 **T W O**

At the coffee bar on the third floor of the lobby levels, Sassy and Racquel sat at a circular white wrought-iron table overlooking the ficus-on-steroids trees.

Sassy curled her permacold hands around the warmth of her coffee cup. "So tell me all about it," Racquel said, her interest as warm as the cup, so warm it made Sassy want to cry. She couldn't speak, and Racquel seemed to take her silence as a need for elucidation. "You mentioned a soap opera's worth of troubles the other day. I seem to remember you telling something about a runaway husband, Alzheimer's, a lost jewelry collection—"

"It was just souvenir jewelry," Sassy mumbled.

"Just?"

"You know. If we—" Damn, she had to stop saying "we." It was the hardest thing to stop thinking in "we" now that she was just a "me." "When Frederick would take me somewhere on a vacation, I'd get myself a necklace or something." She would wear the trinket, whatever it was, for the few days of what she always hoped might become a second honeymoon. Then she would go home to waxing floors, scrubbing the sink, degreasing the stove, and the souvenirs reposed in her jewelry box. Sometimes as she swabbed the john she would think of

her jewelry lying in the dark like paramours, like promises, gar-
nets and zircons nestled in red velvet like the sparkly dreams
casketed in her heart. Just the standard dime-store dreams:
togetherness, faithfulness, love forever, that sort of thing.

"So you had what, a couple hundred pieces?" Racquel
asked.

Sassy didn't know. Not that many. "It's all gone now."

"Along with the souvenir husband?"

"He—" Calling him a souvenir was way too good for him.
Souvenirs were to say that her whole life had not been entirely
wasted. "He took everything."

Racquel nodded her sympathy. "Cleaned out the bank
account?"

"No, not like that." Bank account, ha. "Frederick got
moved up to customer service from the meat department but
he still doesn't make that much."

"Huh?"

"He works at Food World. So I shop anywhere else now."
Sassy struggled for a way to say that it was her selfhood that
Frederick had cleaned out, not a bank account, that she was
emptied, that she felt like last year's robin's nest unwinding in
the wind. "I mean, I was so proud of—you know, the marriage. But he threw it out like—like last week's *TV Guide*."

"What a meatball."

"I knew something was wrong. He kept on saying no, everything's fine, trust me, trust me, she's just a friend. And then
Binky dear calls on the phone and he gets that coo in his
voice."

"That's hard to take."

"Yeah." Sassy managed to smile with simulated courage but
she was feeling the familiar ache. Remembering that fleecy
softening of his voice, remembering sitting at the kitchen table

listening in and looking down at her chapped hands and thinking *how long since he's talked to me that way?* and knowing she'd do just about anything if he just loved her and then trying to tell herself it was nothing, of course he loved her, he was her husband, wasn't he? That was it. She was the wife. She'd been his wife for twenty-seven years. Of course he took her for granted. How silly of her to think there could be anyone else after all this time. She didn't want to be a jealous nag, did she? That would really turn him off. She had to trust him.

Yeah. Right.

"He turned into kind of a jackass," she said.

"No duh."

"I mean, he wasn't always. At first he was sweet. Lots of fun. Boyish." Kind of Huck Finn with a wayward forelock of straw-colored hair, with russet freckled skin. "But I guess he never grew up. The last few years—I don't know how many times I looked at myself in the mirror and whispered, 'I am married to a jackass.'"

Racquel laughed. She had a laugh that flowed like a deep river, that eased the ache in Sassy's narrow chest and made her wonder at herself. The man was a jackass; had she loved him? Or had she just wanted someone, anyone, to love her?

"So he lied to you," Racquel said.

"He sure did. For years."

"What a dingleberry."

With every new epithet Racquel invoked upon the head of Frederick, Sassy felt a little bit better. Racquel had to be only about half Sassy's age, but Lord, Racquel was good to talk with. Racquel was saying for her all the things she barely knew how to think, let alone say, for herself.

A dingleberry. Yes. "A big one," Sassy agreed. "If he'd just *said* something—" All her life, practically, she'd been reading

Ladies' Home Journal, "Can This Marriage Be Saved?" And it always could. But Frederick evidently hadn't read those articles. He never gave her a chance to save it. "If he was going to do something like that," she burst out, "why couldn't he have done it years ago? While I still had a chance?"

Racquel leaned back in her chair, her long strong hands curled as brown as coffee around her cup of cappuccino, peering at Sassy with a shadow of a frown. "A chance?"

"While I still had some looks."

Racquel scanned Sassy in silence, her frown deepening.

"Not that I was ever anything much," Sassy added.

"Honey, you ain't bad-looking."

Sure. Right. Racquel was just being nice. "I wish I could blame him for the gray hairs and the extra pounds," Sassy said, "but I can't. The last ten years or so, I look more and more like my mother."

"So what's wrong with that?"

But—everything was wrong with that, didn't Racquel understand? Women were supposed to look like adolescent boys, not like their mothers. Or maybe it was different for black people?

"Frederick didn't like my mother," Sassy said.

"So how many people do like their mother-in-law?"

Sassy blinked. Racquel had a point.

"Anything in particular wrong with your mother?"

"Right now? She has about one functioning brain cell left."

"Okay, I remember. Alzheimer's. But before?"

Sassy tried to remember. It seemed to her that Mama had been a nice little mama for the most part. She missed her.

"She was just kind of a bird, that's all."

"Aren't we all?"

Given her peculiar personal circumstances, Sassy sidestepped that. "I guess." She murmured with belated wonder, "Frederick made it sound like the worst thing in the world that I was getting like my mother."

"Screw him."

Another nice sentiment. It made Sassy keep talking. For the next hour she spoke of Frederick, Frederick, Frederick, as Racquel listened with unwavering sympathy. She told about how Frederick had invited Binky to his and Sassy's twenty-fifth anniversary party. She told about how he would go places with Binky and tell Sassy casually after the fact to make it all right. She wondered whether Frederick, who was kind of a limp dick anyway, had maintained technical fidelity, sort of like the technical virginity some girls had been famous for in high school, so that he could look her in the eye. She told how Frederick would thank her for being "understanding," then tell her she was crazy for being unhappy, feeling left out he hadn't asked her to go along with him and Bink to the hop, hadn't he told her Binky was just a friend? "What a salami dick," Racquel said. Every few minutes Racquel slipped in amens of this sort, as if she were listening to a Baptist hellfire-and-brimstone sermon. Over the next hour she called Frederick a trouser snake, a frequent whacker, a petercheese, and a slimelicker as well as some other, more routine obscenities. With every epithet that Sassy could not herself dream of uttering, Sassy felt better.

Finally she told the hardest part: how she had sat Frederick down and asked him whether he loved her. He hadn't answered. She'd asked him whether he was in love with Binky. He'd said, "That has nothing to do with this." Then he had said that he hadn't loved Sassy in years. Years. He had just been pretending so he wouldn't "hurt her." And then he had said, "I got to go. Listen, Sassy, if Binky calls, tell her I'm at work, would you?"

"What an *Oedipus*," said Racquel.

"Huh?"

"Think about it. What a jellosnarf," Racquel said with feeling. "I don't believe this guy. What a clueless asshole. You poor thing. First twenty-seven years of him, and then a bird poops on you."

"Speak of the devil," Sassy said, "there it goes." A green-and-yellow flit wafted past their balcony like a figment, like a spark of light landing in a treetop. Perched, it settled its sleek green wings and turned its yellow head toward her. Sassy stiffened.

"The damn thing tried to attack me earlier today," she said.

"It did?"

"Well . . . it tried to land on me. I fended it off."

"It must like you," Racquel said. "I haven't heard of it trying to sit on anybody else."

The parakeet still perched quietly in its tree like a yellow-headed spirit. Sassy felt like it was watching her.

"You just stay there," she told it between her teeth.

Racquel nodded. "Hotel management wants to get rid of it," she said. "It hasn't pooped on anybody other than you that I know of, but it poops plenty. Did you know a bird poops on the average every fifteen minutes?"

Sassy contemplated this. She knew from somewhere that horses pooped forty-five pounds a day. If birds were the size of horses . . . it did not bear contemplation. She shied from the poop stats and backtracked to Racquel's previous statement. "Get rid of it how?"

"Well, they can't exactly shoot it in here. Trap it, I guess. Or maybe poison it."

There began to grow in Sassy a queasy sense of unease. She could tell Racquel all about Frederick, which was a relief, but certainly she could not tell her—no. She could not tell anyone about the bizarre budgie that faced her in the mirror every day. They would think she was insane.

And maybe she was. The idea that they might poison the parakeet troubled her. Okay, she wanted it to leave her alone, but—did they have to kill it? Also—she hadn't quite admitted the connection until this moment, preferring to think that sequence did not necessarily indicate cause and effect, but still . . . it sure looked as if that parakeet had made her start seeing birds instead of people in mirrors. Maybe some sort of weird virus in its poop had instantaneously soaked through her skull into her brain. And if they killed that bird, she might never find the cure.

"They can't do that," Sassy blurted.

Racquel leaned forward, her dark eyes large and friendly, like a puppy's. "You a bird lover?"

"Not hardly." But it began to look as if she was going to have to start acting like one. Reluctantly Sassy admitted to herself that she hadn't been thinking. Damn, she needed that bird.

And it had tried to land on her, she could have grabbed it, but she had driven it away.

"I am an idiot," she said to Racquel.

"What, honey? Why?"

"I just am." Sassy scrambled up, thanked Racquel for the raspberry-flavored espresso, and scuttled out.

The next day around lunchtime, Racquel ambled out on the mezzanine to get away from the bookkeeping and noticed Sassy in her white-and-green uniform sitting at a café table. Racquel peered across the atrium with interest, because this was a violation of hotel rules; uniformed maids were supposed to be seen only when at work, taking their breaks and meals down below. Sassy must have some sass in her after all. Something about the little woman tugged at Racquel's heart, and she wondered what it was. Sassy made her wince with thoughts of what it must be like to be quite so relentlessly middle-aged—but that wasn't it. Pity was boring, and Sassy was not; Sassy was—Sassy was a bit of a mystery.

Sassy sat bold as gold at that café table scanning a large book. A stack of books squatted at her elbow.

Leaving PLUMAGE to the mercies of her employees, Racquel headed over there, her slit grosgrain skirt snapping as she walked, her feather-fringed sash swishing.

Even when Racquel was not conscious of her own secret, it rode in her like the mythic jewel in the head of a toad. Was it the weight of her own secret, Racquel wondered, that made her think that Sassy had a secret?

"Hey, woman," she greeted Sassy.

Sassy glanced up at her with the glassy, unsmiling look of one who has been interrupted. "Oh, hi," Sassy said, coming to after a moment, but without putting down her book. A bright yellow budgie greeted Racquel from its cover.

"*The Complete Book of Parakeets*," Racquel read aloud, sitting down. The other books, she saw, were *Budgies As Pets, The Fact Finder Book of Parrots and Parakeets, Parakeets: A Pet Owner's Manual,* and so on down the stack.

Sassy said, "You would not believe how many colors of parakeet there are." She flipped through her book, reciting. "Green. Yellow. Blue. Aquamarine, violet, pastel, albino, pied." She was growing round-eyed, her small hands clawing at the pages. "Shell markings. No shell markings. Lacewing. Lutino. Opaline, fallow, greywing, cinnamon, crested. And not one of them—" Sassy slapped the book shut and slammed it down. "Not one of them looks the least bit like that one." Her forefinger stabbed the air.

Racquel turned and looked where Sassy was pointing. On a tree limb not far away, the hotel's parakeet-in-residence perched, watching.

Racquel felt her own eyebrows pucker, puzzled. "You need to know what kind it is?" she asked.

A pause. Then, "I guess not really," Sassy mumbled. Racquel turned back to look at her; Sassy looked sheepish. "I guess I kind of got sidetracked into that."

Racquel scanned the stack of books and grinned. "You're obsessed," she said. "I like that in a person."

"I, uh, I was really trying to find out—"

"Does this happen often?" Racquel pursued her teasing. "Do you indulge, like, an obsession of the week?"

Finally Sassy smiled. "The people at the library probably think so."

"Why? What else you been reading?"

"I don't know." She shrugged. "Art history, folklore, trees, Tasmania, whatever. I just sort of browse one section at a time."

Racquel sat back, impressed. "You're educated," she said.

"No, I'm not." Sassy blinked at her, eyes pallid behind her glasses; Sassy needed to start using mascara. Even with the gray hair, she wouldn't look half so plain if she put on some makeup. "I got married right out of high school."

"You don't call twenty-seven years of reading everything in sight an education?"

"I, uh, no, not really . . ." Sassy blinked harder and changed the subject. "What I was trying to find out was how to catch that parakeet. But all it says is wait until night, turn off all the lights, and sneak up on it with a flashlight. That's not going to work."

Racquel made a show of studying the parakeet perched seventy feet in the air. "Not unless you got wings," she said.

"In which case it would be no problem anyway. I'd just outfly it. Hey." Sassy brightened. "Maybe I could hire a falcon."

"What do you want to catch it for?"

"Uh . . ." All of a sudden Sassy jumped up, scraping her books together. "I got to get back to work," Sassy muttered, not looking at Racquel. Sassy fled.

"Huh!" Peering after Sassy, Racquel noticed that the parakeet also was following the little woman with its gaze.

Reporting to work a couple of days later, Sassy carried in each apron pocket a Peterson Field Guide, one for the Eastern United States and one for the Rocky Mountain States. If she'd had more pockets she probably would have brought along Central America too.

Servicing hotel rooms, spreading clean sheets, she yawned and wanted to lie down on the beds, because she had sat up late studying *Birds of the World*; she had gotten only four hours of sleep. Oddly, this made her feel mellow, as if she were swimming in a heated pool. She had never before stayed up so late just because she wanted to. Always before, Frederick had wanted her to go to bed when he did, although not usually for any enjoyable purpose.

Because Sassy had stayed up late in disobedience to her training, she felt druggy and free. When she should have been fetching towels, she stood looking over the balcony, watching the mirrors on the far side of the atrium and promising herself a small pair of binoculars when she got her next paycheck. If she got it. "Whatcha doing, Sassy?" another maid wanted to know.

"Bird-watching."

The woman gave her an odd look and hurried off. Sassy laughed. She actually laughed out loud. That hadn't happened in a while.

She had already identified many of the birds she had seen the day before: a magpie, a quetzel, a great blue heron, a frogmouth, a hoopoe. The names of the birds in her books amused Sassy as much as anything else that was happening: ouzel, brant, limpkin, crake, dowitcher, willet, whimbrel, widgeon, quank. She couldn't wait until she spotted a quank. Racquel was right; she was obsessed. She was going to get her own Peterson, all the Petersons, and record the species she saw on the Systematic Checklist. She was going to join an ornithology club. Her life was a huge joke.

Rats. She had to go to the bathroom.

The Sylvan Tower rest rooms were ultra clean, and Sassy had read somewhere that there were a bazillion more germs on the average dishcloth than on the average toilet seat, but she couldn't help herself; she checked for toilet paper and spread some on the seat, as trained. As she sat, a large pair of ebony feet in strappy gold-stone heels walked into the stall next to hers.

"Hi, Racquel," Sassy called. One of the differences between men and women, she understood from her sociological reading, was that men wouldn't dream of talking to the man squatting in the next booth in the rest room. Too bad for men. In Sassy's experience, some of life's best conversations took place in the shared yet separated intimacy of the john. The stall walls made the place like a confessional, bringing forth confidences, secrets.

"Sassy?" Racquel seemed to be taking some time to get her panty hose down. Struggling with the damn things.

"Right."

"Hey, woman." Racquel's throaty voice wafted warm and comfortable to Sassy as she turned and assumed the customary straddle position. The odor of her bared privates wafted similarly. "How's it hangin'?"

That meant how was it going, Sassy guessed. "Better." Until she said it, Sassy didn't know this was the case. Up until then, when people had asked her how she was, she had said in tepid tones, "Okay."

Racquel said, "Hey, that's good. Is it that your mother's better, or your love life is better, or you've figured out some way to kick Frederick's lying ass?"

Sassy laughed. "My mother's the same, nobody loves me, and Frederick is living it up with his Binky-poo. I don't know why—I just feel better."

"*Nobody* loves you?"

"Not really." Obviously Frederick didn't. "We never had kids." Maybe things would have been different somehow if they had had kids. But that was an old, old heartache. Let it alone. "My brothers don't call me from one year to the next. My mother doesn't even know who I am."

"God, that's a pisser."

Much surprised at herself, Sassy laughed again, because, by the sound emanating from the next stall, pissing was what Racquel was doing.

"Literally," Sassy said.

"Damn straight." Apparently, Racquel didn't get it. "But don't you have *friends*?"

Sassy thought about it. "All the people Frederick and I saw were couples," she said slowly. "I *thought* they were friends."

But apparently they had been more of a social convenience. Now that she wasn't the female half of a couple anymore, she didn't hear from them.

Racquel seemed to understand. "Bummer," she said.

And Sassy laughed yet some more.

Her brittle happiness lasted until she got herself together, exited the stall and reached the sink, where a mirror confronted her.

Oh Lord.

She had tried to reason with herself: it wasn't like seeing a cute little blue parakeet in the mirror was life-threatening. It wasn't even a terrible inconvenience. Not for her. It had been years since she had bothered to fuss with makeup, and her hair just lay there no matter what she did with it. On a scale of one to ten, she had told herself, her parakeet problem rated a one, maximum.

But, oh Lord, she wanted to look in the mirror and see her own homely face. Even though she'd never particularly liked it, she wanted it now; with irrational intensity she yearned for her own reflection. She had lost her mother, her marriage, her home, her dreams—had she lost her self too?

"Panty hose must have been invented by a man." Racquel emerged from her stall, twitching at the irksome waistband under her emerald dress, resplendent under a green-gold peacock boa. Looming on spike heels, Racquel strode over to wash her hands.

With relief Sassy focused on Racquel's reflection, concerning which *Birds of the World* had set her straight. "You're not a toucan after all," she told Racquel. "You're a hornbill."

"Huh?" Washing her hands, Racquel did not look up.

"You're a hornbill." Sassy knew she sounded inane at best and more likely insane, but she didn't care. If she was going to be a bird, she'd be a bird. It occurred to her only belatedly that Racquel might be offended by being called a hornbill, and she amended hastily, "Hornbills are much classier than toucans."

If you considered projectile pooping classy. Which it was, in a way; it kept the nest clean. Hornbills nested in tree hollows and were therefore upper-crust birds. Sassy truly admired Racquel's reflection, a turkey-sized, boldly marked black-and-white bird with a long, heavy down-curved beak, a rather disheveled golden crest, patches of bright red bare skin around its golden eyes, and brilliant cobalt-blue neck wattles. It was a barbaric-looking fowl, yet rendered appealing by long, thickly curling black eyelashes that would have been a credit to any mascara ad. The trademark bill was mostly black, surmounted by an enormous decorative extrusion called a casque—

Sassy caught a quick, astonished breath, her glance darting to Racquel to Racquel's reflection then back again. "Your bird is male," Sassy blurted.

Racquel froze over the sink with the soap still on her hands. Racquel's face went—not pale, certainly, but a different shade of dark. Gray. Slowly she turned her handsome head to stare at Sassy.

"Male," Sassy babbled. "Your, uh, your bird."

"I don't know what you're talking about." Racquel spun away, wiped her soapy hands on a paper towel with shaky haste, and strode out.

"Oh, just *great*," Sassy whispered to herself. Now Racquel was mad.

But—great, that was the one, the Great Madagascar Hornbill. Sassy distinctly remembered from *Birds of the World*—

Sassy returned to work with a mind even more preoccupied than before. During her next break, she trotted out to her car and checked the hefty book she had left on her passenger seat. Yes. The casque of the Great Madagascar Hornbill was unmistakably characteristic of the male.

Male. Racquel's reflection was male.

Bird-watching in mirrors for the rest of the day, Sassy focused on gender. Her own little mirrored parakeet was female, she knew—it had a cute pink cere (the leathery part above the beak where the nostrils were) just like the books said it was supposed to. When a woman in red walked by, the cardinal flapping in the mirror beside her was female, a subtle pinkish olive color. When the boss man Sassy knew to be self-deluded loitered on the mezzanine, the lyrebird loitering in the mirror was definitely male. Some species you couldn't tell, the males and the females looked the same—but otherwise, Sassy saw, all the men had male birds and all the women had female ones.

Except Racquel.

Well. Goodness.

Sassy contemplated Racquel. Tall. Handsome. Straight shoulders. Deepish voice. Large, strictly conical breasts that never seemed to bounce. Always something—a scarf, a high ruffled collar, a feather boa—concealing the Adam's apple area of the neck.

Good gravy.

"I feel awful," Sassy told the maid she was working with at the time.

"You do? Why?"

"I found out something I'm not supposed to know."

"Oh, *really?*" The woman turned to her with beady-eyed interest.

Sassy knew at once that it had been a mistake to say a word. This maid was a catbird. Meow, meow. Sassy turned away and scrubbed hard at a brass ashtray to keep herself from saying any more. But she did feel awful, her chest clotted with a churning cakemix of emotions, mad sad I've-been-had, and she badly wanted to talk to somebody she could trust.

Not Racquel. Lord. She felt hurt remembering that she and Racquel had sipped cappuccino and talked like friends. She felt queasy just thinking about Racquel sitting in the bathroom stall next to her—*sitting*, mind you—and peeing. The last person on earth she ever wanted to see again was Racquel. Well, put Racquel second in line after Frederick.

In the maids' locker room after work, Sassy traded mezzanine duty with somebody else for the rest of the week so she wouldn't have to go near Racquel's shop.

Then she darted out, hunched as if she were battling a headwind, to get away from her insane place of employment. But as she approached the back door, the maids' door, she nearly rammed into a flat emerald-green midriff. Racquel was standing there in the corridor. Waiting for her.

"Please don't tell," Racquel said, keeping her—his—voice low.

Sassy reared back and barked up at him, "You used the ladies' room!"

"Shhhh! What do you expect me to do?" He ran his French-manicured fingertips down his flowing skirt. "Go into the men's like this?"

"*Hold* it!"

"Can't. I'm a coffee drinker." He extended one long, shapely hand toward her in plea. "Sassy, please." He was almost whispering, although the people rushing past were employees on their way home, bolting out the door, couldn't care less about listening in. "Management doesn't know. They'll crucify me if they find out."

As one who had recently been hoisted on a cross made of her own good intentions, Sassy found herself feeling a grudging sympathy. Her tone of voice lowered to a grumble. "What exactly are you, anyway?"

"What do you mean?"

"I don't know enough weirdness to know what I mean!" Talking with this person who blurred her ideas of gender, Sassy felt existential nausea. Seasickness. No solid footing. No bedrock.

Racquel retorted, "I'm not a child molester, if that's what you—"

"Oh, for heaven's sake, I don't *think* that's what I meant."

Racquel took a long breath and let it out slowly. Very quietly he said, "What exactly do you need to know?"

"Why you are masquerading as a woman."

"I like froufrou!"

They stared at each other.

"I like sequins," Racquel elaborated. "I like velvet. Chiffon. Silk, satin, taffeta, tulle. I like high heels. I like long gloves. I like long gowns. And I most particularly like long gloves and long gowns edged with marabou. Or emu. With plumy headgear. Ostrich. Egret. Or a pheasant-feathered mask. Or a feathered choker. And I like—"

"You like fancy plumage," Sassy said.

"Yes, dammit. Don't you?"

"Yes. No. I don't know." He was some kind of big sissy, Sassy decided. A homosexual. She wanted to ask him in a very sophisticated way whether he was gay, but found that she felt too tired to deal with any more unwanted information today. She asked, "What's your real name?"

" 'Racquel' is as real as any."

"Whatever. I'm going home." Sassy sidestepped to walk past him.

He stretched out a hand to stop her. "You going to tell on me?" He sounded like a child caught doing something naughty at recess.

"I'll think about it," Sassy grumped.

"Please—"

"I said I'll think about it!" Once more Sassy tried to get past him. Once more he stopped her.

"Please just quick tell me one thing. How did you know? Did you see through the stall wall in the john, or what?"

"I am going *home*," Sassy said with great decision as she pushed past him, then hustled toward her car.

 **THREE**

The Sylvan Tower's Operation Catch Parakeet required a cooperative effort between Pest Control Professionals, so advertised on their pristine white coveralls, and Climb Any Mountaineers, Inc. The Pest Control people stood on balconies and unfurled what had to be the world's longest badminton nets, but with gossamer-fine mesh, way too fine for badminton nets, really. Mist nets, they called them. Bird nets. The mountaineers rappelled down from higher balconies and conveyed the trailing ends of the unfurled nets to other Pest Control personnel on the opposite side of the atrium. Meanwhile, management sweated, hoping the media would not show up, and with them unwanted attention from the animal rights activists. And meanwhile hotel denizens, including Sassy, gathered on various levels of the lobby to watch. By the end of the day, when the Pest Control Pros and the Climb Any Mountain people had (with the aid of walkie-talkies and much shouting) done their job, giant cobwebby nets crisscrossed the atrium from treetop level on up, and already someone had markered a graffito in one of the men's rooms, Cristo Was Here.

Then everybody went home. Except Sassy.

Her work shift was over. In the maids' locker room she had changed out of her uniform into another sort of work outfit, carefully selected—black sweatpants, a dark turtleneck and a navy cardigan, shabby old black sneakers. Not really athletic shoes. But then, she wasn't really athletic, which was one of the problems on her mind as she hung around the shadowy reaches of the Sylvan Tower lobby: she wasn't up on the latest rappelling techniques. The Sylvan Tower would have made a great playground for a musketeer, a perfect movie set, but Sassy did not feel capable of swinging from a chandelier. Nor was she inclined to attempt any Tarzan-style stunts, even if she were in possession of a grapevine or a rope or something, which she was not.

Assuming that the parakeet was stupid enough to blunder into one of the nets—which seemed a fairly safe assumption, actually—Sassy meant to get it before the Pest Control people did. But how?

Chin on her folded hands on a balcony rail, her tush ungracefully protruding, Sassy brooded upon the difficulties involved.

It occurred to her that she knew somebody who might help her.

No.

But—

No. Absolutely not. She didn't ever want to go near that weirdo again.

Fine. Then look at a parakeet in the mirror for the rest of—

Listen, things could be worse.

Sure they could. Twenty-seven, make it twenty-eight years wasted on a, what the heck had Racquel called him, a jello-snarf—

It was the warm memory of all the inspired names Racquel

had called Frederick that made Sassy mutter, "Oh, good gravy," straighten from her brooding stance, and head toward PLUMAGE.

As usual, the employees were doing the real work; Racquel loitered at the hat display, fondling a soft felt chapeau trimmed with white cut-feather flowers and butterflies, and a wide-brimmed picture hat with a pouf of feather fluff all around, and a toque with multicolored aigrette. Today Racquel was resplendent in a shimmery lavender dress with a banded sweetheart illusion neckline and a peplum.

Sassy blinked as she walked in; Racquel always seemed to affect her like neon. Sassy wondered how Racquel achieved cleavage.

"Hey, woman!" Racquel turned to her, seeming nervously glad to see her. Lavender feathers bobbed above the lacquered, marcellated crest of her hair. *His* hair. Sassy had trouble thinking of him in the masculine gender. He put her off-balance altogether, worse than meeting somebody you couldn't tell *which* it was, and silently but viciously she wished misfortune upon his metallic-sculpted coif; just once she wanted to see Racquel's hair *move*.

"Woman, yourself," Sassy grumped.

Racquel seemed suddenly affected by a nervous twitch under his oh-so-tweezed eyebrow. "Um, talk with you outside?"

"Whatever."

Out on the mezzanine, Sassy said to him, "Will you do something for me, *sir*?"

"Shhhh!" Sotto voce, he said, "If you keep quiet about me, yes, sure I will."

Sassy was by no means sure she should keep quiet. Ever since she had found out about him, her Sunday-school upbringing had been crimping her gut muscles. She eyed him suspiciously. "Maybe I shouldn't. Women go into your changing rooms—"

"If I'd gone to medical school, I'd see a lot more."

"But women know when their doctor's a man. They think you're—"

"Shhhh!"

Sassy lowered her voice slightly. "They think you're a woman, you hand things in to them—"

"I don't. My staff takes care of fittings." Hands hovering in the vicinity of his twin-peaked bosom, he twisted his rings— moonstone, sapphire, amethyst. His fingers were long, strong-looking, and his perfect mauve-enameled nails were decorated with tiny electric-pink primroses with glued-on faux-gem centers. "Anyway, I don't care about seeing women in their bras or any of that."

"You don't?" Sassy put a freight load of doubt in her tone.

"No. I don't. I just—I just like—"

"Uh-huh. I know. Fancy feathers."

"Don't get so damn superior." For the first time some edge crept into his low-spoken tone. "You're a cross-dresser yourself."

"I am not!"

"Yes, you are." He jerked his chin at her; his hair and the rest of him did not move. "You're wearing slacks."

"That's not—"

"Yes, it is. It's cross-dressing. If it's no problem for a woman to put on pants, then why is it such a big deal for a man to put on a skirt?"

Sassy had no idea. "Uh," she hedged, "uh, but, I'm not masquerading—"

"I *have* to. If people wouldn't get so *hysterical*," Racquel grumbled, "I could *go* in the men's room."

This debate was making Sassy feel a bit dizzy. Stress. Just let it go, she decided. Perhaps for the worst reason, because she wanted his help, Sassy found herself believing Racquel. He was gay, she told herself. He wasn't attracted to women. He wasn't going around with a happy dick under that dress. Okay. Whatever. "All right," she grumbled, "okay, fine. I'm a cross-dresser too. Here's what I need you to do." She explained it to him.

"Are you crazy?" he exclaimed.

Not for the first time, Sassy considered this issue. "Possibly. I'm not sure."

"*Why* do you so badly need to capture this parakeet?"

"That's my business."

His metallic-mauve-shadowed eyes widened. "You're not out for revenge, are you? You're not going to *poop* on it or something?"

"Just never mind. Are you going to help me, or do I go to Silly Willy?" This was the self-deluded boss man whom Sassy had seen reflected in a mirror as a lyrebird.

Racquel's broad shoulders sagged. Plaintively he asked, "May I at least go home and change first?"

"Please *do*."

Sassy felt her position of power over another human being hanging unfamiliar and exhilarating in her chest as she leaned on the mezzanine railing and waited for Racquel to return. Blankly staring, she was not really watching for the parakeet, not yet—but there it was. Perched in the nearest tree. Staring back at her.

It had a brilliant yellow head with an orange mask over the eyes. A green body with blue primaries on the wings. A bright yellow butt. A few yellow markings on its long pointed tail. No striations. None of the usual teardrop mottlings around the throat. It looked like a parakeet—no-necked, big-headed, high-browed yet clownish—but its coloration and markings were nothing like those of any of the parakeets in any of Sassy's books.

Of course, with all the new variations the breeders kept coming up with, this was understandable. "Some sort of sport, are you?" Sassy queried it.

The parakeet gazed back at her.

She was not expecting a response. Her questions were rhetorical. "You really are watching me, aren't you? I mean me specifically. You're hanging around me."

The parakeet cocked its head. Perhaps it chirped at her. In the echoing atrium, it was hard to tell.

"You're *stalking* me," she told it. "That's not *nice*."

The parakeet shifted uncomfortably on its perch. Its dainty vermicular toes, Sassy noticed, were mauve, like Racquel's makeup.

"You *did* mess up my reflection, didn't you?"

The parakeet dropped its gaze, looking down and to one side.

"I think you understand every word I'm saying," she told the bird. "You and I need to talk."

"It's not going to move until daybreak," Racquel complained to Sassy. "We might as well go home."

Perched opposite the fifth-floor balcony from which they watched, the parakeet made a hunched silhouette against the dimmed, midnight decorator lighting: with its head facing its tail and its beak tucked between its wings, it slept.

Even though it didn't move, Sassy watched it intently. "How do they *do* that?" she muttered.

"What? Sleep standing up?"

"Crank the head around 180 degrees." Effortlessly. And sleep that way.

"I was watching a robin one time," Racquel said, a droll quirk in his voice, "just kind of watching it hop around, and I said to myself, How does that thing get around on only two legs?"

Sassy laughed. She was trying to maintain a brisk and businesslike stance toward Racquel but she couldn't help it; she had to laugh. Get around on two legs, indeed. And there he stood in platform clogs. Fuchsia open-toed platform clogs with gold-braid trim. And gold-braided scarlet toreador pants. And a scarlet bolero. Racquel's idea of changing his clothes for a covert operation did not seem to include either practicality or subterfuge.

"They're going to wonder what we're doing if we keep standing here," Racquel said. "We might as well go home—"

"They wouldn't notice us at all if you weren't dressed like a road flare!"

"They would too. They'd spot the glare off your glasses a mile away."

"Not as bright as that getup!"

"What did you want me to wear," Racquel complained, "a chador?"

"You could have come as yourself and nobody would know who you were."

"Huh?" In general, Racquel seemed like a genuinely easygoing—guy or whatever, but now he became somewhat wrought. "*Huh?* What did you say?"

"I said, just come as yourself."

"To *what* self do you refer?"

"Oh, never mind. Wear whatever you like. Wear a bellydancing outfit," Sassy grumbled, "made of feathers."

Racquel stared at her, his expression smoothing. "You know," he said slowly, "that's not a bad idea."

Sassy rolled her eyes.

"You really don't want to go home and get some sleep?"

"No." There was a downhill dynamic to these things, Sassy knew from years of sour experience. Go home, go to sleep, and set the alarm clock for four in the morning to get back to the hotel lobby. And then oversleep? And then rush around like— no, thank you. "I'm staying. I don't know when the Pest Control people might show up."

"You still haven't explained to me why you're so fanatical about rescuing this parakeet."

Sassy stared straight at the bird in question and said nothing.

"Well, listen. If we *must* hang around, we could go into the shop for a while."

Not a bad idea. It would get them out of management's sight, yet keep them close to where Sassy wanted to be. "Okay."

Racquel led the way, and trailing behind him, Sassy watched his hornbill flap along beside him in the mezzanine mirrors. Odd. Maybe it was because she had never been in the hotel at such a shadowy time before—but in the darkly gleaming glass she seemed to see, not mirror-image mezzanine behind the hornbill, but forest. She glimpsed the plumy movement of foliage, the snaky outlines of vines in the shadows, the silhouettes of unknowable flowers folded for the night. She could almost hear the rustling of ten-foot ferns, the breathing of trees, the silences and echoing cries of night birds. Her chest yearned. She wanted to be there.

Then she blinked, and her sleepy mind woke up in alarm. What was she thinking? What did she imagine she was seeing? She looked again, and saw the reflection of ficus-on-steroids trees.

Racquel led her through a service door into the labyrinthine, windowless, and blessedly mirrorless guts of the hotel, the gray cinder-block corridors employees used but of which guests were seldom aware. When they reached a steel door marked PLUMAGE, Racquel unlocked it and motioned Sassy in. He did not turn on the lights.

Dim, the shop felt larger than it was. Deep, like—like a forest again. Feather capes and boas hung like willow leaves, swaying in the breeze of Sassy's passing. She liked the way they responded to her, almost as if they were alive.

She breathed deeply of their dry spicy scent and sank into the leather chair where patient husbands were supposed to wait. Her feet were tired after a long day, even though she wore silicone-padded uglishoes to clean. Racquel, however, who wore four-inch heels all day, did not sit down, but roamed the shop with hands lifted like wings, his long fingers questing. He plucked a teal derby from the hat stand, strode over and plopped the topper on Sassy. He crouched in front of her and adjusted it at a coy angle.

"Fetching," he said. "Very fetching. Look at that little pointed chin. You have a face born for hats, Sassy."

He brought a feathered pillbox and tried it on her instead of the derby.

"No," he murmured, "you're more of a farouche type."

He went off again and returned with a highland bonnet trailing pheasant feathers. He crouched and settled it gently on her.

"Oh, that's *charmante. Très charmante.* Come look in a mirror, Sassy."

She shook her head, her chest aching. Drat, she loved hats; why had it been so long since she had bought a hat? But she knew she would see nothing in the mirror except a blue parakeet.

"Why not? Don't you like it?"

"I'm tired. *You* try on hats."

"Can't. That's the only thing I don't like about my look. I can't wear hats."

"Because of all the hair?"

"Yes, because of all the hair." He removed the pseudo-Scottish bonnet and returned with a plumed picture hat worthy of a Renoir. Sassy loved it. She couldn't help leaning forward to accommodate the brim as Racquel placed it on her head, precisely adjusted the angle, and tied the silky ribbon—robin's-egg blue—in a butterfly bow under her chin.

"Oh, that's *it*. You *have* to look, Sassy. Wait. A shawl—"

"No." She started untying the hat to take it off. Racquel crouched in front of her, peering at her.

"Sassy, lighten up," he said gently. "Didn't you ever play dress-up as a kid?"

"Not with a transsexual!" Thrusting the hat back at him, trying to stop this game that was causing her pain, she spoke more harshly than she had intended.

"Transvestite," Racquel said.

"Whatever."

He settled back on his fuchsia heels and gave her a hard stare. "I really irk the hell out of you, don't I? What bugs you more, that I'm a transvestite or that I'm black?"

Sassy was tired, stressed, and in no mood for self-improvement. She snapped, "Actually, what bothers me most is that your hair never doggone moves."

His eyes opened wide, and so did his mouth, and a yawp came out, then rich contralto laughter. "Sassy," he said, and he toppled off his cork-soled clogs, sitting on the floor, laughing some more.

Because he was laughing at her and because he hadn't taken

the picture hat from her, she plopped it on top of his do, where it teetered, its white plumes bobbing and its pastel ribbons curling down over his boleroed shoulders. Sassy seldom laughed out loud, but she had to smile.

"Oh, my sweet black ass." Still chuckling, placidly accepting of his clownish appearance in the hat, Racquel heaved himself up from the floor, stooped over Sassy and combed her limp hair with his fingers. With one hand on either side of her face he lifted her hair into stubby wings, trying to fluff it. He crouched in front of her and removed her glasses, studying her face. He set the glasses aside and smoothed her hair down again.

The feel of his careful hands on her head was heavenly. Sassy sat still, but said, "Racquel, it's no use."

"White woman's hair? It's bad, all right, but it's not quite hopeless. My stylist—"

"It's not just the hair. It's everything."

Still gentling her hair, Racquel asked, "Everything?"

"Everything about me. My hair. My wrinkly face. My pudgy little body. I've got nothing going for me. I'm almost fifty years old, I've been married more than half my life to a man who didn't love me, and now it's too late. Nobody's ever going to want me."

Racquel stroked her hair into place. "Huh," he said softly. "We'll see. We'll just see about that."

"Hey," Racquel said to Sassy as both of them leaned on the mezzanine railing watching dawn turn the atrium glass the colors of mother-of-pearl.

"Hey, what?"

"Hey, I just had a brain spasm. Almost a brain orgasm."

"Lovely."

"About your name. Like, trees are just plants and we name people after some plants, why not other plants? I mean, we name people Rose, Violet, Daisy, Jasmine, Rosemary, Heather—why not Wisteria? Or Dogwood? Or—"

"Or Sassafras, is that the idea?"

"Yes! Why does it always have to be flower names? And why does it always have to be women named after the flowers, not men? I mean, if I had a baby boy, I shouldn't have to just name him Oak or Spruce, I could name him Tulip, or Bud, or Clematis, Clem for short, why not? Why—"

"Shhh!" Sassy hushed him, clutching at his arm.

The parakeet was flying.

Like a green-yellow spark in the creamy dawnlight it flashed up from its treetop—straight into one of the mist nets.

"Ninth floor," said Sassy rapidly, counting up to the balcony to which the end of the net was attached, seeing the parakeet flutter, struggle, thrash itself into a lump of gossamer mesh. "Quick, you run over to the other end and undo it." She darted toward the elevator.

"How come *I* get to run to the other end?" Racquel grumbled.

"Just do it!"

When she reached her end of the net, she could see the parakeet more closely. Still struggling. Tangled nearly into a ball.

"Poor thing," she muttered, feeling a pang in her heart. She knew all too well what it was like to feel entangled, trapped.

The parakeet fluttered once more, then settled into a frozen, panting panic. Too terrified to move. Sassy had heard that small animals were likely to die of shock when they were caught in traps. Mice rescued from cats would still die of shock. "Hurry," she whispered to Racquel, who could not possibly hear her.

There she was—there *he* was, finally, on the far side of the atrium.

Sassy had expected that Racquel would undo the fastenings that secured the net to the far balcony. But evidently Racquel had other ideas. Racquel flourished a massive pair of shears and simply cut the thing loose.

"Whoa!" Sassy grabbed at her end as the net swung down, down—

Its trailing tendrils caught in the treetops. "Oh, no," Sassy moaned, pulling in yards of net which piled like froth at her feet. The bird formed a small, still lump in the cobwebby mesh about ten feet away from Sassy when the net went taut.

So near and yet so far. "Come on, would you!" Sassy tugged, braced her feet against the railing and tugged harder, tugged with all her five-foot-five-inches' worth of strength.

It was not nearly enough.

"They make these things out of fish line or something." Like an unlikely angel, Racquel was there, reaching over her shoulder to grab a double fistful of net. "On the count of three. One—two—"

Three. They both pulled at the net.

It did not tear loose, exactly. Rather, it tried to tear up the tree by the roots, and the tree made some sacrifices to save itself. Leaves stripped, twigs gave way, and the net was free.

Racquel stood back and let Sassy gather in the parakeet.

"Oh, poor baby," she whispered. Even through the wad of netting in which it was enmeshed she could feel it trembling. "Oh, poor sweetie." Sitting on the carpet with the bird in her lap, she began to pick at the netting, uncovering the bird's head. It stared at her with eyes that had gone silver with shock. "Hang on, honey child," she murmured. "Just hang on a couple of minutes—"

"Oh, for God's sake, we don't have a couple of minutes. Security's probably already on the way." Racquel crouched and took the Gordian knot approach, slicing into the net with his shears, cutting the wad of string and bird away from the rest of it. "Come on." He ran toward the nearest service entry.

A few minutes later they were in the back room of his shop, where Sassy sat on a cardboard carton and carefully, oh so carefully untangled the bird in her lap.

She smoothed its wings and held them gently against its body as she freed them, but the parakeet seemed to have no desire to struggle against her or fly away. When she had untangled its tail and, last of all, its delicate legs and feet, it stopped trembling. It nestled in the cup of her hands as she held it against her flat chest. So low that she could barely hear it, it chirped.

"I think that bird is grateful to you," Racquel said.

"I'm grateful to *you*," Sassy said humbly. "Thank you. I wouldn't have been able to—"

"No problem. Hey, stay up all night with a crazy woman, destroy property, risk my sole source of income, why not?"

"Look, don't ever let me blackmail you again. I won't tell anybody about you. I promise."

"Hey." Racquel grinned.

Sassy smiled back and stroked the parakeet. She liked the feel of its smooth feathers, its lightweight warmth against her chest.

"What now?" Racquel asked. "You going to take that bird home?"

"I guess so." It seemed like the logical next step. Insofar as anything about her situation could be called logical.

"You want a box?" Racquel began to poke around his back room, looking for one.

With the parakeet cuddled to her chest, Sassy wandered out

into the shop. With no lights on, but with the early daylight filtering in through the display windows, it was a place of platinum shadow, a tarnished-silver mystery in which feathers fluttered and rustled like living presences whispering.

A thought occurred to Sassy. "Racquel," she called.

"Yo." He appeared with a smallish cardboard box in hand.

It had been a long night of waiting, with plenty of time to talk. After all that talking, Sassy found to her surprise that she trusted this weirdo more than anybody else she knew.

That was just it. He was a weirdo. He was unlikely to pass any judgments on *her*.

She said, "Racquel, do me a favor." As if she had not asked enough of him already. "Look at me in the mirror and tell me what you see."

"Huh?"

"It's too hard to explain. It won't take a minute. Just look." Stroking the parakeet nestled against her chest, Sassy walked a few steps to stand in front of one of PLUMAGE's floor-to-ceiling mirrors.

She gasped.

A resplendent ten-foot winged presence, an angel—no, a great eagle made of thunderstorm—no, a plumy winged tree with a serpent of lightning in its branches and the face of a— God, Sassy couldn't say what it was, its wings and feathering all colors of fire and cloud and rainbow, she was shaking too hard to speak or think, and its featherleaf hands reached toward her and its eyes blazed like ten thousand sunrises and— it called to her, a great melodious cry—

In answer to its cry the parakeet in her arms turned and yearned toward the mirror, gave a wild screech and took wing as if flying to a long-lost love. But somehow Sassy had not let go, and she flew too. Faintly she heard Racquel call, "Sassy!"

but it didn't matter. The bird-presence's sunrise eyes offered to take her in, the parakeet's flying carried her toward them as if on a river of light, and she did not understand what was happening or where she was going but it was all right. Nothing in her entire life had ever felt so right.

Then she felt Racquel grab her arms.

That strong grip stopped her like hitting the end of her bungee. There was a slingshot effect, and the parakeet flew loose from her hands, and everything was confusion. She struggled, thumped down, and found herself sitting on the floor of Racquel's shop still facing the mirror. But there was nothing in it except her blue budgie. It looked distraught.

"What—" Sassy gasped.

"You were heading right into the mirror." Standing over her as if to grab her again if necessary, Racquel sounded stupefied.

"What—did you see it?"

"See what? I saw you dive into the mirror. *Into* it!" Racquel's tone had not changed.

"I wanted to," Sassy murmured, staring without moving.

"You half disappeared. How did you *do* that?"

"I wanted to." Sassy struggled to her feet. "Where's my parakeet?"

"Good God, like I care about your parakeet?"

"Where is it?"

Racquel didn't answer, but Sassy knew the answer.

"In there, right?" She pointed at the mirror.

Whatever "in there" meant.

Racquel took a deep breath. Putting wide pauses between the words, he said, "I—want—to—go—home—now—please."

When in doubt, sleep. Sassy went home and slept as if she had been knocked on the head.

 **F O U R**

$\int$ assy, being Sassy, took her perplexity to the library, bypassing the main reading room, now given over to videos, and finding haven in the reference section, where books reigned. Into the computer she entered:

SUBJECT: MIRRORS.
Subject not found.
SUBJECT: REFLECTIONS.
Subject not found.

For a fleeting but furious moment, Sassy longed for a real card catalog. Lacking that, she took to the nonfiction stacks. "Subject not found, indeed," she muttered as she eventually located *Joy of Mirrors* in the home-decoration section. An hour's further trolling turned up chapters on mirrors in *Ghosts, Fetches and Ghouls, Jung for Dummies*, and *Everyday Magic*.

"Last week it was birds," said the laterally challenged woman at the desk, bemused by this selection.

"It still is, kind of."

"I heard there's a lady in the high-rises has fifty birds in her apartment."

"Mm," Sassy said, and she took her books home. Over the next several hours she learned that glass mirrors first appeared in Venice in the thirteenth century. She learned that mirrors were used for divination. She learned that mirrors were sewn on clothing to turn away the evil eye. She learned more than she ever wanted to know about Snow White, Alice Through the Looking Glass, and Narcissus. She learned that, to the Greeks, a dream of seeing one's reflection in water was an omen of death. She learned that all over the world folk were afraid of reflections and mirrors; the reflection was considered to be the disembodied soul, and could be stolen. She was reminded that a broken mirror is bad luck, that mirrors in a sickroom should be covered or turned to the wall, and that if you look too long in a mirror you're likely to see the Candyman, the Devil, or your husband-to-be, depending on your choice of superstition.

"Same thing," Sassy muttered.

She learned nothing, however, that enlightened her regarding her own situation. After she was finished reading, she went into the bathroom, pulled down the blind, and stared at the darkened mirror for some time. But only her beady-eyed blue budgie stared back at her.

The minute Racquel saw Sassy set foot on the mezzanine, he ducked into an empty fitting room and stayed there. Racquel had made up his mind that he was going to have nothing further to do with Sassy. That woman was just too weird.

The PLUMAGE fitting rooms were top of the line, as befit a classy boutique; they had real doors that locked, and they were not a whole lot smaller than some people's apartments, and they were carpeted. No pins in the carpeting, either.

While he was waiting for Sassy to go away, Racquel kicked off his shoes, then checked his look in the full-length mirror, then put on the red velvet/gold kidskin ankle-strap heels again and checked some more. He loved ankle-strap pumps, twenties-style. He loved the Big Babe Hollywood look. Rita Hayworth, Jayne Mansfield, Hedy Lamarr. Drop-dead glamour. When he was a kid living in the ugliest block in the city he had loved his mama's Sunday dresses and hats, by far the bitchin'est thing in the house or the nabe. He still thought Mama had great taste though he hardly ever saw her anymore. He wished she would come in and shop sometime; he would give her a great discount. Maybe the best thing about having his own shop was that he could get really quality plumage wholesale. Today he had on the gold spiral earbobs with cockatiel danglies, the gold lamé slit sheath with cardinal-wing capelet just covering the shoulders, the gold-and-scarlet quilled—

Somebody knocked at the door.

"I'm not here," Racquel said, assuming it was one of his "associates" with a stupid question about money or something. Dumb girls, when would they ever learn to think for themselves?

"Racquel," said Sassy's plangent voice.

Oh God. The woman had the nose of a terrier. She'd tracked him down.

"Go away," he said.

"Racquel? I need to ask you something, please."

"Whatever it is, the answer is *no*."

"Racquel—"

"Go *away*."

Sassy's tone developed a deckle edge. "May I remind you that I could tell certain things about you—"

"You said you weren't going to do that anymore!"

A long pause. Then in a very soft voice Sassy said, "Oh. That's right, I did."

Such was the pathos in Sassy's murmur that it made Racquel open the door and stomp out. "*What* is it this time?" Looking down on Sassy, Racquel scowled at Sassy's limp hair. Gray. No, kind of taupe. The color of a squirrel, for God's sake. It figured. Racquel had never met a squirrelier person in his life.

"I need to ask you a favor," Sassy said meekly to Racquel's chest.

"I *know* that! Spit it out!"

Sassy explained her request. Thank God the woman had the sense to keep her voice down so the staff wouldn't hear. Racquel stiffened as he listened. When Sassy had finished, Racquel burst out, "Why *here*?"

"I've tried all kinds of other mirrors. They don't work."

Fervidly Racquel hoped it didn't work here either. "Look," he said, "what I thought I saw—it must have been because I'd been up all night. You get tired enough, you hallucinate, you know?"

"No," Sassy said.

"That parakeet's long gone. Probably zipped under the ceiling tiles or into the ventwork or something. Probably dead by now."

Sassy gave him an opaque look that contradicted him more clearly than words.

He could feel his jaw begin to tighten with frustration and subliminal fear. He could *not* have seen what he had seen and she could not be asking what she was asking; it wobbled all sense, all logic, all sanity. He burst out, "Would you *please* explain to me what it is with you and that parakeet?"

Sassy considered, then shook her head. "No."

"Woman, you owe me a hint at least. What's the deal? Did the bird swallow the Hope diamond or something?"

"No, not the Hope diamond," Sassy said with just a hint of a smile.

Racquel was later to learn that when Sassy got that Mona Lisa look on her face it meant that Sassy was putting him on. But he didn't know that yet. He concluded that, okay, he was indeed in the middle of some sort of a warped Nancy Drew mystery, and yes, the parakeet did convey something of great value in its little birdy gut.

He gave a hefty sigh. "Okay, whatever," he grumbled. "If it works, at least I'll be rid of you. Tonight?"

Sassy looked thanks at him, her hazel eyes appearing huge, childlike, behind those industrial-strength glasses of hers. "Yes. Tonight."

Not knowing what to expect, Sassy dressed in layers—T-shirt, sweatshirt, windbreaker, shorts under her sweatpants—and wore her most comfortable shoes. She carried two tote bags tightly packed with basics: graham crackers, peppermints, Deep Woods Off, bread, store brand sharp yellow cheddar cheese, deodorant, granola bars, socks and undies, peanut butter, knife, ibuprofen, Kleenex, a spray of millet with which she hoped to entice the parakeet (all the books said they loved millet), wallet/money/credit cards, Boku Seven Fruit juice in the box, plastic tablecloth by the way of a tarp, Peterson Field Guide.

Although it was eleven at night when she arrived at PLUMAGE, Racquel awaited her still dressed in that same awful gold dress with dead red birds on the shoulders, and those same vampish red shoes. How he could bear to wear that monkey suit and those stiletto heels a moment longer than he had to, Sassy would never understand.

"I *love* your luggage," Racquel said, eyeing her tote bags.

Sassy refused to acknowledge the sarcasm. "Thank you." She brushed past him and headed for the mirror.

The shop spread around her hushed and shadowy, as before. The feathered collars and capes rustled and whispered as before. She stood in front of the same dimly glimmering mirror as before.

Only her blue budgie looked back at her out of the dark glass. Stupid bird. Sassy was starting to think that maybe she ought to give it a name. Hold a mirror up for it to look at and see if it would chirp. Teach it to talk or something.

She sighed and set her bags on the floor; it didn't look as if she'd be going anywhere real soon. Of course it couldn't be simple; why should anything be simple? Maybe it depended on the phase of the moon or something. Maybe it was because of menopause, or something she ate.

Maybe she'd imagined the whole thing, like Racquel wanted to believe. Maybe she was crazy.

No. There was a blue parakeet looking back at her—

Even crazier. Racquel was right. He—

But he had never answered her question, that other time. "Racquel," she asked him again, "what do you see in the mirror?"

"What do you mean?" He slouched closer, his handsome brown face expressively blank. He seemed to be in a sour mood this evening.

"Just tell me. What do you see?"

"I see you, backwards. What the hell should I see?"

But Sassy barely heard him, for in the dark depths of the

glass something swirled—Sassy gasped. It was not a resplendent presence this time, just an intimation, a movement, something lifting into flight between feathery trees, a long flow of hair or mantle or pinion, a comely head turning away. Something about that starlit glimpse made Sassy yearn as if for eternal love. She cried out and lunged after it, hands outstretched, fingers questing.

She dived into the mirror as if into a pool of limpid water, and like water, the mirror closed behind her.

Perched silent, unable to sing, too dejected even to search for food, Kleet contemplated his utter failure. For a short while there had been shreds of hope. But he had left hope behind in the hardair world.

That strange, shining world—he had gone there questing for a mate but had found her not. Instead, he had flown into love of a different sort, he had found Deity—but a wrathful deity who had tested him almost beyond endurance. A deity who had driven him away from the joy of her presence until the fell day when the captive air had turned to mist-vine and entangled him in its meshes.

Then, that hawkbeak day, she had come to his aid. She had rescued him and nested him in her warm branches. With her holy twigs she had smoothed his ragged feathers. She had sung to him. She, Deity.

And he had thought his trials were over.

But then somehow—the One Tree . . .

It was the One Tree he had seen in the oval pool of hard air. And he had left his newfound deity and flown to the One Tree; he could not do otherwise.

Nothing less could have cozened him away from her.

Yet it was nothing. Some strange beckoning, that was all. And here he was, home again, but alone.

Sassy landed on something soft, started to scramble to her feet, then sank back onto her butt and just gawked.

Her first thought was *glory, glory*, before her stuttering mind could find the word for which it was searching: *forest*. Between trees that towered out of sight amid cloud, spokes of lambent light sifted down, not quite reaching the ground. Sunlight? Sassy's mind stammered some more; wasn't it supposed to be night? But she couldn't think; treetops and sunlight rang with wild cries she could not identify, and she gaped up at a vast confusion, gold, green, bright, dark—she could take it in only a bit at a time. A scarlet spike unfurling from a mossy bole. Barbaric jade-green swordblades. Purple-green swags trailing fringes of—liana, grape, ivy? Celadon filigree balls far over-head—mistletoe? Sassy glimpsed flits of shimmer and move-ment everywhere, yellow, orange, azure—but when she looked to see what they were—efts, birds, butterflies?—she saw only misty greengolden glow, heard only the echoing flutelike calls of what might have been birds or—or fetches or some eerie spirit that lived in mirrors. And the trees, so soaring—surely any or every one of them must have been the world tree, the arbor vitae, the tree of the knowledge of good and evil.

"Eden," Sassy whispered. "Paradise lost."

But where—where was the bird-being she had glimpsed in the mirror? And *what* was it? An angel with a flaming sword? And how in the name of heaven . . . where was she to find her parakeet in all this?

Or her lost soul?

The magnitude of what she faced made Sassy sag back and

just lie there on the moss—it was no wonder she had landed on moss, for moss grew shaggy everywhere in the twilight under the trees, on the ground, on boulders and boles and roots that swelled and knotted like muscles. Sassy lay amid moss and ghostly, nodding white plants like Irish clay pipes, and glossy lavender mushrooms, and shoots putting up translucent leaves. Saplings grew whip-thin, yearning toward the distant light, probably doomed to die. It was a shadowland down here, far beneath the paradise up above. Sassy grew aware of a babbling sound—running water somewhere, and also her mind. *Lost,* her mind dithered, *lost scared wet hungry*

"Hush." Sassy got up, comforted herself with the thought of graham crackers, and turned around to pick up her bags. They were of course not there. There was nothing there but moss and more mushrooms, Spam-pink this time. She had left her totes on the floor in PLUMAGE, probably five feet away but it might as well be—

Forever, bleated her brain.

"Hush!" At least there was water. And the water prompted Sassy to put a mundane name to the place so she wouldn't be so scared. "It's *just* a rain forest," she told herself sternly.

Except it wasn't. Sassy had read enough books on rain forests to know that it wasn't. The towering, vine-draped trees made her think of such a primal jungle, but this eden was sweetly cool, not hot or humid or rife with bugs. Some of the immense tree trunks vanished upward into a green so deep it seemed almost black—galaxies of needles. They were conifers of some sort—redwoods? Sequoias? And what about the mistletoe? And what would English ivy be doing in a rain forest?

A black-and-lavender butterfly the size of a robin bobbed by like a Muppet. A misty-gray moth the size of what Sassy considered a normal butterfly fluttered up. Then, from somewhere above, a foot-long pinion the color of dawn floated down, spiraling on the air like maple wings. Within arm's reach in front of Sassy it halted, hovering four feet above the ground, then wheeled so that its shaft pointed away from her.

Sassy gawked at the feather behaving in defiance of gravity. Then, simply because it was beautiful, she reached for it.

The feather scooted just beyond her grasp, then stopped again.

It was silvergold tea rose whisper tawny pink and lustered like nacre. Sassy stepped forward and lifted her hand, but her fingers hovered like the feather; caution had kicked in. What sort of uncanny thing was this? And what might it do to her if she touched it?

The shimmering pinion wheeled toward her, then turned away again, pointing about twenty degrees to the right.

"Am I, uh, am I supposed to follow?" Sassy asked—rhetorically, of course. She was one of those middle-aged women who talked to herself, even in the supermarket.

The feather, however, seemed to hear her. It jiggled encouragement, nodded like a horse, and led off.

"Now wait a minute!" It seemed to Sassy that she ought to take time to think about this. Come up with a plan. Formulate some options.

The feather paused where it was and bobbed on the air like the blip on the monitor of somebody working up to a heart attack.

"Um, okay, okay!" Options, what options? Sassy swallowed hard, swallowing her dithers, and walked after it.

"Look," Racquel told the police detective, "I just know her to have coffee with her."

"Ma'am, that's not what the other maids said." The cop was a no-neck flat-faced man who spoke with a ponderous show of respect but probably knew that any self-respecting woman hates to be called "ma'am." Racquel, of course, knew himself not to be a self-respecting woman and he was trying not to sweat or let fear show in his face or his taut body. The shaky hands were the hardest to control. Damn, he was scared. What might happen to him if he got taken in, searched, what might happen if he went to jail . . . no. Don't think about it.

". . . hung around with you a lot," the police officer was saying.

"For God's sake," Racquel said, "maybe she just went away for a few days."

"For nine days so far? Without calling in to work? Without stopping her mail or canceling her dental appointment? Without telling her landlady, without telling anybody? Did she tell you she was going on a trip?"

Racquel did not answer. He did not know what to answer. It seemed out of the question to try to explain to the officer that Sassy had gone on a little jaunt through the mirror after a stray parakeet.

"On a trip, you think? With two tote bags? Which is what she was carrying when she was last seen, heading in here." The policeman paused to slowly scan PLUMAGE's racks of feather-trimmed gowns with half-lidded eyes, showing no expression. "At 11 P.M. of the evening of February 27," he resumed.

"I wouldn't know," Racquel said.

"I think you do." The cop suddenly looked him straight in the face, and Racquel could not help flinching. "Aren't you usually closed at that time of night?"

"Usually. Maybe I stayed late—"

"Yeah, yeah, to do the books or something. I think I'll have a look around, if that's quite all right with you."

"It's not all right. Do you have a warrant?"

"This shop is open to the public, ma'am. I don't need a warrant." The cop headed for the back room.

"If you stay in the public area." Racquel didn't know why he was arguing. His black-boy upbringing was kicking in, making him mad, making him stupid.

"I can come back with a warrant, if you like," the cop said. "For your arrest."

It probably wasn't true. But the possibility that it was made Racquel sweat, he couldn't think of what to say, and the cop was already through the door into the office/storage area, where Racquel had stowed Sassy's tote bags, figuring she'd be back for them sometime. Hoping she'd be back. Kind of worried about her, but couldn't think of anything he could do about it.

The cop had already found the totes as Racquel strode in. Racquel perched on the edge of the desk so as not to squash his bustle, glad he was wearing his crimson shantung with the cutaway back and the hackle-trimmed band collar; hackles always gave him confidence, and he knew his bare shoulder blades made him look sexy. He watched the policeman kneel and root through the totes, find Sassy's wallet, look in it for ID and grunt with satisfaction as he stood up.

"Still say she wasn't here?" he asked, shooting a hard look at Racquel.

"I just said I wouldn't know."

"And I said I think you do know. I think you better come down to the station with me."

Racquel crossed his legs to draw attention to his gold strappy sandals with escargot heels and shook his head, making sure it was tilted at an attractive angle. Playing it as dumb-blonde as he could considering that he was six feet tall and black. "Sorry, Officer, I can't. I have things to do here."

"You don't seem to understand, ma'am." The cop lowered his head like a charging bull but spoke patiently. "I'm taking you in for questioning. Get your coat."

"I don't have to go unless you're arresting me, do I? And if you're arresting me, I want a lawyer."

The police officer stared at him. The police officer took a long breath and let it out again. "You refuse to cooperate?"

"I'm cooperating! I just told you, I have things to do, you know? I have to get the payroll together. Get some orders off. Clothes don't just stock *themselves*, you know?"

The police officer stared at him. Racquel lowered his false eyelashes to half-mast.

"I'll be back," the cop said. He swaggered out.

Racquel sent his employees home and locked up. Ten minutes after the cop had left, Racquel stood in front of the mirror via which Sassy had made her inexplicable exit, venting his feelings in expletives.

"*Jesus* jumping on the water, what a mess!"

He clicked at the mirror with his enameled fingernails, finding it glassily unyielding. He pushed at it with his palms. He glared at his reflection, noticing that he had chewed off his lipstick and his lips looked like a hamburger bun. This was no time to worry about fixing them. "Mirror, you gotta let me in," he said.

He frowned, then tentatively launched himself at the mirror. His forehead impacted it painfully. He stood back, rubbing it.

"Mirror, come on! I gotta get her back and keep my lovin' tuckus out of jail."

He tried going in hands first and broke a nail. He swore some more.

"Mirror, what's the matter with you? You want the lights off, is that it?"

He tried it with the lights off. He tried to step in, sidle in, dive in. He tried coaxing the mirror and kissing it. He tried threatening to break it, and he would have followed through on the threat except—then what?

He passed from desperation into sweating frustration into despondency. When he reached despair he said, "Damn you," turned his back on the unresponsive mirror, leaned against it, tilted his head back and closed his eyes to think.

As if pushed off the edge of a swimming pool he fell backward into an alternate lucidity.

With a lump in her throat, Sassy gazed up a misty green ravine at a waterfall so ravishing it made her think of drowning herself in its sunbow beauty. Spray bathed her face like tears.

Then, mingled with the music of the torrent she heard another voice singing, a human voice, a tenor so sweet it brought real tears to her eyes. She shifted her gaze to the pool below the waterfall. There, swirling in the eddies and drifting toward her, floated the face and streaming hair of a handsome young man with his eyes lidded but his mouth wide open in song. Face to the sky, he lay with his head upon a sort of curlicue raft—no, it was a harp, a lyre. Sassy stood rapt in the beauty of his song, although she could not understand the words.

At first she assumed that the rest of him was swimming below the surface. But as he drifted closer, she gasped, for she saw that there was no body.

Still, he was the closest thing to a human being she had yet seen. She hated to interrupt the song, but—"Excuse me," she called to him as he floated past her, "where am I?"

His mouth closed, song cut off, and his eyes opened and gave her a lapis gaze which seemed not to understand.

"What place is this, I mean?"

He spoke something brief in a language which clearly was not English. His eyes closed again as he floated on downstream.

From somewhere far, far above, echoing down as if from a distant star, his song began again, but this time in a young woman's wild soprano voice.

Sassy gasped and gawked up where the crowns of the trees forming a lacy jigsaw limned with turquoise—sky so bright it made Sassy blink. That vast riddle of sky and treetops revealed to her nothing. She saw intimations of cobalt and canary which might have been blossoms or birds or god-sized butter-flies or quirks of sungleam amid the greenery or an angel tak-ing a joyride in a chariot of gold. Anything, anything might have been hidden in that immensity. The voice sang like a rebel angel, like a bird of paradise, like a sunbow forming in the murmur of the cataract, like wind from the stars:

> . . . *what you find in shadowland*
> *depends on what you've lost*
> *wanderers in shadowland*
> *abandoned souls in shadowland*
> *eidolons in shadowland . . .*

Sassy heard no more, although the music continued, for percussion joined in as if God were practicing to be a drummer and was using the earth for his bass. Whomp whomp whomp, and with a snap and rattle of vines and saplings, something massive sprinted out of the shadows. Sassy gasped and stepped back as a huge bird ran past, twice as tall as she was, its legs as thick as city trees. It looked like a pinheaded ostrich on steroids. For a moment she thought she was seeing a dinosaur, a thunder lizard. Then she wasn't sure what she was seeing. Whatever it was, so Godzillan was the reverberation of its footfalls that Sassy was not aware of the drumbeat of galloping hooves until the pursuers swept past, laughing: golden youths in Grecian pleated tunics, riding bare-legged and bareback on their finely profiled steeds, as if a vignette from an amphora had come to life. A knight in shining armor would look like a dump truck by comparison.

But no, he didn't. Here came one now.

> *. . . eidolons in shadowland*
> *glory forest limboland*
> *and who you find*
> *depends on whom you've lost . . .*

The song faded away like a rainbow. The bass drumbeat of an extinct bird's running feet faded; hoof thunder faded into distance. Sassy heard only the murmur of the waterfall and the silvery jingle of spurs as the—no, it wasn't a knight after all. For a moment—why had she thought it was a knight? Because the horse wore a silver-studded breastplate? Whatever. It was a white horse, of course, with a lot of Spanish flashiness about it, and on board was a cowboy in a white Stetson and white fancy-tooled leather chaps.

She stood there in a stunned trance, as if she were watching the mother of all parades; what next? She stared shamelessly. The cowboy halted his head-tossing cayuse and touched his gloved fingers to the brim of his hat.

"How do, little lady?" he drawled with just the right crinkle

of smile she remembered from her childhood days watching
Bonanza. Under the wide brim of that white hat he was a suit-
ably weathered, rugged Marlboro Man of a cowboy, with
maybe a touch of Little Joe Cartwright thrown in.

"I'm uh, I'm fine," Sassy stammered. Was that a lie? No,
not really. She felt fine, preternaturally fine, in this place.
"How are you?"

"Just as fit as a fiddle, ma'am. It sure is a purty day."

Like an overtaxed music box jerking into motion, Sassy's
mind began creakily to function on some practical level, and
she realized that here was a person who spoke English. He.
Spoke. English. Finally, somebody she could ask for directions. She babbled, "Excuse me, but—where am I?"

"Somewhere in the territories, ma'am, near as I can figure."

"Oh. Um—the territories?"

"Humdinger of a woods. Why? You lost?"

If he was speaking English, why could she not understand
him? Why, in the context, did "lost" not seem like the right
word for where she was? She hedged. "Uh, no. I'm looking for
a parakeet."

"A what?"

"A little green bird."

He nodded. "Lots of birds hereabouts."

From somewhere deep in Sassy's TV-Western upbringing
rose the correct response. "Yeh. You might say."

"Sure 'nuff. I'll keep an eye out fer it," he told her. "You
haven't seen hide nor hair of a little lost dogie, have you?"

"No." Knights in shining armor or their American equivalent were supposed to help, drat it, but this one was not helping, in Sassy's opinion. All she wanted was a sense of where she
should go, how she should proceed. "I followed a feather
here," she said, "but—"

"A feather!" His eyes widened. "What feather?"

"Just—just a big shiny feather—" Which had taken a notion to zoom back into the treetops, abandoning her.

The cowboy pushed back his hat and scratched his tawny forelock, gazing at her. "Now I wonder," he said very softly. "They say there's something up there . . ." His gaze shifted to the labyrinth of green overhead. "Something big, with wings. Kind of a manito. A spirit no one dares put a name to. Did you see it?"

"No. I mean, I—I'm not sure."

"They say there's no better luck in the world than seeing it." He turned back to her, peering at her intently. "Except if you can catch a feather. That's even better. Then you ain't lost no more."

This was getting way too deep. What place was this? Limbo? Perdition? Sassy bleated, "All I want is my parakeet!"

"Waal, I'll keep an eye out. Kind of a canary bird, right? Green?"

"Green with a yellow head."

"Sure 'nuff. You take care now, little lady." He touched his hat again and wheeled his Spanish stallion away.

"Wait!" Sassy called after him. "What's your name?"

But without turning or answering he rode away, his saddle making cricket noises, his spurs jingling. And what did it matter whether he had a name, anyway? He was just an eidolon. A cowboy. They were all pretty much interchangeable, in Sassy's experience.

Maybe he even meant to help—but he was not going to. Sassy knew better. Men. The big frauds. Riding into the sunset. Where had all the real cowboys gone?

"Poop!" Sassy cried.

.   .   .

Perched in sweetleaf treeplume, hidden in greenfree that matched his own green coverts, Kleet sensed more than heard the faint cry of his deity. It seemed to come from the shadowland beneath the canopy, but—could it be? Could Deity really be such a nearflight away?

Joy lifted his wings. Instantly he flew, searching.

 **F I V E**

his was a place where unicorns ought to live, Sassy decided. As perhaps they did. Perhaps a unicorn had dipped its magical horn in the water she had drunk from the stream below the cataract, and that was why she felt so peaceful. Wandering, with no feather-with-a-mind-of-its-own to lead her, she ought to have been worrying about dire and pressing agenda items such as Something To Eat and Finding The Damn Parakeet and Getting Back To Her Own World, but instead she stood and watched a vast flock of rosy doves flow through the treetops, a river of wings so deep it darkened the turquoise sky. She watched a horseman ride through the forest, a blond giant who wore chain mail and a midnight-purple mantle and severe golden crown; he lifted his gauntleted hand courteously but did not speak. She saw a tawny streak arc tree to tree—a puma? She saw in a valley a young man of ineffable beauty lying amid moss and ferns with his head in the lap of a young woman even more lovely; they gazed into each other's eyes, and Sassy wanted to cry. He wore a velvet doublet and she wore a silken gown, but afterward Sassy remembered nothing about them clearly except their Romeo-and-Juliet faces. Rapt in the afterglow of their passion, she grew aware that she was wandering uphill and down aimlessly, in cir-

cles most likely, but she did not care. She saw a great stag with
antlers like the lifted hands of a god. She saw two Grecian-
garbed women walking arm in arm, their cameo profiles
turned toward each other. She saw intimations of soaring
mountainside through the trees. And everywhere, glimpses of
bright wings. Everywhere she heard the singing of birds
unseen. And she heard the golden notes of a horn. And something, wolves maybe, baying like bells. And from somewhere, a
thin skein of lute music. And—

"Sassy!"

And—someone calling her name?

"Sas-sy! Where the hell are you?"

Sassy stood with her mouth open, blinking as she attempted
to place the voice she was hearing. A voice from another world.

"SASSY!"

With a wrenching effort, Sassy got her slack mouth shut,
then functioning. "Here," she replied. The vocalization came
out as little more than a whisper.

"*SAS-SY!*"

"*Here!*"

Crashing like a charging buffalo, Racquel ran stumbling
toward her between the trees.

Sassy stood as if in a dream, watching him topple nearer, his
arms flapping. In this place she saw Racquel for a moment not
as Racquel but as another bright mystery, another eidolon.
Bird-man, she thought, admiring his proud black crest gilded
at the apex, his flashing eyes and rich curling hackles, his shimmering crimson—dress, she realized with a jolt, back into her
usual perspective. Racquel wore a tight shiny dress slit up to
his thigh, for crying out loud, and ridiculous strappy gold heels
with his painted toes sticking out, and—what in the Lord's
name was that on his back? He tripped, clung to a tree to stay

upright and swung around—Sassy gasped. The back of that so-called dress was bare practically to his *rump*—Sassy saw a hint of *cleavage* down there, and arising from that very spot, a cascade of feathers that took her breath away, an arcing train of sickle-shaped bronze and vermilion feathers apparently boosted from a rooster, trailing almost to the ground. Racquel was a weird piece of work, but that—that tail was glorious, Sassy admitted to herself with a pang. She would not have minded having that tail, if only to keep in the closet.

Racquel righted himself and limped up to her. "Where the hell have you been!" He did not give her time to answer, however. Evidently in a volatile emotional state, he seized her bodily and slung her over his shoulder. Sassy felt his breast against her thigh, conical and unyielding and unnaturally hard. That breast levered her away from his body like a fulcrum.

"Hey!" Sassy kicked, impacting only air. "Let me down!"

Instead, Racquel swung around and strode off with her, panting, "I am taking no chances."

"Stop it!" Sassy pummeled his bare back. From her vantage on his shoulder she was looking right down his—goodness. She closed her eyes and pounded harder. "What do you think you're *doing*?"

"Run off, will you?" Racquel gasped, stumbling over a root or something. "Leave me holding the bag, land me in jail? That's what I get—"

"Let me down before you drop me on my head!"

Top-heavy and losing his balance in a serious way, he dropped her on her tush, actually, as he fell, landing almost on top of her.

Flat on her back, Sassy had the presence of mind to seize a rock. "You touch me again, I am going to conk you!"

"Fine." Lying with his face in a patch of puce mushrooms,

Racquel went slack and closed his eyes. "Kill me and have it done with."

"What in mercy's name is the matter with you?"

In a tone as if spelling it out to a rather dull child, Racquel said, "The cops think I murdered you."

"What? Why?"

"You're a missing person and they found your stuff—"

"For goodness sake, I've only been gone a few hours!"

Racquel sat up and stared at her. "You've been gone a week and a half!"

"No, I haven't! I just got here!"

This could have gone on for a while, and indeed, Racquel had his mouth in motion, protesting Sassy's alternate reality— but Sassy did not hear him. Her focus attracted by flits of green swooping low, and scarlet, and one of iridescent blue, she gazed past him. Her hand softened, letting go of the rock; her mouth softened with delight.

"I'm not the only one who likes your tail feathers," she told Racquel.

"Huh?" He sat up and looked around. "Oh, for God's sake."

On the tree trunk just above him, two huge woodpeckers clung staring at him. Just beyond the woodpeckers, a large bird with fluffy mauve crest feathers perched on a vine, also fixated on Racquel. Something red green brown orange with laterally trailing tail feathers landed on the ground for a closer look. Sparrow-sized bits of cerise flew down. Something erect and brassy-feathered stalked closer between the trees. In the lowest branches Sassy could see blimpy canary-colored birds peering down, and sleek indigo ones with sweeping violet tail feathers, and—birds beyond remembering, and more gathering every moment, all staring at Racquel. Somewhere above, one of them piped a tentative note, but other than that, they all gazed without speaking. Sassy did not know what kind of bird any of them were. Fiercely she longed for her Peterson.

"What the *hell* is that?"

Racquel referred to the erect, brassy bird, which had stalked right up to him and was glaring into his face. Tautly upright, it stood almost three feet tall and looked as hard as steel, with two-inch hooked claws on its black feet. Racquel scrambled to his feet and backed away from it.

Sassy knew that one, at least. "That's a *cock*," she told Racquel. The kind they used in the cockfights in the bad old days.

"I know that!" Racquel stood brushing dirt off his dress with his hands, his voice rising to a peevish squeal. "I know a cock when I see one!"

"I bet you do." Sassy got up also, noting that the cock's hackles were bristling, maybe in answer to the similar feathers Racquel wore around his neck. "I think we'd better be going."

"That's my whole point! You get your sorry little ass back where it belongs and tell the cops let me alone!"

Although too annoyed to say so, Sassy saw the necessity to do this. Also, she was getting hungry. Graham crackers awaited her on the other side. "Whatever," she grumped. "How do we get there?"

"Um, it's over this way, I think." Racquel led off. The birds followed, except for the cock, which lifted its head, gave a clarion squawk of triumph, and strutted, having won the ground. But the rest of them followed Racquel, swooping and fluttering from tree to tree and more flying in to join them, their many wings siffling like a rising wind. Like a roomful of schoolchildren, once they were in motion, they started to talk. Their excited chattering echoed through the forest.

Sassy had no trouble keeping up with Racquel, for he

minced in his heels and tripped on rocks and roots every second step. She wondered whether he had ever been off a sidewalk in his life, then stopped thinking about him. Ambling along in her sneakers, she gazed at the birds, enthralled, living the green blue yellow of the moment, the whisper of wings and the fragrance of orchids. Sassy could not remember when she had ever felt so alive and at peace. Certainly not since Frederick had left. Every moment in this eden healed her of—

Racquel tripped, fell hard on his hands and knees, and bellowed, "I hate this fucking place! Aaaaa!" He reared back. "Snake!"

Sassy stood appalled not so much by his language as by his sentiments. Like a gold-satin ribbon, the snake flowed away between the ferns, more elegant than any necklace Sassy had ever worn. She could have sworn she saw a jewel, a jacinth, nestled between its eyes.

Racquel stood, his crimson silk skirt torn, his knee bloodied, and all his feathers ruffled. "Would you hurry *up!*" he yelped at Sassy.

"I'm not the one tripping and falling," she told him. "Try taking those stupid shoes off."

"And go *barefoot?*"

"You'd probably be better off."

"I *earned* these Guccis, I ain't taking them off!"

"Calm down," she told him.

"I just want to get bloody *home!*"

"Fine." Although Sassy meant to return to this place the minute she had talked with the cops and collected her graham crackers. "How do we do that?"

"It's around here someplace," Racquel muttered, swiveling to stare in all directions. In the trees, clinging to the boles, and on the ground all around him, more various than any Easter bonnets ever made, a congregation of birds turned their heads in unison to watch him.

"What are you looking for?" Sassy asked.

"The mirror."

"It goes away the minute you're through it."

Racquel gawked at her. "*What?*"

"It turns invisible or something."

He teetered toward her. "So how do we get out of here?"

"That's what I'm asking you."

"You mean *you* don't know?"

"How should I?"

"Oh, bloody God."

"Oh, poop," Sassy muttered.

That otherworld cry echoed through Kleet; his heart beat like butterfly wings, beat so hard that it shivered his breast feathers as he sculled mightily at the air.

Perhaps it had been for her, Deity, that the One Tree had beckoned from the egg-shaped hardair pool. Perhaps it had taken no account of him at all. Perhaps that was why he was alone. Perhaps that was why she was here now, somewhere, and not in that other world.

Here—but where?

He flew swiftly, frantically, but at random. Far below him he heard a commotion of many birds but ignored it, for the cries echoed of merriment and mating; Kleet wanted no part of that, he who had no mate. He flew on.

He had found Deity and lost her and now she had summoned him once again and please—

Please, he begged greenplume treefree and azure worldegg as he flew, *Please let her skreek me once more.*

But only watertrickle and leafwhisper answered him. Deity did not call out to him again. Kleet flew until he was weary, searching, but glory forest is vast, shadowland is vast, sky even more so; he could not find her.

Sitting at ease against a mossy tree, Sassy watched the birds, which were in turn watching Racquel rampaging around. There were upside-down-on-the-tree-trunks birds like nut-hatches with curved bills, something like a pheasant with a fluffy white turkey tail and a grotesque cobalt-blue head, something with a puff of yellow plumes on its back, a jay not blue but green, little shrimp-colored birds, a pair of knobby-legged storks, two big hen-shaped birds with blue faces and punk featherdos, two cassowaries—there were many many birds, but not the one Sassy was looking for. There was a pair of hyacinth macaws, but there was no parakeet.

The macaws perched side by side on a bowed sapling, mak-ing kissy noises through their beaks and nibbling at each other's faces. Sassy looked away. Nobody was likely ever to nibble her face again. Nobody was going to love her ever again.

Arguably, nobody ever had loved her, except maybe her mother. Who now no longer even recognized her on the rare occasions when she forced herself to visit. Alzheimer's was hell.

"If you would stand up and *help*," Racquel yelled, "we'd stand a better chance."

Sassy sighed. By "help," Racquel meant blunder about try-ing to run into an invisible mirror. He had been doing so for some time. Sassy had suggested going to find somebody, the young couple perhaps, and ask for directions, but Racquel wouldn't hear of it. In certain ways he was quite typically male.

"I know it's around here someplace," Racquel grumbled,

feeling at the air, the broken feathers of his bustle rattling. "Sassy, c'mon!"

Sassy rolled her eyes and got up. Ambling dreamily, she made modern-dance moves at the air in order to placate Racquel. She felt none of his urgency, except that she was starting to get really hungry. "How did Alice do it?" she called to him.

"Huh?"

"Alice. How did she get back through the looking glass?"

He halted to look at her. "I read that book."

"So did I, years ago, but I don't remember."

"Neither do I. Dammit!"

A pause while they stared at each other with knotted looks, straining to remember how Alice did it.

"Dammit," Racquel grumped. "Hell. It was kind of a stupid book."

"That's what I thought."

"Yeah. It was just clever, that's all."

"Clever and political. Satiric."

"Yeah. I didn't give a rat's ass what happened to Alice."

"That's the way I felt! I'm glad there's somebody else in the world who feels that way."

The conversation had drawn them closer to each other until they stood face-to-face, surrounded by birds that continued to be fascinated by Racquel even though his feather-studded hair sculpture, Sassy noticed, hung broken and draggled like his tail feathers. "Your hair moved," she remarked.

"Oh. I guess now your life is complete."

Only later Sassy sensed providence in this sarcastic comment. Then, she knew only that she felt something, or someone, watching her—she, Sassafras, not her feathered friend. She looked past Racquel's left shoulder and saw. Shy, behind all the others, in the shadows between the trees something

human-sized gazed back at her. Sassy felt her heart startle like a
deer and leap like a skylark as she saw a face like a magnolia
petal, dewy smooth oval blush and cream, strange yet strangely
familiar. She glimpsed hands lifting toward her, upsweep of
dawn-colored wings, a shimmer of robe—or was it a cloak of
heavenly feathers trailing down? She did not care; she noticed
without knowing that there were no feet, that the presence
floated, not touching the ground—but her gaze was all for that
face too shadowed, too far away to recognize. She gasped,
yearning. She reached out to run toward—

As Racquel turned to see what Sassy was gawking at, he
caught the edge of his gold strappy sandal on something and
lost his balance. Automatically Sassy grabbed for his hand to
help him, and as he fell backward through a flat place in the
air, he pulled her with him.

After four days had gone by and he hadn't heard from Sassy,
Racquel went to see her.

He took something new from the stock, a feathered and
sequined baseball cap, to try to make her laugh. Racquel had a
feeling it was going to be hard to get Sassy to smile. Not that it
hadn't been pretty damn funny when they came back, landing
practically on top of the cop, who was there with his ever-
loving warrant searching the place. But then the cop was so
shook up he'd blundered into the mirror and knocked it over.
And it broke. Broke to smithereens. And Sassy just stood there
and cried.

Getting out of a taxi in front of Sassy's apartment building,
Racquel sighed, because he was breaking a promise to himself.
He had sworn he was going to stay away from Sassy from here
on out. But God damn, she had turned to him and cried in his

arms. Sobbing against his artificial bosom. He swallowed hard just thinking about it.

He went in.

Damn, how can people live in these places? *It's not as bad as where I grew up*, Racquel reminded himself, waiting for the elevator. No dark broken steps, no winos, no smell of urine. But the cinder-block walls painted institutional beige, the mustard-brown vinyl flooring, the low acoustic-tile ceiling, the posterboard signs No Soliciting No Loitering No Recreational Wheeled Conveyances No Public Displays Of Affection—might as well say No Living. Racquel wore fuchsia to defy places like this. Specifically, in this instance, he was wearing a fuchsia tunic fringed with dip-dyed cassowary over a bias-draped plum skirt. And a touch of cassowary at the neck. The right accessories meant everything.

No functioning security system in this place, either, he noticed as he knocked at Sassy's door.

"It's open." Her voice sounded wan.

He went in, walking through a front room piled with books to find her sitting at her kitchen table amid more books, mostly about birds. She did not get up to meet him. She barely looked at him.

"Hey, woman." He slapped the glittery baseball hat onto her head. She did smile, and she took it off to see what it was, but she did not show enough interest to head for a mirror and admire how it looked. And she was cute as hell in that hat, dammit, with her heart-shaped face, her big eyes and her little pointed chin. Even her big honkin' glasses were cute under that hat. But she did not put it back on, just laid it aside.

"I haven't seen you around." Racquel sat down at another chair at the table, which was one of those tasteless aluminum-tubing-and-plastic laminate kitchenette affairs, with aluminum-and-plastic chairs to match. Heinous.

"I lost my job," Sassy said.

"I know. Doesn't mean you can't come see me."

"I haven't felt like going anywhere."

Racquel moved a pile of books to the floor and studied her. Sassy looked like she didn't give a rat's ass about anything. No makeup—of course, when had he ever seen Sassy in makeup? How long had she been letting herself go? Since he had known her, anyway. There she sat all slumped, with her hair not combed. Wearing sweatshirt, sweatpants, and they didn't even match.

"I'm almost sure it was ivory-billed woodpeckers I saw," Sassy said.

"Huh?"

Sassy pressed her hands on the large book lying open before her as if pressing flowers. A bird book, of course, with big colorful pictures. "Ivory-billed woodpeckers," said Sassy. "And Hawaiian honeycreepers. And a moa. I saw a moa. And those were passenger pigeons I saw flying over." She spoke in a monotone, like a grieving person telling the story of how it happened, the cancer, the motorcycle accident, whatever it was. "And those weren't hyacinth macaws. They were Spik's macaws. There's only one left alive in the wild. I saw two."

"What are you talking about?"

Sassy closed her book softly, as if putting a baby down to sleep, and turned the cover toward him so that he could see the title: *Rare, Endangered, and Forever Gone.*

"The last ivorybill anybody's seen was in Cuba in 1988," she said. "But I saw a pair."

"Where?"

"You know where."

Faced with her steady gaze, Racquel started to babble. "Sassy, that—it can't be real. We just think we're remembering the same thing. It's like when people drop acid together—"

She gave him a look so flat and weary it hushed him. "That parakeet," she said. "The one that was in the hotel. It's not an escapee from some pet store. It's a Carolina parakeet." She showed him the picture. Green body, yellow head, orange eye patch. Blue primaries on the wings. Yellow rump patch. Yep.

"So?"

"They're extinct."

Racquel pressed his lips together and looked at the linoleum floor, against which Sassy's bare feet curled together like white, shivering puppies.

Sassy said, very low, "The voice said that what I found would depend on what I'd lost."

"Voice?"

"Voice from—wild, from the treetops. Near the waterfall."

Racquel was sorry he had asked. He didn't want to know any more, and it was no damn good for Sassy to keep brooding about it and grieving about it. The mirror was broken. She couldn't go back there, and it was a damn good thing, because "there" was insane. He looked up at her and said, careful to keep his voice gentle, "Sassy, you've got to come out of it. Think about living in *this* world."

She did not reply immediately. He could see that his words made little impression on her. But finally she said, "What for? So I can go back to cleaning hotel rooms?"

"You can get a better job." With a Vanna White gesture Racquel indicated the stacks of books. "Look at all the stuff you know. You ought to be one of those ortho-knowledge-ists."

Sassy barely smiled.

Racquel let himself get serious. "Damn it, Sassy, what you've lost, you've lost *here*, not in some freaky fairyland. *Here.* Now. But you gotta fight back. Put that hat on, woman."

She looked at it, but did not make a move toward it. She said, "I don't wear hats."

"Why not?"

"I just don't. They're not who I am."

She sounded quite sure. Racquel studied her almost in admiration; she knew who she was, weirdness and all? There was only one of her?

"It's a pretty hat," Sassy added as a polite afterthought.

Racquel asked, "So who are you?"

"Huh?"

Jeez. She was the one who had brought it up. "Why don't you wear hats?"

"I'm too old."

"Since when?"

"And I'm too plain."

"Sassy—"

"Just let me alone, Racquel, would you?"

"No." He sat back in his chair staring at her. God, she'd lost even more than he had thought. "How are you going to get it back if I let you alone?" He could help her; he knew he could.

"Get back what? My husband?" Sassy soured her mouth to show that she was bitterly joking. "No, thank you."

"Not your damn husband! I'm talking about *you*, Sassy! I'm talking about being a woman." Racquel's passion jarred him to his feet; he couldn't help it. Jesus, being a woman—it was the biggest, best, most beautiful project anybody could undertake, worth devoting a lifetime to, which is what it usually took, what with foundation garments and cosmetics and depilatories and everything you had to know, yet there sat Sassy born with the gender he had always wanted, and—how had she lost that sense of herself? How had it happened that she just didn't care anymore? Racquel blurted, "You got so much going for you, Sassy, I just want to shake you! Don't you sometimes, just sometimes, want to wear something besides *sweatpants*?"

She blinked up at him without answering. Cute little face. Cute little pointed chin.

Racquel made himself sit down across from her again. "Look," he said quietly, "here's what we're gonna do to get you feeling better about yourself and everything in general. Skin first. Some apricot scrub maybe, some shower gel, some body splash. Then the hair. Jesus, Sassy, white people can have any color hair they want and get away with it; why should you settle for gray? I got a hairdresser just waiting to get her hands on your hair. Then get your ears pierced—"

Sassy's head jerked up with the most spirit she'd shown all day, and her hands flew to her earlobes. "I am not!"

"Yes you are, so you can wear all kinds of earrings. You just wait, couple months you'll be going back for more holes. Then your nails, a manicure—"

"Who's supposed to be paying for all this?"

She meant that as an objection, and Racquel wasn't going to let it fly. "I can do your nails myself. Hell, Sass, I'll do them right now." He shoved books to one side. "Where's a dish towel?" He grabbed one off a hook and laid it out. "Gimme your hands."

"Racquel—"

"Give it a chance, Sassy." He took one of her hands and started massaging her fingers.

Sassy's eyes widened. But the massage stopped her protests, as he knew it would. He knew it felt too good to pass up.

"Kick-ass little hands," he told her, rubbing, ignoring her

chapped skin for the time being. "Dainty. Sweet. I bet you got sweet little feet too. Stretch them out here." She did, and he looked down past the edge of the table to study them, feeling genuine envy rising in his chest. "God, Sassy, your feet are *perfect*. Not a bunion on them, or a corn, or anything." What a bite. She must have worn sensible shoes all her miserable life.

"Oh, that's good," said Sassy in dulcet tones. "I know what I'll do. I'll just walk on my hands and wave my feet in the air."

"I'm serious, woman." Goofy little twit, she had no clue how sexy feet could be, but she was going to learn. Racquel went to the sink and ran water till he got just the right hot temperature, filled the dishpan and squirted some Dove in it, brought it over and set it on the floor by Sassy. "Soak."

"Huh?"

"Stick your feet in there."

While they were soaking, he found an emery board in his capacious handbag and shaped Sassy's fingernails, stroking the tips, never sawing at them. His own nails were French-tipped gels this week, but he figured Sassy wasn't ready for that, or for fiberglass or silks or all the rest of it. He stroked her natural nails into gently rounded ovals. These days most nails had shovel tips, but Racquel preferred the classic oval. Sassy's nails came out almost the shape of her face. Racquel massaged her hands again, with lotion this time, put extra lotion on her cuticles to soften them, pushed them back with a Q-Tip, then cleaned the lotion off her nails with polish remover and brought out undercoat and several colors of polish from his purse. Even though he had his nails professionally done, he still bought polish and carried it around for touch-ups and because he liked the colors. He carried extra jewelry in his purse too. Feathered earbobs, mostly. Just because.

"Iced Teal," he read the nail polish color names off to her,

"Malachite, White Jazz, Mango, Road Flare, Lagoon, Tropical Butterfly."

"What ever happened to pink?" Sassy asked.

They settled on Lagoon, which was a sort of sky-blue-water color with a silvery sheen. As Racquel was stroking on the second coat, Sassy asked, "Racquel. You got anybody?"

"Huh?"

She spelled it out. "Do-you-have-a-sweetheart?"

"No."

"A significant other?"

"No."

"A relationship, a partner, a lover, a husband, a wife?"

"What are you, a thesaurus? No. None of the above."

Silence while he completed the job. Then she asked, "Are you looking?"

"Sure."

More silence. He moved his chair, laid the dish towel in his lap and said, "Put your feet up here."

She did so. She asked, "Which gender?"

He looked her straight in the eye and told her the truth. "Any gender at all."

$\int$ assy found herself being surprised by a tiny prickle of pleasure every time she caught sight of her own wetly gleaming fingertips and toes. The fact that she was pleased by something so frivolous as a manicure and pedicure surprised her doubly. She had tried to make Racquel take the feathered baseball hat away, but he had insisted on leaving it, and the sight of it nesting on her kitchen table pleased her in some secret way she could not understand. She would never wear the thing, so what was the sense of keeping it? Such nonsense. Neither a useless hat nor an equally useless set of painted digits solved any of her problems, but—a sleekly plumaged canary-and-periwinkle baseball hat sectioned by rows of violet sequins—it was nice to look at, that was all. Who could resist just looking at it?

Greeting her budgie in the mirror the second morning after Racquel's visit, Sassy said "Hi, stupid," smiled, and went to have her coffee. She gazed at her own hands as they curled around the mug; with enameled nails, her hands felt different, more substantial and significant. It wasn't like she had never worn nail polish before, but—jeez, she couldn't remember when. It must have been a long, long time ago.

She looked across the table and felt herself smiling at the hat too. She reached across the table and put it on, liking the way it hugged her head. Bet it looked cute on her too. She had almost forgotten how it felt to like hats. She wished she could look in a mirror and see—

No. Some hard, dark feeling in her gut gave her to know that hats were not for her. She took off the feathered cap and set it on the table.

The dark internal pressure formed into a memory: she and Frederick walking through Valu-Mart and she stops at the hats and reaches to try one on. Not to buy, she knows they can't afford to buy any, but Frederick says "NO" as if it's somehow disgusting that she wants to look. She grabs a hat anyway and smiles at him from under the brim, but he glowers as if the sight of her offends him.

It was obvious that she did not look good in hats. Or that hats were not right for her. Or that she was not a person who should wear hats.

Obvious. Yes.

She contemplated this for a moment, finishing her coffee, then went and looked in her closet and her dresser. Somehow something pretty should have been there, but she found nothing except sweatpants and elastic-waisted jeans.

She put on an ocean-blue sweat suit to match her water-colored nails, searched her supply of anorexic head scarves for one that had some faded blue flowers in it, and got her coat on. She knew she should be heading out to look for a job but she wasn't. Instead, she went to see Racquel.

When she got to the Sylvan Tower, no one looked at her. Good. That was the kind of person she was. Not the sort to attract attention.

Racquel was wearing a dress the same color and glare as the fog lights on some rich guy's BMW, and his grin when he saw her lit him up almost as bright. As she walked into PLUMAGE he called, "Hey, it's Sassy! *Sweet!*"

A lot went without saying. Sassy knew he knew that she was there partly to thank him for giving a damn about her. And partly because she hadn't been very "sweet" the last time she saw him.

But he also seemed to take it that she was there to continue an already-begun course of self-improvement. He showed her some new belts, gold chain with gilded feathers dangling from the links. He showed her the feather-tufted earrings she could look forward to wearing when she got her ears pierced. He showed her a silver-straw picture hat with a single black ostrich feather curled around the brim, rhinestones studding its vane. "Wouldn't you like to wear that?" he asked.

"No. Not really."

"What is it with you and hats, Sassy? I *know* you like them."

Sassy said, "I look ugly in hats."

"You do not! Sez who?"

Frederick. But Sassy said only, "I just do."

"Frederick told you that, right? What a turdball."

"No, he didn't! He just—I don't know."

Sassy studied her blue Lagoon fingernails, which Frederick probably would not have liked either. Meanwhile, she felt Racquel studying her.

Finally Sassy said, "He was just sort of negative in general about hats and stuff."

"And stuff?"

"Like—I don't know. Boots, leggings, fancy belts, that sort of thing. Plumage."

"What a snarf," Racquel said.

Sassy shook her head. "He was just being a husband. Stuff like that costs money. He was good in lots of ways, he fixed stuff around the house, brought freebies home from the grocery, and there was never that much money, and he was the one who had to pay the bills—"

"He's still a jellosnarf. Didn't he want you to have *anything* nice?"

"I—I had my jewelry—"

"And nothing to wear it with."

"It was me," Sassy said. "Trying to look—" Feminine, attractive, sexy, all turned out to be words she could not quite say. "Trying to look that way, I couldn't carry it off. He just kind of let me know I couldn't do that."

In a very low tone Racquel said something Sassy could not quite catch. Something that rhymed with duck. Then he asked, "You weren't supposed to wear anything you liked?"

"I think it was more—I wasn't supposed to wear anything that made me think I was attractive."

"Good God."

"I wasn't supposed to . . ." Sassy found that she could not quite conceptualize the way Frederick didn't want her to feel sexy. When she had started to look like her mother, that was it. He had made it quite plain that he detested her mother. "I don't know what he wanted," Sassy said to her hands. "Mostly he obviously didn't want *me*."

Racquel said softly but quite plainly, "Well, fuck him with a salty dick."

This sentiment startled Sassy so badly that her head jerked up and she started to giggle.

"I mean it." Racquel faced her steadily. "Fuck him. He made you feel like dog doo, Sassy."

Racquel's wholehearted sympathy was making Sassy's eyes go hot and moist. She swallowed hard. "I—I thought it was just part of being a wife."

"Oh. Uh-huh. Like a wife isn't a person?"

"Well, I felt like, as long as he was faithful . . ." Sassy turned away to look blindly at feathered chains, because even after a year she found herself still unable to comprehend Frederick's infidelity. After she had devoted her life to him—which, in hindsight, seemed like a pretty stupid sort of devotion, but she had been doing what she thought she was supposed to. He was supposed to be her prince. Even after she had slowly come to know that he was not a prince but a jackass, still, he was her very own jackass, and she was still willing to give everything she had to the covenant—but it didn't seem to matter to him. He went and tossed it off like—like spitting out a hawker. How could he do that?

Sassy still just couldn't understand.

Without looking at Racquel she said, "I think the man on horseback might have been King Arthur." A hero and a faithful husband. "Who the lovers were I don't know." But she expected they were faithful too, because she knew what she had lost.

If the forest was Paradise lost, then the shadowland beneath the trees was Perdition. The place where lost dreams dwelt.

Racquel said gently enough, "Sassy, stop it."

"No. I can't. Racquel . . ." Sassy made herself turn to face the tall—woman, half the time she still couldn't help thinking of Racquel as a woman. A woman and her best friend. Almost her only friend. Looking up to meet his eyes, she asked him, "Are you going to get the mirror fixed?"

He pressed his lips together in a worried magenta line and shook his head.

"Get a new mirror put in the same frame, I mean?"

"Sassy, do you have any idea how much it costs to get an oval mirror cut?"

She stood looking at him.

"Anyway, I can't. The frame's broken. Sassy—let it go."

But she couldn't. Somehow she had lost her self, and it had gone in there to join the other lost things.

"I've been thinking, it was probably some kind of chemical got in the ventilation system. Trippin' us. Doesn't it feel like that to you, too? A brain party? A freaky dream?"

She couldn't be angry at him, because he was right, it did. If it had not been for the goofy parakeet looking back at her from the mirror she wouldn't be here, begging him, because what had happened before did feel like a dream, fading day by day, some of the jewel-bright details dulled, turned to dust, lost, and—all the more reason she had to get back there soon, yesterday was not soon enough, or she would forget, it would all be lost to her.

Lost.

She could not face more loss. She turned away.

"Sassy, honey," Racquel said, "you've got to get over it."

There was so much warm concern in his voice that she couldn't speak or look at him; she could only flee.

"Sassy," he called after her as she darted out of the shop, "let it go. Move on."

Racquel checked his look in the plate-glass window of Food World. Hair, check. Lipstick, check. Boobs firmly in place, check. Face intact. Dress straight. Chartreuse looked marvelous against his skin. Scanning himself in the glass gave him confidence, and somebody had to do something, obviously, although Racquel had no idea what he expected to accomplish by going here; he just wanted a look at Sassy's toad of an ex, that was all. Shifting his bustard-trimmed shawl to a more becoming angle around his shoulders and twitching his fitted skirt down around his hips, he sashayed in.

It didn't take long to locate Frederick. A man with yam-colored hair was stationed at one of the cash registers. Racquel strolled around and took a look at the tabloids—**Boy in Coma Grows Wings, Jacko Nose Heartache, Diana Living in Barbados with Elvis**—also taking a couple of glances at the cashier. Freckled all over. Name tag said FRED. It had to be Mr. Hummel.

Odd-looking dude. Round-shouldered, kind of amorphous. Something about him reminded Racquel of a toy, a stuffed animal, one of those gingery bears with the arms put on with pins so they could move. Racquel couldn't see why Sassy loved the guy. But then, why did anybody love anybody? Sure as hell Racquel had nobody who loved *him*.

He picked up a basket and made a rapid round of the store, grabbing bagels, rice cakes, boneless chicken breasts, herbal stress tea, nail polish remover, cotton balls, yogurt and, at the register, *Cosmopolitan*. FRED was still there. Racquel stood in his line and watched him wait on a young couple with a baby, a teenage boy buying gum and popcorn, a middle-aged woman in nursing whites. Somehow FRED managed to run them through the process without once acknowledging their existence as human beings. He scanned their groceries without speaking. He handed them their change and said "Thank you" but his eyes never focused on them.

Not Mr. Personality, Racquel thought, although willing to make allowances. It had to be hell standing behind a cash register all day. The man was on automatic pilot—

"Hi, how *are* you, miss?"

Startled, Racquel realized that FRED was speaking to him. More specifically, Frederick was bespeaking his boobs. The man's watery greenish eyes were focused now, for sure—focused on Racquel's chest, before scanning up to Racquel's face. "You doing okay today?" Frederick asked brightly.

"Um, sure. I'm fine."

With his freckled hand Frederick selected an item from Racquel's order. "Oooh, Dannon blueberry yogurt," he declared as he scanned it. "That's really good for you."

"Uh-huh."

"Fresh bakery bagels," Frederick murmured intensely as he selected the next item. "Have you tried bagels with sugar-free raspberry preserves? They're *yummy*."

Racquel felt his mouth stiffening into a reflexive smile. He was no stranger to male attention, and usually he liked it, but not this time.

"Nail polish remover." Frederick paused before scanning this item and studied Racquel's hands. "Aaah." He gazed warmly into Racquel's face. "You take good care of your nails, don't you, miss? They're *very* attractive."

Racquel showed his teeth, nodded, and did not reply.

Frederick scanned the nail polish remover. "Cotton balls. Oooh. Those are to go with the nail polish remover."

The nail polish remover and the cotton balls were for Sassy. And her ex-husband was hitting on him.

Racquel grew aware that a considerable line had formed while Frederick chatted him up, scanning his order in slow motion. Judging by the sardonic looks on the people behind him, nobody was missing what was going on.

"Rice cakes," Frederick rhapsodized. "You—"

"I'm in a bit of a hurry," Racquel interrupted, teeth clenched.

"Absolutely!" Frederick hopped to it like a fuzzy bunny. "You're a busy professional girl, and it's obvious from your *appearance* that you're a *perfectionist,* you're under a lot of stress," he babbled. "Herbal stress tea."

Blessedly he had little to say about the boneless chicken breasts or the *Cosmopolitan.* In vibrant tones he informed Racquel of the total. He took Racquel's money and handed Racquel the change. The groceries stood in a pile on the counter. Frederick stood beaming at Racquel.

Racquel stared back at him, his teeth aching from smiling.

Frederick's face lit up with a stupendous thought. "Would you like them in *bags?*"

Racquel nodded.

"*I'll* put them in bags for you!"

"Please."

With a feeling as if he had just encountered a centipede in the basement, Racquel watched Frederick bag his order. What a crotch the man was. Racquel would have staked his boobs that Frederick had been hitting on younger women for years. What this man had put Sassy through . . . Racquel knew what he wanted to do to Frederick. But it was not something he ever permitted himself to do. It was dangerous.

Frederick held the plastic grocery bags out to him by the handles, leered at him and said, "You come back, miss. Have a *nice* day."

Racquel did it anyway.

As he took the bags, he leaned closer to FRED—the man caught his breath and ogled in response. Racquel leaned almost close enough to kiss. He bestirred his mouth from its ghastly rictus. He spoke.

"You look like *my* kind of guy," he whispered to Frederick in a deep, gritty voice, unmistakably the voice of a male.

Without bothering to wait for a response, he minced out, his drop-dead red sling-back heels clicking all the way.

. . .

Just to be doing something, anything, that might help her solve the mystery of her own life, Sassy went to see the woman in the high-rises who had fifty pet birds.

It was not hard to find her. Just ask, then follow the smell.

Although distinctive, and whiffable in the hallway, the odor was not unpleasant. It was a warm, lizardy fragrance, as sere and crisp as feathers. It made Sassy think vaguely of sand dunes, palm trees.

A Magic-Markered sign on the door said LOOK DOWN, with the OO of LOOK colored into downcast eyeballs and an emphatic arrow pointing floorward. Sassy was looking down, seeing nothing but indoor-outdoor carpeting, when the door was opened by a large, homely woman with complexion problems and stringy hair. At that point it was difficult to look down, because the woman, clad in a clingy T-shirt, had a parakeet walking around on top of each of her generous breasts. It occurred to Sassy that this woman was outdoing Racquel, wearing the living plumage.

Sassy blinked. "Um, hi. I was wondering, um . . ."

At that point Sassy lost her voice, because one of the bosom birds pooped, and the poop ran down the tightly stretched rib-knit of the woman's shirt, forming a drip in the nipple area.

"You want to see the birds?" She seemed not to notice at all that she had just been pooped on, and she had a warm smile. "Look down and watch where you step. Come on in."

Walking in, Sassy joined a promenade of other bipeds. Birds—parakeets, cockatiels, parrots, and other Psittacidae—swaggered on the floor as well as shrieking from atop the cages which had taken over the apartment. Cages sat on the TV, flanked the shabby sofa, stood in stacks and ranks along walls and on the counter of the kitchenette, but Sassy saw no birds actually occupying any of the cages; instead, budgies whirred through the air and perched on lamp shades, a large scarlet macaw ripped apart a *People* magazine, a cockatoo monopolized the coffee table.

"Sit down," the hostess invited, raising her voice to be heard over squeak whistle chitter squawk screech chirp twitter coo and the relentless dinging of some bird's bell toy, all counterpointed against Michael Jackson from a staticky radio. A medium-sized mostly yellow bird landed on the woman's head as she gestured toward the sofa. "Make yourself comfy. Just make sure ain't nobody under you."

Sassy sat, exchanging glances with the cockatoo. Parakeets clustered on a shelf in front of a mirror hanging on one wall. Two smallish peachy-faced had-to-be-lovebirds pressed against each other, beaks open and interlocked. The parrot dinging the bell stopped and glared at Sassy. "Shut up!" it said. "Who farted?"

Without appearing to notice, the bird woman settled herself at the other end of the sofa, removing the bird from her head; it perched on her hand. She brought it to her face— Sassy cringed at the sight of the bird's large black hooked beak an inch from the woman's eyes; she wouldn't want that bird so close to her eyes, even though she was wearing glasses. But the bird woman puckered her mouth and let the bird nibble at her lips.

"Kissy kissy," she said. "This is Pookie; he's a conure. I'm Lydia. What's your name?"

She was looking cross-eyed down her own nose at the conure exploring her mouth; it took Sassy a moment to realize that Lydia was speaking to her. "Oh! Uh, I'm Sassy. Sassafras."

"Who farted? That's stinky," said the scowling parrot.

"That's Ezekiel. He's a Congo gray. He's very intelligent. You can have conversations with him. I mean, he likes to talk dirty and all that, it's like talking with a three-year-old, but no worse than your average male." A parakeet had walked up from Lydia's boob to her shoulder, where it was nibbling at her earlobe. The big woman fit Sassy's idea of a welfare recipient: Goodwill clothes, skin pasty from a diet of pasta, and maybe not too bright. "Kissy kissy," she said, tilting her head toward the bird.

"That looks like it feels good," Sassy said to be polite.

"It does." Lydia transferred the conure to Sassy's shoulder, where it started at once to preen Sassy's hair. It better just damn stay on her shoulder and away from her face—but actually its ministrations did feel good. It was more physical attention than Sassy had received anywhere else in years, except—except lately from Racquel, messing with her hair, painting her fingernails.

"Birds give me more loving than any man ever did," said Lydia.

The conure transferred its attentions to Sassy's ear, nibbling around the edge. This also felt good, until the conure clamped down on her earlobe with its hooked beak. "Ow!" Sassy yelped. "Jeez." Racquel wasn't the only one trying to put holes in her ears.

"No no," sang Lydia. "Say no no."

Sassy put her hand up to remove Pookie from her shoulder; he bit it. At that moment Sassy realized that the bird woman's complexion problems, which she had taken for menopausal acne or something, were not that at all; all those red spots were bird bites. Blood blisters.

"These birds beat up on you!"

Lydia smiled, really focusing on Sassy for the first time.

"They give me little ol' love hickeys now and then." There was something so innocent about her homely-faced gaze that Sassy looked away, feeling somehow abashed.

The Congo gray parrot who had been ringing the bell, Sassy noticed, was now straddling it and rubbing the nether regions of his belly on it, his eyes shining like silver. The lovebirds were at it too. There seemed to be no place safe to look. Necessarily, Sassy shifted her eyes back to Lydia, reminding herself that she, Sassy, considering the way her life had been lately, had no leeway to think this woman was crazy.

Lydia, smiling at the world in general, noticed the masturbating parrot but did not alter her smile. "Ezekiel," she said, "knock it off."

"No!" yelled Ezekiel, increasing his tempo.

Sassy blinked. The bird had not actually understood and responded to Lydia, had he? He had just said a word he happened to know. Coincidence.

"Ezekiel," said Lydia just as placidly, "you're being rude. We have company. Stop it."

"Fuck you," said the parrot, but at the same moment his feathery face achieved an intensely stupid expression. He shuddered, then relaxed. He stopped.

"Thank you," Lydia said.

"You're welcome," said Ezekiel.

Sassy felt her jaw slacken. She blurted, "You really can have conversations with him?"

"Not just him." Lydia turned her ineffable smile on Sassy. "But with the others it works better if I speak their language."

Sassy did not know what to think or believe.

"Though I have a terrible human accent," said Lydia. "And I'm not very bright. I talk bird like a three-year-old." One of the many budgies whirred over, and Lydia put up her hand for it to land on, clicking a few bird-sounds at it with her tongue. The parakeet chirped back. Lydia nodded and remarked to Sassy, "He just wanted to people perch. They love it and so do I. I love their little warm feet." She made kissy noises at the budgie. "Parakeets are sweeties," she told Sassy. "They're my favorites. They're clowns, with their little round heads and the way they dress up. They come in more colors than peacocks or anything. And they ain't as moody as the big birds."

"I should hope not," Sassy said. Her ear still hurt from where the conure had bitten it. She rubbed it.

"What I like about parakeets, they lead an active fantasy life," Lydia said. "Look at them there at that mirror." Sassy looked. Lined up on the handy perch in front of the looking glass, white yellow lilac green blue gray aquamarine, the parakeets gabbled, each fixated on its own reflection, evidently preferring it to the company of others of its kind. "You would not believe what they think they see in there," said the bird woman. "They talk and talk." Sassy could hear this. The parakeets not only talked; they chirped, whistled, cooed, fussed, whispered, tsked, cried out in alarm, attacked their own images or made kissy love to them. Once again Sassy found that she did not wish to witness such nuzzling—or perhaps it should be beakling. Billing. Whatever. She did not want to see such a public display of affection, birds kissing themselves in obvious enjoyment of their own reflections, while she went lacking even her own homely face in the mirror to love. She looked down at her own hands, studying her wetly lustrous fingernails to comfort herself. Damn, the nail polish was already beginning to chip—

Something looked back at her out of the polished oval nail of her middle finger.

Sassy gasped. It was—her, the one with wings and a

strangely familiar face. Bolder this time. Sexy glance askance, full-lipped Julia-Roberts smile. She seemed to see Sassy, to know that Sassy had seen her, and she tossed her head, sending auburn hair flying, as she turned away, flinging up her arms amid a flutter of gauzy sleeves. Then Sassy was looking at her winged back. Sassy saw her gamboling across a sun-rayed flower-rich forest glade, her feet never touching the ground— if there were feet; Sassy could never remember afterward whether she saw feet. It was all a dancing blur in the tiny blue pool of her fingernail. But one thing she saw quite clearly. The girl, whoever she was, gave her a backward glance and a grin, then flipped up her swirling robe. The brat mooned her.

Sassy jolted upright, aghast, and lost sight of the vision. She peered at her fingernail, but the girl was gone; she saw nothing but nail polish. "Poop!" she cried.

"Huh?" The bird woman blinked at her, then smiled and glanced down at her poop-streaked self. "Oh. Yes," she said, "they do that because they love me."

R acquel was just heading out to keep his
weekly hair appointment when look out world, here came
Sassy like a dumpy comet shooting across the mezzanine, with
annunciation in her face. Racquel kept moving, because he
didn't want to be late, but Sassy grabbed him by the peplum to
slow him down. "It's something about *ovals*," she declared in
egg-shaped tones. "It might not be just your mirror. It could
be my fingernail if it was big enough. It could be *whatever*
oval."

Damnation, was she still talking about that damn broken
mirror? Racquel didn't understand what she was all excited
about, and he didn't want to. She needed to just get over it,
damn it, so he wouldn't have to think about it anymore and
worry whether he needed to see a shrink. More sharply than he
intended to, he said, "Sassy, I don't have time right now. I'm
supposed to be getting my hair done."

She released his peplum but did not step back. "Where?"

"Up top." He tilted his head back in a vague reference to the
top of the sixty-seven sunlit vine-draped stories of glassy
atrium and the hidden world overhead, where the elevator
shafts disappeared, the greenery closed in and the canopy

began: the locked suites, the rotating restaurant, and Rapunzel's salon.

Sassy demanded, "Does *she* have an oval mirror?"

"Maybe." Racquel didn't remember. He ran for an elevator, wondering how those women on TV did it so gracefully in heels; it must take years of practice. Sassy, given the advantage of sneakers, kept up with him and followed him in.

They had the elevator to themselves. Racquel watched the hotel slide away outside the glass, but became aware that Sassy was watching him with an intensity of expression that made her look almost cross-eyed in addition to four-eyed behind her glasses. Racquel remembered a childhood friend who used to do impressions of a hen about to lay an egg; it was the same expression. Sassy was about to ovulate something more.

"*What?*" Racquel asked.

Sassy breathed, "Does *she* know about you?"

Instantly, appallingly, Racquel understood exactly what the goofy little woman meant. Hairdressers knew everything. Hairdressers might as well be psychic. *Did* his hair tech know?

He had no idea. He felt himself gawking at Sassy. "Christ," he whispered as the elevator jolted to a halt at the top floor. Then he raised his voice fiercely. "God damn it. Don't say things like that."

He saw her smirk as she followed him off the elevator and across a hushed expanse of moss-green carpet into the skylit salon.

The Rapunzel was generally acknowledged to be the city's hair-care acme of luxury and relaxation, although actually the piped-in zephyrs-and-birdsong music made Racquel nervous. But he came here anyway, because these people understood the drop-dead principle. With some satisfaction he watched

Sassy's mouth form an ingenuous O as she took in the ambience: deep velvet sofas and easy chairs instead of a "waiting room," glass tables bearing cordovan-leather-bound back issues of *Vogue*, Art Nouveau lily lights, orchid-scented mist fountain in the shape of a golden naiad, life-size Grecian-style statues of Marlene Dietrich and Hedy Lamarr. If Sassy was looking for an oval mirror, Racquel reflected, no, there wasn't any—at least not in this room; there were several salons honeycombed within Rapunzel in order to preserve the privacy of the clientele.

"Racquel, darling," the blond receptionist greeted him from behind the French provincial desk. Her rosy blossom of a mouth smiled upon him, but her heather-blue gaze was fixed with consternation upon the potbellied little woman standing there in her dreadful sweat suit, peering through her glasses.

"That's Sassy," Racquel said. "She's a good friend of mine." Although right at the moment he was more than a little pissed at her. His mixed feelings made him grin as a thought possessed him. "What you see before you is the world's most neglected hair," he confided to the high-maintenance woman at the desk. "Tell you what." He knew he was never likely to get Sassy to come in here voluntarily again. "Think of her as the ultimate challenge. Take her in hand. See what you can do with her. It's on me."

More surprised than protesting, Sassy found herself seated in the consultation salon, surrounded by bulb-lit Hollywood mirrors and hairdressers—or hair technicians, as they referred to themselves, not to be compared to the gum-cracking hairdressers down in the strip mall. Sassy respected the distinction;

this place was certainly not like any beauty shop she had ever been in before. Her Wal-Mart jacket now hung from a filigree coat tree, and she could feel several hands fingering her hair.

"Oh, dear," said the woman who had led Sassy back there from the front salon, the one with blond hair rippling down in bangle-decked spiral tresses almost to her knees; Sassy had pegged her as Rapunzel—but wait, there was the sultry-faced black woman with many, many pencil-thin beaded braids flowing clear to her feet. And the pouty brunette, also with long, glorious ringlets. And the redhead—

"Excuse me, which one of you is Rapunzel?" Sassy asked.

They laughed like songbirds, and one of them, an elegant black woman, folded her six-foot height to smile into Sassy's face. "I am," she said, incongruously, for her hair was cropped close to her classical Egyptian head.

"You *are*?"

"Actually, I'm Romaine." The woman gave her a stellar grin. "Another kind of lettuce. Close enough."

"Your mother named you after *lettuce*?"

"Better than if she had called me Chicory Endive."

"There's no Rapunzel," said the brunette, who seemed impatient to move on to business. "It's just the salon name."

"Oh, dear," said the blonde again. "Sassy, darling, have you ever in your life used conditioner?"

"No."

"Excuse us a moment."

They huddled and whispered. Sassy did not even try to overhear, because she was distracted by the many mirrors, the multiple stolid blue budgies looking back at her and the various flitting birds that belonged to the hair techs; Sassy saw (usually in triplicate) a yellow-billed cuckoo, a puffin, a rose-breasted grosbeak, an indigo bunting, a mynah, a titmouse, and several others she could not identify. She wished she knew what they were, and she wished she could figure out which bird went with which perfectly surfaced woman—which one, for instance, was cuckoo, and which one was a titmouse. But the birds hopped and fluttered so much that it was hard to tell.

Quite out of the blue, and with a pang made half of anger and half of heartache, Sassy wondered what kind of a bird Frederick might be. A vulture? A bustard? Likely she'd never know. Certainly she wasn't going to go ask.

The Egyptian beauty, Romaine, had come back and was speaking to her. ". . . three-step conditioning treatment," she was saying, "and then we think a blunt cut, work some of those outgrown layers together to give a more unified fullness you can keep up with just glaze and root lifter. And then, of course, coloring. With your skin tones, we'd suggest something in the warm range . . ."

Not blue? Wasn't she old enough to be a blue-hair? Faced with her cream-and-cobalt mirror budgie, Sassy found herself uninterested in the hair-color samples, bundled like soft paintbrushes, that Romaine was showing her. Pecan, chestnut, hazelnut? Tree-turd colors. How boring. Who wanted to be a nut? And what was the point when all she could see was—okay, that stupid bird in the mirror was a pretty bright blue, but why couldn't it be a sunny yellow instead? Or something less commonplace? Why not aquamarine, violet, albino, lacewing? Or a rare crested parakeet? Or—why did she have to be a stupid budgie? Why not a crested cockatoo, a fighting cock, a—

"Is something wrong?" Romaine asked, peering at her.

"No! No, um, I'm just . . ." Sassy realized that she wasn't dealing with this Rapunzel situation very well and it wasn't going to get any better. Too many choices always confused her thinking. "I'm just, um, tired." Rapidly Sassy considered how best to get herself out of this muddle without hurting Racquel's feelings. "I'm fine. I, uh, just give me a, whatchacallit, a conditioning treatment or something."

"Are you sure?"

Sassy was. Quite sure. As she followed Romaine out of the cubicle, Sassy found her thoughts veering back to fighting cocks and Racquel and his plumage, his cock-tail bustle so admired by all the jungle cocks and ibises and motmots and jacamars and barbets and honeycreepers and bee eaters in the forest of dreams she had lost, so many kinds of birds in the world, so varied their plumage, so much one could be, and why was cocktail the name of a drink anyway? *If I had a tail,* Sassy thought, *what kind would I want?* Mockingbird? Macaw? Quetzel? But why limit herself to birds? How about a squirrel tail, a cat tail, a lion's tail? Why not? A switchy twitchy lion's tail poking out through her sweatpants, tawny slinky with some piercings, some gaudy gold tail rings, throw in a scrunchie or two? Sure, if people had tails they'd accessorize them. Tail perms, tail jewelry, tail wigs, and tail toupees. Put a ponytail on a pony tail—

Stop it, Sassy told herself, starting to feel dizzy. *If anybody knew, they'd think I was crazy.* Tail, indeed; more like a mind skidding out of control, in a tailspin. Ha.

Ouch. Stop.

She blinked and forced herself to pay attention to where she was going, with Romaine walking her back toward the spalike room with the sinks in it. Blinking again, Sassy noticed the blond receptionist opening the door of a cubicle to go in, and for a moment Sassy's mind actually focused, halted by the sight of Racquel in the chair. Racquel as she had never seen him before: Racquel with a plastic apron around his neck to cover his sweetheart bodice and his hair hanging like a wet mop. His face, bereft of its sculpted coif, turned toward Sassy, and for just a flash, despite his lipstick and his glitter-lilac eye shadow, she saw him as a man. He made a good one.

But that was not what stopped her in her sneakertracks. Okay, she saw Racquel, but at the same time she saw what stood, in a golden Art Nouveau scrollwork frame, beyond him: an oval mirror.

With a wordless cry she darted into the room, almost knocking over a hair technician or two.

"Oh, no you don't!" Wet hair, plastic apron and all, Racquel lunged up from the chair to stop her.

But Sassy did not stop. She saw nothing in the mirror except Racquel's big barbaric hornbill looking mad as a wet hen, but she plunged on anyway. Barely noticing Racquel teetering on his heels toward her, barely hearing his shout, she hurtled for the mirror and dived straight in. And when he grabbed at her, off his balance, such was the force of her momentum that she took him with her.

Motionless, with head thrown back and mouth agape, Sassy watched the brown crow-sized bird dancing on the diagonal trunk of a broken tree. She was not the only watcher; other birds of the same sort clustered on nearby trees, looking on, some of them plain brown—those were the females—and others with yellow plumes flowing down from their flanks; those were the young males. But the plumes of the older males, the dancers, were largest, and lifted, fountaining over their backs in a sunny cloud. Sassy saw now that two of them were dancing—on a sloping branch of the same tree another brown yellow-headed bird waltzed to the same heartbeat music that

Sassy could only imagine. The first dancer spread his wings and gave a bugling cry; the second answered it, and both speeded their dance as some of the lesser-plumed watchers joined in, exalting their heads and wings to dance in place as faster, faster, calling back and forth, the two lords of the dance fluttered and spun into a frenzy, then into a sort of swooning trance. Their movements slowed, they shuffled, they abased their heads and wings into a deep bow, their filmy plumes cascading over their heads. Crouching, legs hidden beneath their chests, beaks gasping and gaping, they trembled, their plumes aspiring and catching the sun, perched like shivering blossoms.

"What the *hell?*" said a harsh voice.

"Shhhh!" Sassy shushed Racquel, but it was too late. The plume-flowers folded; the birds took flight.

Racquel grumped, "What *was* that?"

"Some kind of bird of paradise, I think." Sassy spoke gently, because Racquel had shown himself to be a bit overwrought.

"Paradise, hell," Racquel muttered. He'd lost one shoe back in the beauty salon, so he was limping around barefoot and carrying the other one like a weapon; his hair was a sodden mess; and all he wanted was to find his way back to what he called civilization.

"They called them that because they had no feet," Sassy said, aware that she was not explaining very well. The European explorers of wherever-it-was had seen stuffed skins first, and the natives had taken off the legs and feet and sewed shut the holes, and the Europeans had thought the so-beautiful birds came from some celestial region where they flew all the time and never needed to perch. Or poop, probably.

It must have been nice to be so naive, able to believe. Sassy wanted to say so to Racquel, but he was not listening anyway. "Nice feathers," he said grudgingly as the birds disappeared between the trees. But then he turned on Sassy. "Would you for crying out loud get your saggy butt in motion and help me find the goddamn mirror?"

"Racquel, it's no use." Sassy forgave the insult to her butt, because Racquel was genuinely upset. "Face it," she told him, keeping her voice soft, "you don't have a clue where it is."

"Well, damn it, if you hadn't dragged me off the minute we got in—"

"I thought I saw the parakeet."

For a moment she thought he was actually going to rend his garment. Instead, he tore off his plastic apron and threw it on the ground. "*FUCK* the parakeet!" he cried when he could speak. "May a bird of paradise fly up the parakeet's nose! I wish I'd never heard of the goddamn parakeet, I wish I'd never seen the goddamn parakeet, I wish the goddamn parakeet never existed!"

Sassy opened her mouth to say that she wished the same, but realized, with a widening of her eyes, that it was not true.

"No," said Racquel in a supreme frenzy of bitterness, "I wish I'd never met *you*. Chasing a Caro-fucking-lina fucking para-fucking-keet into a madland," he added, subsiding somewhat, "and I'm eternally screwed."

Despite the insults to her person, Sassy felt compunction. He deserved an explanation, she decided, regarding the para-fucking-keet. "Racquel," she told him, "sit down."

"On the goddamn ground?" But he sat, probably because he had worn himself out. Sassy made herself comfortable on the velvety moss and faced him.

"If I can tell you this," she said, looking into his eyes, "I can tell you anything."

She briefed him, fumbling for words to explain her predicament—a budgie in the mirror instead of herself? How could she expect him to care? It was laughable. Ludicrous. So ridiculous she could not look at him any longer as she spoke. She looked at her own hands, the celestial-blue polish chipping off her fingernails. But she felt him silently listening.

"Good Lord," he said, very low, when she had more or less finished.

She took a long breath of relief because he was not laughing at her.

"That's scary," he said.

She had not expected such understanding, especially given the mood he was in. He was so wonderful, damn him and his fancy feathers, he made her want to cry. She swallowed hard before she could speak, and she still didn't dare to look at him, lest she come undone. "All the folklore says that a person's reflection is the soul," she said to the ground. "Like, a water spirit might snatch your reflection in a stream and take your soul away. Or in a room where someone died, the soul went into the mirror and you had to cover the mirror or it might take your soul too."

"Stop it. You're giving me the shivers."

"But do you believe me?" She still couldn't believe it.

"If I wasn't sitting here, I'd say no, you're crazy."

She nodded. "I felt like I was crazy. Like there was nobody I could tell. I mean, where could I go for help? You don't go to your family doctor and say you're seeing a parakeet in the mirror. He would have put me in the wacky ward."

"Sassy," Racquel said, "look at me."

She did; she looked at him, seeing maybe more than he wanted her to. There he sat in that drag-queen dress, and it wasn't even his best effort, a kind of muted red-orange taffeta-and-illusion thing with only a few lime-green feathers overlying the bustline. He couldn't compete with the courtship display Sassy had just witnessed. The birds weren't following him around today.

He gazed at her levelly. "Sassy," he said, "I know there's something about mirrors. I mean, obviously. We're sitting here. But listen. As far as I'm concerned, if you're missing your soul, it's not the parakeet that took it away. It's that ghoulish ex-husband of yours."

Mating season.

Kleet perched alone, well hidden amid treeplume, and did not sing. At this singproud pairdance time, Kleet felt his loneliness most keenly. It was always with him, for he had no flock and no hometree. There were many birds in the sweetleaf treetops, but in all his fledged life he had never seen another parakeet like himself. He remembered no nest, no motherkeet, no parentkeets of any kind. He remembered only flying through the forest and then the sojourn in the strange and wondrous hardair warmworld where there were many good things to eat and much music, songnotes out of strange textured nestholes—and Deity.

Deity, his warm walking treebeing. His chest warmed and swelled at the thought, stirring his breastfeathers.

Yet—still, even after the advent of Deity, he had found no sweetkeet.

He had encountered no parakeets at all.

His breast quivered, and he offered to Deity a small chirp: *Please?*

Surely Deity—surely Deity could not mean him to live the rest of his life alone? Now that he had encountered Deity, surely all would come to him, surely he would find a female to make his life complete, surely she would allow him to touch bills with her and nibble at her headfeathers and display to her his plumage and strut flirt tease step on her tail and—mate with her—

All around Kleet, suntop treeplume rang with the caws and warblings and chirs and whistles and skreeks of wingmales calling for mates. But Kleet could no longer find courage to lift his head and sing forth his own sweetmate song.

Please, he asked Deity again very softly. *Please?*

Racquel was getting footsore, Sassy saw. He was limping. "It's not much farther," she told him.

"You sure?"

"No," she admitted. "Actually, I think we should be there by now." She was trying to lead them to the waterfall-to-die-for and the river in which she had seen the head of Orpheus, faithful lover of Eurydice, drifting and singing. She was doing this not because Racquel had showed any interest in sight-seeing, but in an attempt to locate the cowboy, or for that matter, anyone who spoke English. She hoped that a friendly native guide might be able to point them toward one or more of the items on the loose operating agenda they had agreed on, including, but not limited to, Find Food And Shelter, Find An Oval Mirror, Get Me The Hell Out of Here (Racquel's top priority) and Find Parakeet (Sassy's goal, but far down the list for Racquel, who continued to favor ear piercing as Sassy's next move toward establishing identity).

"Face it," grumbled Racquel, picking his way ouchily over the moss, "we're lost."

"Well, naturally. This is the forest for lost things." Despite all common sense and her already-hungry belly, Sassy felt breezily at ease here, with sunlight sifting down gold into silvergreen shadows and birds flitting and singing all around. More—she felt profoundly at peace here, and loopily happy, so much so that her good humor was evident and Racquel was finding it hard to bear.

He scowled at her. "Give me a break."

"Okay. We might as well sit down."

"That's not what I meant."

"But it's no use going on if we're lost."

"We won't get anywhere by sitting on our butts!"

"Sit on the ground, then. Just sit already. I want to look at your feet."

He rolled his eyes but did as she said. Sassy sat down also, lifted his sizable feet into her lap and studied the soles, suddenly and shamefully aware that she was not sure what color they should be on a black person. Was ecru the equivalent of pink? She didn't see any bleeding cuts, but there were some raw-looking patches. Racquel hadn't complained, but he had to be really hurting. "Look," she said to him, "you stay here. I'll go back and get that plastic thing you left—"

Racquel gave her no opportunity to complete her thought, a vague one postulating plastic slippers. "No, you don't! You're not leaving me. I know how that goes."

He spoke with such vehemence that she knew it would be no use to argue with him. She thought some more. "Well, we can pull off the hem of your dress—"

"We're not ruining my dress!"

She sighed, hitched out from under his feet, rose to her knees and for no conscious reason began to comb his long hair with her fingers. His eyes widened, but otherwise he did not react, so she kept combing. His hair was dry now, its texture pleasantly coarse, like that of a horse's tail. It made her think of the Rapunzel hair tech with many many braids, and because her fingers wanted to, she began to braid Racquel's hair.

After a minute he tilted his head back for her, and his shoulders eased downward, relaxing as Sassy braided tiny plaits around his face. She wished she had bright cotton strings or slim ribbons or something to wrap around them, but the braids stayed even though she had not even a thread to bind the ends. This should have surprised her, but did not; in this world small miracles seemed possible. Not far away, standing in the shadows, two tall white cranes were—voguing, that was what they were doing, in hypnotic slow motion, their long necks and great wings dipping and aspiring in the graceful postures of their dance. Right by Sassy's face something iridescent flashed by, then another in pursuit; there was a rainbow whirl and tussle in the air. Sassy did not look to see whether they were fighting or mating. Same thing sometimes. Anyway, she did not want to watch birds court or mate anymore. It hurt. She was finding too much of what she had lost.

Braiding, she worked her way around to the back of Racquel's head. He sighed. Not moving, he said slowly, as if to check his reality, "Anytime you look in a mirror, all you see is a blue parakeet?"

"Yes."

"And other people's reflections are birds to you too? I'm a—whatchacallit?"

"Hornbill."

"And that's how you knew I was—"

"Male. Yes."

Silence. The rainbow wrestlers flew away. Above Sassy some bird was calling, calling. Intent on Racquel's head, she did not look up.

With just a hint of pathos Racquel asked, "What does a male hornbill look like?"

"Strikingly handsome," Sassy replied at once, laying it on thick. "Savagely elegant. Shining black with bright barbaric wattles and an absolutely daring bill. And," she added, "the most adorable eyelashes."

Racquel contemplated this in silence as Sassy finished a fringe of braids around his neck. She had forgotten how much she liked braids. Maybe she'd grow her hair long, she thought, so that she could braid it every day. Old ladies were supposed to keep their hair short, but so what. She would wear hers long and gray and she would braid it in plaits and pigtails and buns over her ears and she would decorate it with yarn and flossy bows and fake flowers. And it would give her fits, probably. It would never be as thick and user-friendly as Racquel's. She plaited coils at his temples and there was still plenty of hair left to play with. She stroked it up to the top of his head and began French-braiding a sort of Heidi crown for him.

She asked him, "Do you have any brothers?"

"Two."

"Older?" She was kind of hoping that he had one much older, a lot like him but of a masculine persuasion and maybe widowed.

"Younger."

"Oh." Damn. "Do you see them much?"

"No."

The flat word dropped like a stone. Sassy could almost hear it cavitating all the birdsong in the air.

"I got nothing in common with them," Racquel said more quietly. "They're brothers."

It took Sassy a moment to figure this out. Of course his brothers were brothers—oh. "You mean like in a gang?"

"Street brothers, yeah."

She didn't dare to ask anymore, but he went on anyway. "My parents, I got nothing in common with them either. I mean, they're okay, I see them at Christmas and whatever, but—we can't talk."

Sassy picked up a tiny iridescent blue wingfeather from the ground and tucked it into his hair.

 **E I G H T**

R acquel," Sassy asked, "what have you lost?"

"Huh?"

She stood still to give him a break from limping along after her. In the green twilight between the trees, deer grazed on the moss; one of them was pure white and looked soft-focus, as if it were posing for a Breck shampoo ad. Two ibises stood on the rocks like spirits; overhead two small pomegranate-colored birds fluttered and giggled, beak to beak, while others called, out of sight in the green labyrinth above. Sassy wondered whether Racquel was seeing it with the same yearning that she was, or even seeing the same scene. What he found depended on what he had lost, and she knew that he must have lost something; everyone has lost something. Life was loss, in her experience. "What are you finding?"

"*Huh?*"

"Here. In—"

"In this damn jungle?"

"It's not a jungle!"

"Yes, it is." He glared at the deer. "Look at them. Graze, graze all day, but wait'll you lie down to sleep and they sneak up and stick their horns in you." Before Sassy could recover from speechlessness, Racquel shifted his glare to the ibises.

"Those ten-inch beaks, you know what they're for? They're for picking your liver out after the horny sneaks kill you."

"Racquel, they are not!"

"Are too."

"You big baby, nothing is going to hurt you!"

"Says who? What they got such big beaks for, then? I tell you, something is going to kill us if we don't die of starvation first." His glare widened into a stare of desperation. "Tell you what. You grab one of those funny-looking birds, and I grab the other, and we wring their scrawny necks—"

"No!" Sassy recoiled from him the way she would rear back from a snake. "Don't say things like that!" Unthinkable to kill the bird-spirits of this paradise; didn't he know that?

"—make a fire," Racquel was saying, "and—screw it, forget the fire, I'll eat them raw."

"You're talking just like a man," Sassy told him. Oddly, seeing him as a man made her willing to forgive him. Men were supposed to be insensitive and require humoring. "Get a grip, doofus. Raw ibis is never served in the finer restaurants." Mushrooms were, however. And mushrooms grew everywhere, their moonstone colors underfoot nearly as vivid and various as the birds overhead. Feeling an eerie sureness prompt her, Sassy bent and grabbed several periwinkle-blue ones, caps, stems and all. Straightening, she took a large bite out of one. "Manna," she declared, offering a handful to Racquel.

"Are you crazy?" he yelped, flinching away from her. "That could be poison!"

"It's good. Like blueberry bread." Sassy ate greedily as Racquel watched her with white-rimmed eyes like those of a spooked horse, as if he were waiting for her to topple in agony or perhaps to emulate Alice in Wonderland in sudden feats of gigantism. Sassy did neither. She devoured all the mushrooms, belched with satisfaction, and told him, "They're really very good." Remembering he was a man, she added, "Meaty. Like portabella."

"I'm happy for you." Judging by Racquel's sardonic tone, he had more to say, but he was interrupted by a jingling sound and the muffled rhythm of hoofbeats. The deer lifted their elegant heads and bounded away, and with their harness ringing two young men came riding on swan-necked white steeds, richly caparisoned, and the youths rode them in cloth of gold—afterward Sassy could remember little of their clothing definitely not purchased at Wal-Mart, for her gaze was caught on their warrior faces, scarred yet deeply innocent, and alight as if all their sorrows were over. *Lovers*, Sassy thought with hot angst prickling her eyes. Lovers in the most fundamental sense—they loved each other. *Faithful friends, faithful comrades, faithful lovers.* One of them looked at the other and smiled for no reason. He carried a curling horn, an elephant's tusk rimmed with silver.

"Hey!" Racquel bawled at them, flailing his arms and pointing at Sassy. "She just ate the freaking mushrooms!"

The warrior youths turned, smiled, and lifted their right hands in courtly greeting as they rode past. One of them called something in some liquid, melodious language.

"Wait!" hollered Racquel.

But they rode away. "Roland and Oliver," Sassy said as they jingled into the shadows. "I think." Judging by Oliver's horn. In the *chanson* it was called an *olifant.*

"Like I care?" Racquel folded to the ground, letting his legs spraddle ungracefully in his skirt, his despair visible; he clutched his braided head in his hands. "It's probably next Tuesday by now at home."

Sassy stood wondering where there might be a pearlescent pinion to guide them. That was why she had eaten the mushrooms, she realized with a flutter of insight; their nacreous mottlings were like those of the feather she had followed her first time in shadowland. And the mushrooms were good, she knew they were good—but was she to wander lost, eating manna, for forty years, or eternity, or what? Where was her yahweh, her guide? To see a feather was good luck, the knight in a shining Stetson had said; to catch one . . .

She looked up, searching the distant treetops for a sign, but saw nothing except birds in love.

Limping along, his astonishment deepening to match his despair, Racquel kept watching Sassy as she watched the treetops and turquoise sky, the labyrinthine green of creepers and mistletoe, the gigantic oaks and pines and—and mimosas for all he knew. The orchids far overhead, the lapis-lazuli frogs clinging to the leaves, the black-and-scarlet butterflies bobbing in sunrays, the moss-colored shadows, the birds. He watched the way she gazed, her face rapt and deeply innocent, as if her troubles were all over. There was something almost supernatural about Sassy in this place, something ethereal about her face, as if she could stay here and be a cataract running between the rocks or a songbird in the green canopy or one of those people on a horse, an eidolon.

Looking at Sassy, prompted by her uncanny certainty as well as by the emptiness of his belly, Racquel decided to go ahead and eat the damn mushrooms. Right by his bare sore feet he found a cluster of fungi wearing little wisteria-colored caps like toques and asked Sassy, "This kind?"

"Yes, those are good. Sit down a while."

They both sat. The mushrooms tasted like coffee cake or maybe more like boysenberry Danish or a bran-apple muffin; in any event, they made him want a cup of espresso, and of course he couldn't have it. Too bad. Sassy didn't say a word while he ate; Racquel glanced over at her and saw her staring up at a pair of those little blue parrots she said were the most endangered bird in the world. The way those two looked, dancing cheek to cheek on their branch, they were about to take care of that problem by making more.

"You watching to see how it's done?" Racquel asked a lot more harshly than he intended to.

Sassy gave him a sideward look and a half smile. "I don't know why I'm watching."

She was probably thinking about that uxorious louse Frederick.

"It kind of hurts," Sassy said. "Lovebirds."

Racquel didn't know what to say, so he promptly opened his mouth and barfed out something stupid. "Huh. He'll leave her the minute he's done with her." Whichever one "he" was. The two blue—macaws, that was it, macaws were different than parrots somehow—the two chambray-colored birds looked exactly alike.

Sassy had turned back to watching them. "No, he won't," she said. "They mate for life."

That eerie sureness of hers again. Almost frightened, Racquel blurted, "How do you know?" and realized that he sounded rude.

Sassy did not react to his tone even to look at him. She gazed at the blue macaws nibbling each other's faces as she said, "Most birds, you'd be right, the male would up and leave. Most birds, the female is plain and the male is the gaudy one, a dandy."

"Hey, I like that in a male."

"I figured you would." Sassy gave him her sidelong smile again. "The female is plain, so she gets to sit on the nest; she blends into her environment. Just like the typical housewife."

"Another endangered species."

Sassy swiveled to gaze at him as if he had said something amazing. "Darn," she said, her voice hushed. "You're right."

One of the blue macaws turned coyly away, sidling along the branch; that would be the female, Racquel opined to himself. The other one fluttered his wings and nipped at her tail.

"So anyway," Sassy said, focused on the macaws again, "with most birds, the male gets the freedom. Just like with people."

Racquel didn't like her bitter tone. "He has to bring home some worms now and then, doesn't he?"

"Bring home the bacon. Traditional hubby."

"Aren't there birds where the wifey gets to bring home the bacon?" Odd, Racquel realized; he knew scads about feathers, but almost nothing about birds. There was an aphorism somewhere in that thought, like not seeing the forest for the trees.

Sassy said in a low voice to the forest, "I think there's one species somewhere in South America with the female brightly colored and the male sits on the nest."

The female macaw had taken a pose like a sculpture in blue lapis, proud-breasted, proud-winged, tail up and head thrown back so far that head and tail nearly touched.

"But those two are colored alike," said Sassy with a wistful note in her voice. "And birds like that, like the Canada geese, hawks, swans—you can't tell the difference between males and females, and they share everything. The nesting, sitting on the eggs, the feeding, everything. And they mate for life. They're faithful."

Racquel blurted, "What the hell makes you think you're

missing a soul?" It seemed to him that she had more soul than most people.

She gave him a startled look. "Well," she said after a moment's hesitation, "I'd forgotten that I really do like hats."

She did? That was a change of key. Of course, Racquel now realized, she couldn't see herself in the various hats he had tried to put on her.

"Oh!" he said.

"And braids," Sassy added.

Well, those were serious matters to have forgotten, okay. But still—

Racquel's attention was diverted as the male macaw advanced on the poised female, his eyes shining like tiny silver dollars. "He's getting ready to stick it in!" Racquel cried with enthusiasm as if he were Joe Husband watching a football game. Too late, he realized that he sounded a trifle crude.

Sassy gave him an expressive look, very Jane Housewife, but said merely, "They're not *that* much like people. Male birds don't have a stick-it-in. They have cloacas."

"Huh?"

"Cloacas. Kind of a vent. A hole. The only ones who have— you know—" She actually blushed. "Some waterfowl," she murmured. "Ducks."

Racquel could barely conceive what she was trying to say. He cried, "*Only ducks have dicks?*"

Sassy blushed harder. "Yes."

"But—*why?*"

She gave him that look again and turned away without replying, standing up to turn her back on the mating macaws as well.

. . .

For a timeless time, as they walked on, Sassy thought about something Racquel had asked: why did she think she was missing a soul, and not just a reflection? She had not known how to answer Racquel's question; it was hard to describe the emptiness—not just the loss of Frederick, but a great loss made up of many small losses over the years. She had ended up explaining it to Racquel in terms she had thought he might understand— hats, hair. But there was more, far more. She vaguely remembered that she had once been a person who liked organza, eyelet, daisy lace, dotted swiss. Who had taken a pair of bell-bottomed blue jeans and put a scalloped flower-embroidered hem on them. Who had preferred filmy nighties to flannel ones. Who had wanted to have someone rub her temples when she had a headache and give her a backrub whether she had a backache or not and—and love her, all of her. For a moment she ached anew, remembering what it was to have that body-love in her. But she could not remember well enough to say it. These days she seldom even noticed that she had a body.

She remembered how she would try to give Frederick a backrub and he would pull away.

Riding in her heart where dreams of goodness used to be, there was only a knot of bitterness.

Racquel was probably right. It was probably Frederick who had emptied her of her soul, not some parakeet.

"Now I'm thirsty," Racquel said.

Sassy peered at him, bemused by his tone; he wasn't complaining. He was just stating a fact. Really, he hadn't complained much once he got past the first shock, Sassy realized. Even the way his feet had to be hurting, he just padded along. He had physical courage. She admired that.

"Now that I'm not hungry anymore, I'm thirsty," he amplified, apparently thinking from her stare that she hadn't heard.

"Well, we should look for water then."

As if her voicing the thought had made it happen, a silvery gleam appeared in the distance, amid greenshadow.

"Was that there before?" she asked Racquel.

"Huh?" He looked where she pointed. "Hey!" He limped rapidly toward it, leading the way downhill between green-velvet boulders the size of sofas to the pool.

"Whoa," Sassy said.

As if she had ordered him to halt, Racquel stood there. For a moment they both just stared, for it was strange to find such a pool in the midst of wilderness. It looked like the reflecting pool from some royal garden. Edged with cadet-blue and gray-green and shrimp-pink stone—some sort of quartz, Sassy thought, or marble, or maybe even jade, she did not know, and she made herself a mental note to drop by the library and take out some books on rocks when she got home—if she got home . . . Edged with stone of the subtle colors Sassy loved, the pool nestled in a glade, a smooth-lawned sort of glen, and all around it grew nodding white flowers similar to daffodils. It was odd, those garden flowers, and the pool without a stream leading into it or out of it, and the glade—a man-made dell, it seemed, a gently rounded dingle, a clearing, although not so large that it would let in sunshine except at high noon. Sheltered all around. Not a breath of air moved, and the pool lay glassy still in greenshadow, and even the birds made no sound in that circular glade in the cup of which the rock-rimmed pool lay as if in the palm of God's hand, a perfect oval looking glass for the sky.

Between Sassy and Racquel and the pool stood a six-foot freshly painted signpost bearing messages in several languages, the English of which decreed: DANGER. NO SCRYING.

Eyes wide, Racquel asked, "What the hell is scrying?"

"It's some sort of magic . . ." Sassy tried hard to remember; she had read something about scrying in one of her books on mirrors. "It's a kind of divination with mirrors or shields or anything shiny. I think you have to be a virgin to do it."

"Well that lets me out," Racquel said without missing a beat. "How about you?"

"Give me a break."

"Hey. If I'm not a virgin, I can't scry, can I? So no problem. I'm going to get my drink." Surprisingly quickly for a guy with sore feet he headed past the sign toward the pool.

"Racquel, wait!" Sassy called. This place gave her pause, as the old stories used to say.

Racquel did not wait, but sang falsetto, "It's my party, and I'll scry if I want to, *scry* if I want to, *die* if I want to . . ." He did not continue the song. On his hands and knees among white flowers at the edge of the pool, he went very still.

"Are you okay?" Sassy got herself moving and headed toward him. "What do you see?"

"Nothing." He cupped his hands and lifted water to his mouth.

"Racquel—"

But nothing untoward happened. He drank. Sassy stood beside him as he dipped his cupped hands again and again. With ripples spreading, the water looked like—like water, nothing more. Pretty. Intricate, the way the circles of wavelets interlocked, like a wedding-ring quilt in shades of shadow-green and aquamarine.

Racquel finished drinking and lumbered to his feet. "What did you see?" Sassy asked him once more.

"Nothing much."

"Racquel, come on."

"I just saw myself. My reflection." With her gaze on him, he sighed, and added, "Except I was a guy."

"You mean it showed you the truth about yourself!"

"Truth? What's so damn true?" Racquel stumped off.

Sassy stood where she was, her lips parted, hearing her own heartbeat in her ears—it sounded like a washing machine on the heavy-load cycle. While uninterested in the philosophical ramifications of Racquel's existential bleat, she stood enthralled by other thoughts. Possibilities. If she looked in the pool, might it show her her true self? Instead of a blue budgie, might it reflect her own familiar Sassy-face, wrinkles and wispy hair and the hint of baby-fine mustache on her upper lip and the skin tabs growing on her eyelids and—good, bad, all of her? Her gut went watery with yearning at the thought. Even if it was just for this one time and never again, she had to see.

She turned. The pool lay glassy still again, showing nothing of its own depths, offering a glinting image of nodding narcissus flowers and treetops and a glimpse of azure sky, as if waiting for a god to look down from the latter and ask, Water, water in a pool, who's the very greatest fool?

Trembling, yet smiling at the same time, Sassy knelt on the smooth flat pastel-colored rocks at the verge.

She looked.

She gasped.

Paprika-freckled, Frederick smirked back at her from the surface of the water.

He smirked, and then he grabbed her. Sassy screamed as everything toppled into an eddy of blackness.

Racquel whirled when Sassy screamed, catching just a glimpse of the arm snaking out of the water. Sort of like the lady of the lake except the hand looked kind of hairy for a lady and it held no sword; instead, it seized Sassy by her limp gray hair. Before Racquel could react except to scream in his turn, there was a splash and Sassy was gone.

Yelling, Racquel ran to the pool and dived in after her.

The shock of the cold water turned everything black for an instant, and in a crazy flash he thought he was dead, he had broken his fool neck against the bottom of the pool without noticing—then his vision cleared and he found himself swimming along its stone-cobbled belly. Finding Sassy should have been easy; this was a pool only a bit larger than your average hot tub, and its water was glass-clear. But Racquel found only a few bored-looking koi down there. He surfaced, gasped for breath, and dived again, unwilling to believe it. He swam underwater the short length of the oval twice before he could encompass the truth: Sassy was quite simply not there.

Streaming water, he scrambled out, hyperventilating, cold to the heart, yelling "Help!"

How anyone could help, he had no idea.

"Help, somebody! She's gone!"

What happened next he would remember unto the final moment of his life.

He stood amid broken white flowers, crying out for a miracle, and upon shining wings it came flying down.

Racquel stood in abeyance of all functioning, his soul open as wide as his mouth and eyes, his knees weakening, watching it swoop down out of treetops as distant as heaven and condescend to him. It had the human form of a skinny young woman with a great-eyed, heart-shaped gamine face—but she could not be human; she was too ethereally beautiful, and she had pearly rainbow wings worthy of an archangel. She was all flutter and flow, Rapunzel masses of auburn hair, gossamer gown flowing down—even in his extremity of wonder, Racquel noted that floating gown and wished he had one like it to wear with great wings like a cape and damask Victorian slippers. But he saw no shoes on this being. No feet, either. Either the gown hid them, or she had none. She did not stand on the ground; she hovered in front of him, scanning him up and down.

She said, "Your dress is hanging oddly in the front."

"Huh?" Racquel regained his functioning to some extent and looked down at himself. "Shit." He had lost his boobs. Expensive custom-made silicone black-boy boobies, they were probably lying at the bottom of the pool. Where Sassy should have been but wasn't. What the hell was going on? Utter confusion supplanted much of his panic, because—

"Sassy?" he whispered to the apparition bobbing in front of him. "You—you're dead?"

"Do I look dead?" she retorted with more spirit than Sassy ever showed.

"But you—you're an angel." She looked like Sassy with wings. She *was* Sassy, ineluctably she was Sassy, although she appeared several decades younger and dynamite good-looking.

"Hell, no. I'm no angel."

Sassy never swore. Boggled, Racquel blurted, "You—you're not her? Are you Sassy?"

Her tone quieted. "I'm all the Sassiness she's lost. Poor Pavlovian wimp." As she spoke, her great wings gently fanned to keep her steady. "It's about time she came looking for me."

"Um, she's not looking for you," Racquel babbled before his stunned brain could unfreeze itself and stop him. "She's looking for a parakeet."

"A pair of *what*?"

"A, um, a bird."

"Huh. Well, screw her." She scanned him again, noting the

way the wet dress clung in all the wrong places, and mischief sunrose in her eyes. She said, "I should think poor old Sassy would be past that by now."

"No! I—she—" Racquel felt himself reddening and took refuge in the immediate. "Look, something pulled her into the pool." He pointed. "But she's not there."

"I didn't think she was fool enough to dare the pool!" The winged one's eyes widened with a sort of respect. "Or gutsy enough."

"I drank from it and it didn't hurt me."

"Well, ain't you the doo-doo." She gave him a bored look and started to turn away.

"Wait! What are we going to do about Sassy?"

"When she thinks to look for *me*, she'll be back." The Sassy-bird turned her lovely back and soared away.

Racquel bawled after her, "But what *are* you?"

"What the hell do I look like?" Her scorn floated back to him. "I'm a freaking bird of paradise!" She disappeared into the stained-glass mist above the treetops.

Racquel stood for what might have been a moment or an hour gazing after her.

 **N I N E**

Sassy staggered to her feet and found herself, dripping wet, up to her knees in one of the goldfish basins at the Sylvan Towers, with koi nipping her ankles and a number of hotel guests staring at her through elevator glass.

This would have been distressing enough, but as her eyes focused behind her bleared glasses and her mind found a take on the situation, it got worse. Life tended to do that, in Sassy's experience; whatever would be least bearable in any given situation was most likely to happen. Murphy's Law, thus:

Just beyond the rim of the basin, dapper in a suit from Sears, stood Frederick.

With his hands in his trouser pockets, he rocked on his heels in a manner he had always considered fetching. "Sassy!" he said with a nervous smile. "I, um, good to see you again."

It was such an awful moment that Sassy could only stare at him.

"The cops called me down here," Frederick explained. "When I found out you were missing, I was *concerned.*"

Deep within her gut Sassy felt a sluggish anger stir. He was concerned about her? How nice. Where was his concern for her when they were married?

"I was *quite concerned,*" Frederick iterated earnestly, with a touch of martyrdom because he was not getting the desired response. "Are you okay? What are you doing standing in that fishpond?"

Sassy's entire body clenched like a fist and went arctic cold. With her arms wrapped around herself, she began shivering so hard her teeth chattered. Like a squirrel she gabbled, "Whu— whu—whuuu—"

Frederick removed his suit jacket and with exaggerated tenderness placed it around her shoulders. His touch made her gut stir again, queasy. She flinched away from him.

"Whu—what did you grab me for?" she cried.

He stepped back and eyed her cautiously. "I didn't grab you, Sassy. I just put my jacket on you. You're cold." His helpful, explaining tone made Sassy want to scream. "You need to get out of that fishpond," Frederick continued, speaking slowly and carefully and clearly as if to a lunatic. "Get into some dry clothes." He started to offer his hand, then appeared to think better of it, as if she might bite.

Sassy thought of diving into the knee-deep water to get back where she had come from, and if she had thought it might work . . . but she knew better. She would just traumatize the fish and break her fool neck. The situation was beyond redemption, at least for the moment. She sighed, stepped out of the fishpond and stood dripping on the floor. She wondered whether her car was still in the parking lot. Where were the keys? She couldn't think.

"So where have you been?" Frederick asked.

She stared at him without answering.

He waited a while, then said, "Well, you can't just stand there. And you can't go outside like that. You used to work here, right? Is there somebody you can borrow dry clothes from?"

She watched his mouth move as if she were observing a museum exhibit, something alien feeding, a starfish, a sea urchin. She heard his words only as background noise.

"I think the cop is still interviewing downstairs," Frederick said. "But maybe not."

It all felt like a bad dream. Maybe it was. Sassy closed her eyes, took a deep breath and opened them again, but—damn—everything, Frederick was still there.

Interpreting her silence as incomprehension, he expanded—literally; under his cheap white shirt his chest puffed, lifting his wide tie, paisley, like big blue sperm swimming around. "They *thought* maybe I could help them find you," he declared, "and I *did*. We'd better go tell them. Come on." He turned away.

She stumbled after him. Years of conditioning made her follow even as she thought *I want to go home*. But how? Clothes soaking wet. Car probably towed. Sassy opened her mouth and tried to ask about the car, but all that came out was a wordless bleat.

Frederick turned back to peer at her with freckled benignity. "Is something wrong?"

She spoke with sudden clarity. "Nothing you'd understand." He seemed to think that he had wandered by and found a madwoman standing in a fishpool, but Sassy knew well enough what had happened. When she had seen his face in the water, he had seen her, and there she was. It made sense. She had always been his good little reflection.

Racquel stood shivering in his wet dress, thinking of throwing himself back into the pool permanently, with a rock on his chest, when the feather floated down like a silver sword of Zorro slicing a long, lazy zigzag in the air.

Silver? No, not silver but all the pearly colors of dawn. Gawking, Racquel suspected he knew whence that foot-long pinion had come, and he forced his gaze away from the feather to stare up at treetops and distant deep sapphire sky. But he saw no sign of her.

Then the feather halted at the level of his chest and just out of his reach, wheeling like a weathervane—no, a feathervane. Ha, ha. And he had no one upon whom to inflict the pun, damn it. Where was Sassy? What was happening to her?

The feather pointed away from the oval pool, up the slope of the dingle and into the forest.

Racquel had a feeling that if he left this place behind he might never find it again. And it was his only link to Sassy— but there was nothing down there except koi and two chocolate-colored silicone boobs like giant Hershey kisses out of the wrappers, and he was not going to dive for them because he was too cold and bummed and it was all too goddamn weird and he had no clue what to do to get Sassy back.

The feather bobbed on air, waiting for him.

Goddamn helplessness, anyway. "Lead on, Macduff," Racquel grumbled, and the luminous pinion apparently did not mind being so titled, because it did lead on, and he followed.

Through greenshadow, over mossy boulders and through icy trickles of water, through rifts of mushrooms the colors of wild rose and wisteria and tamarind the thing led him. It seemed to be a kindly feather; it waited for him when he followed too slowly, which was most of the time. For what might have been hours or a few minutes he faltered after it, limping until he stumbled. After a while the ambient light turned all the colors of the mushrooms and then some; the shadows grayed into twilight. Something as gray and silent as the shadows ghosted past; owl. There on a low branch sat another one, perched fluffy as a feather duster. Sassy would know what kind. Probably some damn extinct or endangered owl. Spotted owl, maybe. Cute little thing—until it turned its weird ring-gold eyes on him. Then he shivered, cold in his wet draggle of dress. Birdsong quieted into twitterings and owl call; night was falling. In the dusk the feather shone like sterling silver.

"I can't make it much farther," he told it. He could see the feather, but not his footing, and with every step his feet hurt like very hell.

The feather jiggled in response and darted on. Racquel sighed and slogged after it.

Just as dusk became dark and he really could not go on much farther, he saw the light ahead, a modest amber glow tucked down into a cup of the forest. Campfire. People. Food, maybe. Rest. Without reasoning any farther, without considering whether these putative people had ever seen a black guy in draggled drag before, he staggered toward the firelight.

In the lower-level men's room, Sassy swabbed johns in an incandescent fury, hating herself for wearing once more the decent and obeisant poplin uniform of a maid, hating herself for meekly stepping back into this—this—she could not think words bad enough to describe this job that involved cleaning up unknown men's bathroom mistakes and the occasional flaccid condom. At first when they had offered her "another chance" at the job, she had said no thank you. Just wanted to go home, wet clothes or no wet clothes. Leaving Frederick still looking for a cop to brag to, she had gotten as far as her car, which was glory hallelujah still there in the employee lot—but no key. Duh. Not thinking real clearly.

Back inside, hiding in the maids' locker room, she had phoned her landlord to beg a ride.

"Where you been?" he had asked kindly. "You're evicted."

Evicted?

Yes, he'd put her stuff out on the sidewalk. No, there wasn't any of it left. Yes, he had rented her apartment, to an exotic dancer complete with a rainbow of ostrich-feather fans. Judging by the landlord's tone, he found his new tenant more interesting than he had ever found Sassy.

It had taken Sassy's bleary brain a while to absorb this, then another while to postulate some options: share a bed with her mother at the Alzheimers' home? She almost felt incompetent enough, but not quite. Sleep in her car? Needed the key. Sleep in a Sylvan Tower broom closet? Damn, it was that or the street.

And to sleep in the Sylvan towers she had to accept the all-too-excremental maid job.

Moreover, there was another practicality to be considered: being employed at the Sylvan Tower, at least she had access to the locked floors and Rapunzel's oval mirror.

Unfortunately, it was nighttime now; the salon was closed. She was going to have to wait until daylight. But the minute the place opened—God, please let it work. She had to get back, she had to get back to the eden of lost dreams and find Racquel.

At the thought of him, Sassy lost the rhythm of her scrubbing and stood with her johnny mop dripping on the floor, her throat aching. Poor guy, he was footsore, he had no shoes, nothing to wear, and he'd never meant to be there to start with. So far PLUMAGE seemed okay, his employees were keeping it open, but—poor Racquel, what he must be thinking of her. She had to find him and bring him back before he lost everything too.

Briefly Sassy wondered about finding the parakeet that had gotten her into all this. But then she dismissed the thought as low priority. So she'd go around with a budgie for a reflection, so what? Racquel mattered more.

Finding Racquel mattered even more than figuring out what to do about Frederick.

Frederick, who was going to be back, she could just tell. Frederick, all too cordial. Frederick, smiling and clueless. Frederick, intent on what he did best: messing up her life.

Sassy flushed the john, wishing for a brief, savage moment that Frederick's head were in it, and moved on to the urinals, where she had to replace the sanitary cakes; eww. Why did they have to make such foul things the color of paradise sky? Sassy took care of them quickly and moved on to the wash-stand, where she was wiping the countertop when Frederick walked in.

"*There* you are, Sassy," he enthused. "I've been looking all over for you."

Sassy made no reply. She couldn't; this inappropriate man's mere presence in the vicinity racked her insides so badly, even after more than a year, that she just wanted to crawl under the sinks and hide. And she wanted to claw his eyes out, except she lacked proper claws by today's acrylic standards, and at the same time, quite illogically as he was the one who had caused all her pain, she wanted to run to him for comfort and cry on his shoulder. And she hated her own weakness for feeling all of this yet doing none of it. She stood dabbing at the soap dis-penser with a drippy old sponge.

Frederick walked over to the urinals and stood there—for a moment, her mind going rapidly but ineffectually like a ham-ster in a wheel, Sassy thought that Frederick meant to use the facilities, flip it out in front of her and pee on the nice fresh cerulean-blue cake of deodorant she had put in there; how dare he? It was the crowning thought to immobilize her entirely. Her hands, slimed with soap, faltered to a halt.

Leaning upon a urinal, Frederick scanned her and said with his best Don-Johnson boyish smile, "You're looking good, Sassy."

She still hadn't spoken a word, and she wasn't about to start now.

"I mean it," he told her, increasing his earnestness quotient. "You're looking real good. Have you done something with your hair?"

Unbelievable. The jackass was hitting on her.

Hitting. On. Her.

God have mercy. Next he'd be telling her she'd lost weight.

"You look younger. Have you lost some weight?"

Christ, Sassy's mind cried out like a bird of paradise, *what has become of my soul? Why can't I just throw the sponge at him?*

Frederick lost his shy-boy smile and began to look puppy-dog hurt that she hadn't responded. "Look, Sas," he said, gruff yet vulnerable like Bruce Willis, "you know it's not easy for me to say, but I—I'm really sorry if I hurt you."

If? *IF?*

Sassy's chest, on the rack of mixed emotions, screamed so loudly that finally her mouth moved, if only to whisper. "So what's happened to Binky-poo?"

"Huh?" Frederick affected a moment of nonrecollection. "Oh. The Bink transferred to Mexico."

Now he was doing the other Bruce Willis, showing no emotion. Sassy's grip tightened on the sponge till it spurted. The jerk. He'd left her for the wispy-blond chickie-poo and now the chickie had pooped the coop or whatever it was chickies did when they left, his anorexic sweetie was gone and he didn't even *care*?

Of course she, Sassy, wasn't showing much emotion either. Oblivious to her clenched hand, he stepped closer to her. "The Bink was just a physical thing," he told her, keeping sincere eye contact just the way they had taught him in management class.

Just physical? *Just?* It had been years since he'd shown any physical affection for her, Sassy.

"You, uh, you're more than just a squeeze. I mean, I married you. That ought to mean something."

Sassy's mind shrilled with sarcasm. *Yes, it certainly ought to, it did mean something to some of us.* Snappy comebacks, right when she needed them; damn it, why could she not speak?

"What I mean," Frederick said, standing too close, speaking gravely to the top of her head, "getting married, that's not for temporary even if sometimes you think so, you know?"

Sassy blinked several times rapidly, trying to wake herself up from this—was it a nightmare or a dream? In his boneheaded way, Frederick seemed to want her back. Back to familiar life. She could have a home again and know who she was. Be a wife again.

"I'd like it if you and me could get back together," Frederick said as if he were proposing a pleasant social evening.

But—but instead of joy, Sassy felt an ache like a red-hot stone nesting in her chest, so hard and stinging it made her stir her mouth to whisper again. "You threw out twenty-seven years . . ."

"But I *did* hang in for a long time," Frederick said, nodding. "Why don't we try again, huh? Another twenty-seven, what do you say? We could go away for a couple days. Go up to Allentown, hit the factory outlets, get you some new sweaters or something."

Earnest about the factory outlets, he had stepped even closer to Sassy, close enough to touch. Sassy wanted to press against his obtuse, cushy chest and cry. She wanted a home instead of a broom closet. She wanted him to take care of the bills. She wanted his warm lumpen weight snoring in the bed next to her at night again.

She also wanted to take the johnny mop and ram it right down his throat and ditto the sponge up his nose for good measure. And she wanted him to reach out for her but she had the weird feeling he was more likely to grab her by the hair. And if he did either of the above she wanted to slap his face just as hard as she could. She wanted to kick him where it would hurt. Afraid of her own feelings more than anything, she stepped back, and the blue budgie sitting on air in the mirror caught her eye; it perched bolt upright and cigar slim, its round head turned toward Frederick in silent screaming alarm.

Frederick's advance had placed him in front of the mirror also. Sassy glanced at the place where his reflection should be.

Then she blinked. Then she stared.

"Or some shoes," Frederick added. "Whatever you want. C'mon, Sassy, what do you say?" urged Frederick in his best Santa-Claus tones.

"You have no bird," Sassy blurted. She saw no reflection in the mirror where he should be. Nothing at all.

"*Huh?*"

She looked at him. "You have no bird," she repeated loudly and clearly because evidently he hadn't heard her. "None whatsoever."

Not even a budgie. Jeez.

The life of a homeless person was looking better every minute. Sassy slapped her wet sponge back into its bucket on the cart and wheeled on out.

Son of a gun, Sassy thought. Son of an iron ironic cannon on Fort Custer or somewhere, the Sylvan Tower was hosting a fashion convention, and one of the cutting-edge Paris couturiers had taken it into his head to attempt pow-wow chic. In other words, plumage. Variations on the fan-shaped feather bustles worn by fancy dancers at Native American events. Exotic, elegant, pencil-thin models strolled a runway in the second-lobby-floor ballroom, and watching from the back, Sassy saw glorified turkey tails affixed to "the head" (worn with a prairie-style broomstick-pleated muslin frock and Mediterranean cork platform heels, as the announcer pointed out), shooting à la Flash Gordon from the tips of "the shoulders" (with fawn-colored slubbed silk accented with genuine porcupine quilling and fourteen-karat gold jingles authentically imprinted to simulate snuff-can lids), worn like canary-and-turquoise concave wings (with Pueblo-inspired quilted vest and faux-fur-fringed anklets), and occasionally even where a bustle belonged, on "the derriere" (of synthetic-doeskin miniskirts, mostly, with beaded headband and spike heels and for God's sake don't try to sit down). Elegantly seated on fake fur thrown over the hotel chairs, the convention attendees took notes and applauded each successive model more enthusiastically than the last, oblivious to the activity in the back of the room.

Standing in back, however, Sassy took it in: the Native American protest. A few members of the something-or-other nation, Sassy missed which one, were there in business suits trying to point out misappropriation of their people's heritage and traditions. ". . . crassly insensitive commercialism," one of the Native American men was saying to a bored-looking TV reporter when Sassy started listening in. "My people are tired of being exploited by European culture." Mercifully, he skipped the long history thereof. "Even if it were done with respect—but I see no respect here. I see cultural rape."

Only half-listening, Sassy noticed with bemusement that he did not look like a television Indian at all. Neither did any of the others. They looked like people, that was all. Their skin color was not red; it was mostly dun or indeterminate. One of the women had blond hair. One of the men had the high cheekbones and black-braided hair Sassy would have expected, but one of them had brown curls, and the spokesman was bald, round, and looked like a mid-level CPA.

He said, "The eagle feather is not a fashion statement to be mocked; it is a sacred adornment of the kachinas, by whose permission my people have been permitted to borrow, not own, the eagle feather for our ritual dances. If—"

The news reporter perked up and lifted his microphone. "You say the feathers are supposed to be worn for dancing?"

"Yes. But not ballroom dancing." Why was a formal dance called a ball? Sassy wondered, and her mind veered for a moment into thoughts of basketball, volleyball, elegant couples in black tuxes and gowns spiking it over the net. ". . . ritual based on the mating dance of the prairie chicken," the Native American spokesman was saying.

Sassy gave him her full attention. So did the reporter, motioning to his cameraman to wake up.

"Could you show us?" he asked.

"Certainly," said the man with stony dignity. He glanced around at his companions, who nodded. One man turned to a tray on a stand, removed the water glasses from it, and began to pound out an exceedingly basic rhythm with his hands; a few heads in the fashion-show audience turned. Then more, as the balding man in the business suit crouched and began a slow, shuffling dance.

The others joined him. Together they circled, bent and swaying, to the drummer's muffled rhythm. People stared, and the TV reporter and the cameraman looked very happy with their news bite; they looked as if they wanted to laugh. But Sassy felt no inclination to laugh. She felt her nape hairs prickle with awe and a recognition she could not name. She could almost see the drooping wings, the tails fanned in display, the naked pathos of shuffling scaly feet, claws dragging in the dust, the eyes half-lidded, the heads abased in self-abnegation.

She wished Racquel were here. Where was he? Damn, he belonged here with her, now. She didn't care whether he wanted, as she did, to dance the prairie-chicken dance, or whether he might be more interested in the beanpole of a model pirouetting at the end of the runway in her Venetian chopines, her stick-slim Navajo-patterned skirt, her squash-blossom silver jewelry and the sequined vermilion feather peplum surrounding her waspish waist. She didn't care whether he wanted to dress like that; indeed, she rather expected he might, being Racquel. She liked his plumage. She missed him.

As the dance ended, Sassy found herself face-to-face with the black-braided man.

"Do prairie chickens mate for life?" she asked him.

He stared but gave her no answer.

The cop caught up with her in the employee lounge, as she sat at the sticky table staring at the snack tray and wondering whether she dared to filch a packet of animal crackers, whether the security camera was really just a dummy the way some of the maids claimed.

There he stood stiff as a brick on the other side of the table from her, and it was the same flat-faced no-neck cop she'd knocked over popping out of the mirror last time, which surprised Sassy. If she'd bothered to think about him at all, which she hadn't, she would have thought he'd have passed the entire Missing Persons of Sylvan Tower embarrassment off to some other cop by now. Judging by his expression, she bet he'd tried.

He took refuge in the usual formalities to begin with. "Mrs. Hummel?"

He knew quite well who she was. "I'm not married," she said, surprised by the anger in her own voice.

"Um, Miss Hummel. I'm investigating the disappearance of—"

"Of me."

Her interruption jarred her out of his routine. "No, not this time. Nobody filed a missing persons on you."

Lovely. "But Frederick said you'd been asking him about me."

"In regard to your known association with another missing person. Mr. Shelton."

"*Who?*"

He pressed his lips together, puffed out a disapproving breath, then said, "Mr. Devon Shelton. The proprietor of the PLUMAGE boutique."

"You're looking for *Racquel?*"

"He goes by that name," said the cop with acid in his tone, "yes."

"He's on the other side of the mirror. Uh, she is."

"I am aware that Mr. Shelton is a transvestite," said the officer stiffly. He had not sat down. He wanted no part of any of this. "I spoke with his family."

"Is that who filed the missing persons report?"

"No." The single flat word.

God, did he have a lover after all? "Who did, then?"

"His assistant manager. Miss Hummel—"

Sassy sat up straight and peered at the cop. "But you talked to his parents? Are they worried about him?"

"*Miss* Hummel—"

"Just tell me this one thing and I'll answer your questions. Please. Do they care about him at all?"

The cop sighed and looked at the floor. "The mother does. Maybe," he muttered. "Miss Hummel." He glared up at her. "When did you last see, um, Racquel?"

"It's hard to say. It feels like several hours, our time. But then, it was day there and it's night here. It might only be a few minutes."

He stood with his tablet poised, but his pen hovered motionless. His flat face showed some whitening around the nostrils and mouth.

"He was right beside the oval pool," Sassy added.

"Oval pool? What oval pool? Where?"

"I told you. On the other side of the mirror."

"Miss Hummel—"

"Not the one you broke," she explained. "Any mirror will do, except it has to be oval. And large enough," Sassy added as an afterthought. Her mind was circling like blue butterflies over cow dung. Frederick. Where to sleep, how to get something to eat. A mother with a son she'd named Devon. It didn't matter. Racquel, stranded in the forest of lost dreams. Cops looking for him.

"Do I understand you correctly, Miss Hummel? You are saying—"

Sassy's circling mind settled on a scary thought, *oh Lord, Racquel,* and she interrupted again. "Did you tell the hotel management about him?"

The cop's fleshy cheeks had gone watermelon-pink, in pinto contrast with his whitening nose. "I'm the one asking the questions, thank you. You say you saw Racquel, uh, Mr. Shelton only a few minutes ago. Do you know where he is now?"

Sassy said quite truthfully, "No."

"No?"

"I wish I did." She needed a friend just then, and the feeling rippled in her voice.

Nevertheless, the cop glared. "Miss Hummel, I'd appreciate your cooperation."

"I *am* cooperating!" Sassy wondered why she was not afraid of him. Too bummed by everything that had happened, probably. Too flattened. Wooden. Compared to the turmoil Frederick made of her insides, this cop was nothing. A cream puff.

"I ought to take you downtown."

"Go ahead!" At least then she'd have a place to sleep. "You know I'm telling the truth," she added. "You were there when we came back—"

She could not have made a worse mistake with him. His pink face went the color of a pickled egg. He dropped his tablet and his command of grammar. "Youse were hiding behind that mirror or something!" he roared. "Trying to make a fool of me. Youse—"

"Fine. It didn't happen," Sassy said.

Her dead calm, more dead than calm, startled the yelling out of him. He stared at her.

"And if it didn't happen, I'm not here, right?"

She felt so wooden she almost believed it herself.

"None of this happened," she said.

The cop swallowed. "That's a good idea," he said.

Sassy said, "I don't exist."

"Okay, miss. Um, sure," said the cop in a thin voice out of keeping with his thick neck. His skull under his buzz haircut must have been not as thick as it appeared. "Fine by me." He backed toward the door. "You don't exist," he agreed, and he was gone.

It was the black Egyptian-cat-goddess hair tech at Rapunzel's front desk this time. She greeted Sassy with wary-eyed reserve. "Oh. Uh, hello again."

"Hello." Sassy felt suddenly very much aware that she was wearing the selfsame sweats as before, a bit rumpled from drying in the maids' locker room. She had slept on a lumpy sofa in the employee lounge, and she had slept badly. Her hair felt stringy. She wondered whether she might request a complimentary shampoo.

Probably not. The young woman, what was her name, Romaine, seemed eager to be rid of her. "You came back for your coat, right? I'll get it." She fled toward the back.

Sassy had forgotten all about the coat. She had so little left that when the girl brought it to her it felt like a celestial gift. She put it on at once and comforted her hands in the pockets—whoa. Car keys! That, and she actually had a few dollars in there.

Not that car or money would be of any use to her where she wanted to go. She asked, "Actually, what I came for—may I see your oval mirror for a minute?"

"No." Romaine sounded most unprofessionally abrupt.

"I have to." Sassy darted past her, heading for the cubicle.

"No! You can't."

Sassy ran, lunged at the cubicle door like a sprinter lunging for the tape, flung it open, then stood there as the young woman clunked up to her in her platform heels.

"You can't," Romaine repeated.

Sassy could see why. The mirror wasn't there—only a startled hair technician and an older woman in a perforated plastic dye bonnet. The latter was starting to look pissed off.

"We got rid of it." Romaine pulled Sassy away by the arm and closed the door. "You'd better leave, ma'am."

"You got rid of it?" Sassy repeated, as blank as a parrot.

"Not me personally. Management. Ma'am, this way." The young woman steered her toward the exit. "I'm asking you to leave the premises—"

"They were that afraid somebody else would dive through it?" Sassy was still grappling with mirrorlessness.

"—without any further disruption." Romaine shoved her toward the door.

Sassy left.

That day she cleaned rooms with a lack of luster, shedding her uniform to grab a shower and shampoo in one of the bathrooms as she was scrubbing it, for which infraction she received an unsatisfactory rating from her shift supervisor.

Camped out on the sofa in the lounge that night, she could not sleep at all, and it was not just a matter of through traffic and lumpy upholstery. It was not just a matter of having been chewed out. It was not just a case of being homeless and almost penniless. It was not just being divorced and having to contend with Frederick—

Well, maybe it was partly Frederick. The thought of him jolted her up off the sofa and sent her wandering through the Sylvan Tower's filigree lobby in the dim light of 2 A.M. lonely.

She could almost hear the place breathing, it was so quiet, so glassy still under the great vault of the atrium, so shadowy beneath the feathery trees. Sassy leaned on a wrought-iron balcony railing and stared down six stories into the fishpools swimming with warm glints like amber stars; goldfish, or the rippling reflection of neon? Sassy couldn't tell. She couldn't see any reflection of herself, not even a blue budgie.

Frederick. The nebbish. The narcissus without a reflection. Man without a self.

He stole my soul. Over the years. He's a black hole soul sink.

Vaguely Sassy wondered why he didn't have one of his own. Maybe there weren't enough souls to go around. That made sense, the way population increased. Each generation had more people than the last, so if you believed in reincarnation, which made more sense than wings and a harp when you thought about it, if souls got passed down then some people got born without one. And then what to do? A resourceful person would probably grow a perfectly nice homemade soul from scratch, but someone like Frederick—he would just want to snatch somebody else's soul like one of those nasty water spirits snatching somebody's reflection. A soul snatcher, that was what Frederick was. A malevolent lurking soul snatcher. Stealing hers because he had none of his own.

Racquel was right about him.

The thought of Racquel put a point like a spearhead on Sassy's despair. Was he okay? Would she ever see him again? Did he hate her for getting him into this bizarre mess called her life?

She had to get back. Back there. Back to her paradise, his perdition.

Please.

Sassy had long ago stopped believing in God—although she did somehow believe in the soul, she knew in her heart that creatures were more than just hunks of meat moving around, she even felt that trees were more than just oversize broccoli, and maybe that was sort of the same thing as believing in God—for whatever inchoate reason, she tilted back her head to gaze up at the sky as if that might somehow help. Except she could not see sky. She looked up, up at dusky atrium soaring above her, balconies, vines, canopy of glass the sick tongue-gray color of the city night, plumy tops of ficus trees—her heart turned over with yearning. She had never, she realized, been in the forest of lost dreams at night. What was it like? Did tree frogs sing, or human voices, or spirits? Were there wild cries echoing, the crackings and whistlings of night birds, the caroling of foxes and wolves? Somewhere did a flute sing? Did stars nest silver in the treetops? And the moon—was it a curling white feather in the sky there, a single sickle feather from a white cock's tail?

For a moment she could almost see the moon, the stars flocked in the treetops like sugar doves, she imagined it so ardently that it all melted together, the ficus and the glory forest and the canopy overhead and the canopy of leaves she remembered—but then it was just the Sylvan Tower again.

Just for a moment . . . but now it was gone.

And everything was too hard, too glass and steel and smog and smell of disinfectant cleanser, and Sassy couldn't bear it. It wasn't fair.

Head thrown back, she cried out, not caring who heard her.

"Oh, poop!" she cried to the uncaring realm of locked floors and suites.

In the listening silence that followed, the echoes of her angst faded away.

But then, as she sighed a breath that solved nothing and lowered her head, there came another sound. A feathery whirring bore down on her out of the shadows.

Skreeek!

It cried out even more loudly than she had. And joyously. Sassy felt almost sure she heard joy in that wild cry. Startled, she flung up her arms as a warm plop of bird poop annointed on her shoulder—startled, but not afraid this time as she felt her visitor landing on the temple of her glasses.

"Hello?" She put up a hand cautiously and brought it down with a parakeet thereon.

The parakeet.

Its little warm feet gripped her forefinger. It fluttered its wings to keep balanced but did not fly away. It tilted its yellow head to look up at her face, and its beak emanated a sound too tender to be labeled a mere chirp; it was a bird-whisper such as it might have breathed to a lover.

"Goodness," Sassy said. "Mercy. What in the world am I supposed to do with you?" But she felt warmth start in her heart and radiate to her face, she felt herself blinking and smiling because—because there still was a connection between her and—there. How, she had no clue, but on her hand perched a visitor from the lost realm of her soul. And she was no longer so alone.

TEN

It was hard to remember that she had thought all her troubles would be over once she found the parakeet. Now he was here, but she didn't know how to get him to restore her own proper image in her mirror, and moreover she didn't much care. Reflections just didn't seem so important anymore. All she cared about was getting back to the forest, and back to Racquel.

It turned out to be surprisingly impossible to find an oval mirror. Throughout the rest of that night and the next morning Sassy ransacked the Sylvan Tower for one, searching the locked floors and the boutiques and even the storerooms, while the other employees cast sidelong glances at her, like there was something wrong with being obsessed? Something odd about being homeless and prowling with a parakeet following you everywhere? Wherever she went, it flew along with her or rode on her shoulder, accenting her sweatshirt with its poop.

Sassy was experiencing an exalted form of desperation which made her care not whether people stared at her or whether there was poop on her sweatshirt. The only point of light in her life right now was the parakeet. Its devotion made her feel warm and humble. On her way around the lobby's sixth level, she held out her hand and it landed on her. "Twee!" it cried at her with a fey joy. "Twee! Twee! Twee!"

"Okay, I'm Twee," Sassy agreed. "And what's your name?" She spoke rhetorically, like a doting pet owner, but the parakeet answered with a cheep.

"Kleet?" said Sassy onomatopoetically. "Okay. Kleet, I am starting to think it is a conspiracy. They took all the oval mirrors away."

By noontime she could no longer joke about it. Hunger and exhaustion and discouragement caught up to her, and she ducked into the mezzanine ladies' and leaned on the edge of a sink, feeling like she might either puke or cry. "Kleet," she asked—for the parakeet had ducked in there with her, of course—"what am I going to do?"

"Twee! Twee! Twee!"

Sassy looked up, and her despair softened into a bittersweet smile. Wings fluttering ecstatically, Kleet was greeting her blue budgie in the mirror. After his first three shrieks he gabbled tenderly, beak to beak with Sassy's reflection. Her poor budgie, it looked as glum and hassled as she felt, its cobalt feathers rumpled, and it looked as if it wanted to swoon in Kleet's arms. Or wings. Whatever. Just behind the glass, it— she—pressed close to him as he crooned and twittered and tried to nibble at her cheekfeathers.

"Kleet," Sassy said, "you're smarter than people. They can't even see her."

They look at me and all they see is a dumpy dumped housewife with squirrel-gray hair.

As if he could hear her thought, Kleet whirred up suddenly to perch atop her much-impugned head. "Twee! Twee! Twee!"

Sassy put her hand up and brought him down where she could look at him. She loved the feel of his vermicular feet gripping her finger. She loved his round eyes in the sides of his no-neck head. She loved his feathering, as yellow as daffodils, as green as Eden in sunlight.

"Twee," he said to her earnestly.

"Kleet," she wondered aloud, "what are you trying to tell me?"

In all his short life Kleet had never felt so loonishly happy, so blessed. She had called to him once again, his deity, she had called to him from the hardair world and the force of her clarion summons had startled him from his sleep, he had flown to her, he had found her again, and—this was the dayspring of Kleet's great joy—she had extended her pale holy twigs to him in greeting. She had allowed him to perch thereon. She had spoken to him by name.

And as if this were not ecstasy enough, Deity had shown unto him an azure princess of a parakeet—it was the first time Kleet had ever encountered one of his own kind, and she was female and so fair, so lovely melting blue, and—true, she was sealed away from him behind the mystery of hard air, but—but would she not soon, somehow, be his mate?

"Twee!" Kleet sang in rapture and rejoicing and holy praise. "Twee! Twee! Twee!"

His was a living deity. A tree that spoke and walked. A very descendant of the One Tree.

Long ago, in the Great Time, Kleet knew, there had been the One Tree whose feathers were all colors, not like the mostly green feathers of the sleepy trees today. The One Tree's feathers were iridescent blue like jays and yellow like canaries and bronzegold like pheasants and flashing red like tanagers and flamingo-pink and toucan-orange and hummingbird-puce and green like—like parrots, of course. And parakeets. And like parakeets and linnets and larks and nightingales, the One Tree sang. There were no birds back in those beginning times, and no other trees except the One, but the One Tree sang like every bird that was ever to be and grew great enough for every tree. And as the One Tree grew and sang, it lifted its branches and took flight. It darted up like a skylark, it soared like a sea hawk—but it did not leave the earth. The One Tree's roots grew to the core of the world, and such was the greatness of the One Tree that when it flew, the whole world flew with it.

Kleet knew these things, not because any mentor had ever told him, but because they were true. From his hollow-cored bones he knew them.

But, his bones told him, the One Tree became lonely. Flying through the vastness of being, the One Tree found many worlds, worlds like eggs and worlds like stones, worlds made of fire or ice or fog or dew, worlds with many sorts of creatures living on them—but never another world with One Tree like itself. With each world it found, the One Tree grew lonelier.

Then out of the solitude of the One Tree there came the First Winter and the Great Molting.

Kleet understood the loneliness, the solitude. He had felt them.

Sadness had made the One Tree shed all its plumage. And that was the end of the solitude of the One Tree. Each feather shed by the One Tree flew up and became a bird, each according to its color or colors, all the many birds in the world, far beyond numbering. But the molting of the One Tree did not stop there. When all its feathers had dropped, the One Tree itself began to molt apart, twig by twig scattered far, far by the winter wind, branch by branch falling, and finally splinter by splinter cracking like a great shellbreak, until every part of the One Tree was leveled to earth.

And each twig, each splinter, each branch, grew into a tree, all the many trees in the world, far beyond numbering.

Trees were dwindled, diminished remnants of the One Tree, Kleet knew, sleepy stupid things that no longer sang or flew. Still, many trees molted upon the coming of winter, remembering the One Tree.

And many birds still flew to trees for comfort, remembering the time when Bird was Tree and Tree was Bird. Sitting in the heart of Tree, singing, Bird knows itself to be the spirit of Tree.

Sitting upon the warm lifted five-twigged limb of Sassafras, singing, Kleet knew her to be Deity. BirdTree.

"Twee," he sang her praise. "Skreek. Skreeeeek! Kek kek kek Twee!"

And she sang back to him, skreekings he understood not at all, although the music of her singing swelled his breast fit to burst with joy. Deity sang:

> *"Birdie, birdie in the sky,*
> *Why'd you do that in my eye?"*

"Sassy! Hi," Lydia said. "Come on in."

Surprised that the big poopy woman remembered her name, Sassy smiled mistily. She hadn't thought Lydia would know her; these days she didn't think anybody knew her or cared. She carried Kleet nestled to her gravitationally challenged bosom under her coat, because it was cold out, and she had been feeding herself and Kleet on junk food filched in the employee lounge, she was missing work, not that she gave a flying leap, and she had spent her last few dollars on gas to get to Lydia's apartment. But Lydia's greeting made her smile.

She didn't feel like making small talk, though. As soon as she had stepped into the apartment (watching the floor so as not to trample other bipeds) and Lydia had closed the door behind her, she opened her coat to show Lydia the parakeet clinging like a honeycreeper to her sweatshirt.

"Twee," said Kleet.

"Oooh!" said Lydia, her homely voice hushed like dawn-light, her homely face soft and bright like sunlit forest mist as she gazed at Kleet, as Kleet gazed around him.

"Kek kek kek!" With a cry that for once was not "Twee," Kleet flurried into flight, zooming toward the other parakeets.

Lydia wore, swear to God, the same rib-knit too-tight poop-on-the-boobs T-shirt as before. But Sassy felt no revulsion this time. She took off her coat to reveal her own sweatshirt spangled with poop.

"He loves you," Lydia said.

"Are you sure?" Sassy felt not so certain. True, Kleet liked it when she sang, and she could not recall that anyone else, human or bird, had ever liked her singing. But Kleet had not yet bitten her. Sassy sported no blood blisters on her face.

Yet—of all the angsts she had been experiencing since Frederick had so rudely snatched her away from where she wanted to be, for all of her desperation, she had not felt that old famil-iar misery labeled "Nobody loves me." There was Kleet.

And there was Racquel.

Oh. *Oh.* Momentarily Sassy felt her breath stop.

Nah. Just a brain spasm.

"Sure I'm sure. He adores you." Clearing a cockatoo and two baby parrots off the sofa, Lydia sat down. Sassy started to sit beside her, but then another brain spasm seized upon her.

"Lydia," she requested, "do me a favor, would you, and come stand in front of the mirror?" She wanted to see what sort of a bird the big, soft-spoken woman was.

"Sure." Lydia shooed away a conure that had landed on her head and heaved herself to her feet again.

An owl, Sassy bet herself as she led the way to the wall mirror with the parakeet shelf in front of it. Lydia would be an owl or maybe a dove, something soft gray fluffy and otherworldly and wise.

There was no need to fight the parakeets for mirror space; they were all clustered at one end of their perch, bunched around Kleet with mighty chirpings. Peering through the huddle of budgies to make sure Kleet was okay, Sassy did not look at the mirror until she and Lydia stood in front of it.

Then she looked, and gasped.

"Lydia!" she yelped.

The plain-faced, bosomy woman wheeled to peer at her. In the mirror, plain bosomy Lydia mirror-image did the same.

"I can *see* you!"

It was Lydia in the looking glass all right, clear down to the streaks of bird do on the shirt. Not an owl or a dove, and not a no-birder, like Frederick, and not a surprise-birder, like if she had turned out to be a vulture or something, but—just Lydia. Herself.

Lydia had to be the most complete, whole person on the face of the planet.

Sassy was so excited to see a human being with a self-reflection that she flapped her arms and jumped as if she were trying to take off and fly.

"Whatever blows your skirt up," said Lydia, her gaze not owlish after all, but far more serene. Utterly accepting.

Sassy grabbed her hand like a child. "Can you see *me*?" she appealed. "In the mirror," she added; it was terribly important to get this right. "Can you see me?"

Lydia looked, then stared. "I'll be danged," she said.

"What? What do you see?"

"A blue parakeet. Where'd that come from?" Lydia swiveled her head to check on the parakeets still gathered around Kleet, then looked back at Sassy's blue budgie in the mirror again.

Sassy yelped again and bounced some more. In the mirror, her blue budgie lifted its wings and danced.

"Is that *you?*" Lydia asked as if somebody had got a name tag wrong.

"You can see me!" Sassy caught hold of both her hands and danced a half circle around her, swiveling her about-face. "Nobody else can see me. Lydia, you're the one. I knew it." Sassy towed her toward the sofa, scattering macaws and a lovebird or two. "I knew it. You're the one who can help me get myself out of this mess I'm in."

At the rim of the benighted hollow Racquel froze, seeing three things at once: the campfire, with its promise of warmth; a haunch of something that was definitely not mushrooms roasting over the gentle flames; and sitting around the fire, fletching arrows and waiting for their dinner, the men. Seven or eight of them. Unmistakably heterosexual men, even though they wore tunics and—whatchacallums, leggings, cross-gartered and too baggy and patched to be considered tights. It was the ill-fitting hose and something about their oafish posture that tipped Racquel off, the jutting angles of their lumpen shoulders and their bristling jaws. And if there was anything that frightened Racquel more than death or taxes, it was men. Hets. In gangs.

He had blundered right into the great all-time original boys' club, he realized. And all the boys sat with their glinting steel knives in hand and their bearded faces turned his way, staring at him.

And there he stood, unmistakably a guy in drag.

He shivered with more than the chill of his wet dress and bare legs in the nighttime breeze.

One of the men nearest to Racquel stood, looming and shadowy in the firelight, his knife a bright blood-colored slash in the firelit night.

Shaking, Racquel started to inch away.

"A Moor, by my troth," said someone almost in a whisper.

"Aye, a Moor!" said someone else in the same wondering tone. "Shipwrecked, perhaps."

The man standing close to Racquel beckoned. "Welcome, stranger," he said with more presence of mind than the others were showing. "I am Robin Hood and these are my merry men. Welcome to our revels." He swept his arm toward the food and the fire.

Relief flooded Racquel, clashing with his fear so badly that it shook him worse than ever. He felt his knees weaken and give way. Shadows seemed to wheel around him; he could see nothing but firelight and shadows. He collapsed where he was.

"Is he alive? Is he breathing?"

"He's fainted."

"Do Moors faint?"

"He's half-naked, poor fellow. Half-starved with cold."

"Get a blanket, Tuck."

"Brandy? Do we have any brandy?"

"No, Robin drank it all."

Amid hubbub, Racquel felt many hands taking hold of him, heaving him up and carrying him closer to the fire. Blessed warmth. Someone was rubbing and chafing his hands with something coarse and sweetly dry. Someone else was rubbing his legs and feet.

"His poor feet, they're all blood."

"Get that wet—what is that, some sort of robe? Get it off him."

Limp, Racquel felt them tugging his dress open and struggling to remove his empty bra.

"What sort of a corset is this?"

"Some kind of baldric that Moors wear."

"It's religious, perhaps. To carry relics in."

"What is this—" The voice grew hushed; Racquel felt someone pulling down what was left of his panty hose. "His skin comes off like a snake's!"

"Don't! You'll hurt him."

"It's already off."

"As fine as if an angel molted it."

"He seems all right underneath."

"Odd-colored but everything's there."

Naked, and not so much semiconscious anymore as opting out of all this, Racquel felt them wrap a blanket around him.

"Somebody get some water warming for his feet."

"Will, rip me some bandaging, would you?"

"Can't anybody find any brandy? Or some mead? Anything?"

"I told you, Robin drank the lot of it."

"Pepper, then. Find some pepper to put up his nose."

Racquel took exception to the idea of anyone's stuffing pepper up his nose. He opened his eyes and tried to sit up but was surprised to find that he could not do it. An odd noise came out of him, a sigh that was more like a moan.

"Wait a bit. He's coming around."

Two men sat him up, one on each side, their arms behind his

back, supporting him. Robin Hood himself placed a cup of
something good to his lips. Warm meat broth. Racquel stared
into Robin's eyes, as friendly as a golden retriever's, as he drank.

"Thank you," he whispered when, after he had gulped most
of the broth, Robin took the cup away.

Robin's jaw dropped. "He speaks English!"

"The Moor speaks the King's English!"

"A few words of it, at least."

"I have heard of birds that speak English."

Racquel said to the men helping him, "I can sit up by myself
now. Thank you."

"More than a few words!"

"But listen to the quaint foreign twist he gives his speech!"

"How came he here?"

Racquel said, "I have lost . . ." But how to explain to them
in a way that they would understand what he had lost? "I have
lost my—my companion." But they would think he meant a
man. And maybe they would not understand how emotion
was making him watery inside, rocking the boat. "My—"
Friend? Yes, Sassy was very much his oddball friend, but she
deserved a stronger word. "My sweetheart." These men
belonged to a more innocent time; maybe they would not
attach a sexual handle to the word.

They smiled, but not nastily. "The Moor came here with his
leman!"

"A dark damsel, belike!"

"This I must see. We must find her."

Robin asked Racquel, "You have lost her? How?"

"She disappeared into the oval pool."

The hubbub ebbed into an owl-feather silence. Racquel
could not tell whether they understood the oval pool or not.
They all sat in a circle around him gazing at him, and the only

movement was the tawny flickering of the firelight on their green jerkins and beard-shadowed faces.

Slowly Robin said, "She came here from—from another land? Like you?"

"Yes." Realizing that an incorrect assumption might ensue, Racquel added, "But she is white. Like you."

"Ah." Robin's acceptance was casual and complete. His men murmured a similar acceptance, then sat in silence again.

"She's still here in a way," Racquel said. Heartache made him say it even though he felt they could not possibly understand. "She's in the treetops somewhere. She's so beautiful. Like a spirit. Robed like an angel. All shining, with great wings. A feather guided me here."

"Ah!" This time it was a gasp, a sharp breath sucked in like undertow, and Robin drew back from him. All the others had gone rigid, and in their faces he saw—fear? Awe?

Worried that he had committed damage of some sort, Racquel tried to undo it, babbling on. "I mean, that's sort of her, but sort of—I don't know. She's just a little gray-haired hotel maid really. Older than I am. Kind of dumpy. Her name is—"

"Shhhh! Hush!" Robin lurched forward and seized him by the shoulders to stop him. The contact made Racquel realize that Robin needed a bath, but there probably wasn't an awful lot of opportunity in this place for personal hygiene. Anyway, despite his shabby shirt and touches of visible grime, Robin struck him as a nice-looking fellow, not handsome exactly but emanating goodwill with as much ease as he exuded body odor. "You are not strong enough to say that name," Robin whispered with greatest concern. "None of us dare."

"Wha?" The query was startled out of Racquel more by Robin's grip than by his words. Robin softened his grasp and his tone as he answered.

"You are a blessed one," he murmured. "To see her is the greatest of luck and blessing. To touch—" He drew back again. "You have not touched her, have you?"

Racquel thought about this, and concluded that he had not. "No."

"Then you are not yet an immortal." Robin essayed a smile. "Come, eat of the King's venison, my Moorish friend." His smile warmed. "Eat, rest, sleep. In the morning we will speak more of your trouble. Perhaps my men and I will be able to help you."

 E L E V E N

"**B**ut how did it happen?" Lydia asked, placid but puzzled. "I mean, why?" Sassy had told her how. Parakeet poop on the pate.

Sassy shook her head, indicating ignorance. "I don't think it could have happened to you."

"Huh? Why not?"

"Because you're so—so complete." Sassy did not know how better to explain her growing sense that she needed to be put back together again, re-membered, because she had been Frederickized. If she had not given herself so wholly to the marriage—make that given her *self*, given Sassy away— then none of this would be happening to her. And that would be—

That would be kind of a shame, actually.

Son of a gun.

Fondly she glanced across Lydia's bird-possessed apartment at Kleet, who sat twittering and cooing with his new budgie buddies. "I used to think he did it to me for some reason," she said, pointing at Kleet with her pinkie to be polite. "But why would he?" Now that Kleet was her companion she could not imagine that he had ever intended to harass her. "If he did, I'm sure it was some sort of weird accident."

"Well, let me ask him," Lydia said.

It was a concept so simple yet stunning that it took Sassy's breath away. With her mouth feeling for air she sat where she was. Lydia, however, heaved her poop-streaked bulk up from the sofa and crossed the room, treading nimbly around perambulating conures, to the perch where Kleet gabbled. She offered him her pudgy forefinger and he hopped on readily. Pivoting so that she created a kind of privacy with him, away from the other budgies, Lydia lifted him to within a few inches of her eyes, pursed her lips and whispered a series of kissy-sounding chirps to him.

"Twee!" he cried, lifting his head. "Twee! Twee!"

"Tree?" Lydia sounded puzzled. "He says you're his tree," she reported to Sassy.

"*Huh?*"

But Lydia had turned her attention back to Kleet, who was emitting a jazzy riff of soprano tweets. "He's very serious about this," Lydia murmured, listening intently. Sassy could see that he was; in his excitement Kleet fluttered his wings, nearly lifting himself off Lydia's finger. His twittering rose to a whistling crescendo, then subsided. Lydia nodded, puckered her lips and clicked her tongue at him.

"Thank you," she added, apparently for Sassy's benefit, as Kleet had already turned away and taken flight, zooming back to his perch by the mirror.

"Well." Lydia plodded over to sit by Sassy again, looking a trifle bemused. "Kleet's stuck on you like he's stuck with glue. He says you skreeked him and he skreeked you back. He worships you, and I mean that the way it sounds. If I'm understanding right, you're a kind of tree-goddess where he comes from, which I guess is that place behind the mirror you told me about."

Incapable of comprehending most of this, Sassy bleated, "*What?*"

"I think he wants to mate you," Lydia went on, "or he wants you to find him a mate, or something. I couldn't follow very well."

"He can't mate me!"

"Honey, I'm just telling you what I think he said."

"Since when do birds mate with trees? And how would he know about my name anyway?" A tree name, for gosh sake. Once more and with feeling Sassy deplored her mother's choice of nomenclature for a helpless newborn.

"Your name?"

"Sassafras."

Lydia sat up straight and said in humble, breathless tones, "Well, I'll be licked."

Sassy complained, "I don't want to be his tree. Did you ask him how I can get my own reflection back?"

"He don't have no idea you got one. He don't understand about mirrors. I mean, look how parakeets talk to mirrors."

True. To parakeets that was another parakeet or something in the mirror. On the far side of the glass, like visiting somebody in jail.

"A mirror is just hard air to him. Air you can't fly through. Except sometimes you can, it looks like."

"Aaaak," Sassy said, because for an eyeblink she was Sassy yet not Sassy, she was a plain brown hen bird stuck with a dandified mate, or no, now he was no mate and she wanted not sure what, world egg, world tree, yellow green scarlet azure sun bright plumage tree world, she wanted to see, to be— "Aaak!" The flutterflight of her own thoughts startled her like a grouse going up. "I'm going crazy." She grabbed her head in her hands, fingers dug into her stringy hair. "I'm so confused."

Lydia balled her hand into a fist under her chin and leaned on it, her elbow on her knee. Fist, chin, elbow, knee, all settled together into comfortable rondures; Lydia looked like she could stay that way all day, studying Sassy. Sassy emerged from her own hands, met Lydia's barn-owl gaze and didn't know what to say.

"How'd you get that way?" Lydia murmured.

"What way?"

"Kind of ash-gray."

She should talk. She wasn't the healthiest thing herself, kind of dough-colored. Sassy said, "I feel okay," which was amazingly true. "Crazy, but okay." Although with everything she'd been going through it was a wonder she felt okay. And no wonder she felt crazy.

"Not like you're sick," Lydia said without moving. "More like you're kind of thinned out. No aura to you. Or maybe it's that you're mostly aura and not much else. You're kind of shadowy."

Sassy blinked and checked her face with her fingertips. Was it possible that her appearance had changed and she didn't know it, now that there was a budgie in her mirror? Her face seemed to be all there, but how could she know anything for sure anymore?

"I thought so the first time I saw you," Lydia said, "but I didn't like to say anything."

And now that she had said something, it was mostly incomprehensible. Sassy demanded, "What do you mean, shadowy?"

"What I mean is, like you said, I don't think Kleet could have skreeked you if you'd been right to start with."

"Would you speak *English*? What do you mean, no aura?"

"No color," Lydia muttered, though perhaps not in reply to Sassy's existential yawp. She looked distracted. Uncurling like an oversize grub from the sofa, she made her massive way into the kitchen. Through the door Sassy could see only Lydia's blue-polyester backside, but she could hear her rummaging. She studied the polyester snaggles on Lydia's butt for a moment. Then Lydia turned and, rather like a manatee beaching, emerged from the kitchen, presenting a shoe box with both uplifted hands.

"Can you believe I used to peddle Maybelline?" With the air of one laying an offering on an altar she placed the shoebox, which said Hush Puppies, Quiet Your Barking Dogs, on Sassy's lap.

Sassy looked at her, then opened it. It was like opening somebody's crayon box jumbled with yummy hues. Tiny sample-sized tubes of cheek color, eyelid color, lipstick—Sassy had not known that lipstick came in so many colors. Involuntarily she gave a gasp of delight, quickly revoked as she wondered what good the stuff would do her. She didn't wear makeup, for the Lord's sake. The last thing she needed right now was lipstick.

"Take 'em along," Lydia was saying.

"What for?"

"Put some on you. Might help."

"I can't!" Sassy sounded like a whiny child, even to herself. She softened her tone. "How am I supposed to put makeup on?"

"Oh. Duh." Lydia rolled her eyes as she remembered that Sassy could not see herself in a mirror. "I'll put it on you, then." She dumped birds and books off the coffee table, then settled her cushy butt on it, her plump knees against Sassy's bony ones. "Take those glasses off," she said, and when Sassy didn't move, Lydia lifted the eyeglasses off Sassy's head herself and set them on a corner of the coffee table. To Sassy, everything blurred, going soft-focus and prismatic like the romantic scene in a movie, the room a rainbow of parrot macaw lovebird. She gazed entranced yet she hated being without her glasses. She hated being helpless. Lydia was pawing in the box then rubbing something onto a forefinger. "Let's put some color in your skin first."

As she lifted her hand to dab, Sassy pulled back. "Lydia, this is silly."

"Is it as silly as seeing a budgie in the mirror?"

Sassy sighed and closed her eyes, letting Lydia paint her.

At the first touch her face felt more real. Which was odd, because there is nothing more fake than makeup—is there? But Sassy belayed such thoughts, halted mental activity of any kind, her focus all on the soft dab stroke feathertouch of Lydia's fingers smoothing creamy quiddity onto the skin of her brow, temple, cheeks, chin. It felt wonderful. Sassy closed her eyes and soaked it in as if—as if—starved, that was it, like a plant starved for rain, like—*Most of my life*, Sassy realized with a pang of hindsight, *I have been starved for touch.* Such a simple, nurturing thing, human touch. Such a peaceful, right thing, to sit back feeling Lydia coloring her eyebrows almost hair by hair, hearing only her own breathing and the twittering of the birds, many many birds. *Forest,* Sassy thought hazily. *Canopy. Ivy, ferns, butterflies drifting up like black sparks.*

Lydia said, "Open your eyes a minute so I can see what shadow to use."

Sassy blinked. For a moment everything looked strange because it was not the forest, just Lydia's apartment. Cages. Ripped magazines, poopy newspaper. Ezekial dinging his bell. Dirty birds.

Lydia stared into her eyes with a frown that deepened into a trembling pout as if Lydia wanted to cry. Very low, Lydia said, "Sassy, do you *have* an eye color?"

"Of course." Didn't she? "Kind of greenish, last time I noticed."

"When was that?"

"When was what?"

"When was the last time you noticed?"

"I guess it's been a while." Might have been years ago. Sassy didn't want to think about it. She closed her eyes again.

It might have been a brush or a Q-Tip or Lydia's gentle fingertip feathering the color onto her eyelids. So soft. So pleasant, like holding a kitten. Funny, she felt younger. Sassy sat for a moment not wanting to let the feeling go when Lydia said, "Okay, all done."

Then she opened her eyes and said, "Lydia. What you asked me before, how I turned into such a nebbish—I think it was a wife thing."

The big woman stared back at her with stolid noncomprehension.

"Frederick was always hitting on hoochie girls," Sassy explained.

"Hoochie girls?"

"High-maintenance skinny baby chickies. At first I tried to compete, but—it all seemed so shallow—after a while I just kind of said, I'm your wife, deal with it. I mean, I never *said* that. We always tried to pretend he wasn't doing anything wrong. I just said it with the way I looked."

"Huh." Lydia glanced down at herself, then looked straight into Sassy's face and grinned. "I never been married. What's my excuse?"

Sassy looked at Lydia's eyes. Warm, shining brown, like woodland pools. "You're not missing anything important."

"Take your word for it. But how come nobody ever wanted me?"

Huh. Was it worse to be wanted then dumped, or never to be wanted at all? For a moment, forced outside her dismal focus on herself, Sassy felt weightless, relieved, and at the same time her heart went out to Lydia.

"Men are stupid," she said.

"That kind of sums it up, don't it?"

No, it didn't, really. It was unfair and she knew it. But—such being the case, why did it feel so good?

It felt so terrific that she said it again, theme and variations. "Men are jerks."

"Amen. Can't live with 'em and can't live without 'em."

Although Lydia had lived without 'em, evidently. "I guess in a way you've had it worse than I have," Sassy said.

Lydia shrugged. "Life shouldn't be no pain contest."

It was a sentence worthy to be expensively framed and hung on a prominent wall. But before Sassy could absorb it or respond, "Twee!" cried a familiar voice. "Twee! Twee! Twee!" Kleet, skreeking his excitement, zoomed to her head, landed in her hair, and pooped.

"Too bad you can't see how nice you look," Lydia said.

"I'll take your word for it."

"I put green eye shadow on you."

Put that together with red lipstick and probably Kleet thought he was seeing a Christmas tree. "Thank you," Sassy said.

"I wish I could do something about your hair." Lydia meant its limp-squirrel look, probably, not the bird poop; all she had to do about that was hand over a Kleenex.

"Kleet seems to like the general effect just fine," Sassy told her.

· · ·

Crossing the lobby of the Sylvan Tower after dark, with her shoe box full of face-crayons tucked under her arm and Kleet hidden under her coat, Sassy wondered what kind of job Lydia had done on her, how she looked. Judging by the way the guests idling at terrace cafés turned their aristocratic heads to stare at her, she had to look clownish, if not downright demented.

Demented seemed preferable. And if they didn't think she was demented now, they were going to know it after they saw what she had decided to try.

She needed a *big* mirror.

Passing the elevators, she stopped as she caught sight of the massive neon-lit decorator mirrors that sheathed the shaft. Their darkly golden depths called up within her a resonance she could not name. She had not meant to make her attempt in such a public area, but—who cared. Parting her coat to let Kleet perch on her shoulder, she opened her shoe box, letting the lid drop to the floor. She chose the brightest lipstick she could find—Flame Cerise, the label said—and wielding it like a sword of fire, she swept it outward and upward to the fullest extent of her arm as she red-limned a large oval on the mirror.

She liked it at once, her hefty lipstick oval. Not perfect, more of an egg shape, but—egg, ova, ovum, oval, wasn't it all the same thing? Fertility. Life. She grabbed a different lipstick, Tangerine Coral, and added scallops and curlicues to the rim of her oval. So far, so good. No one was bothering her yet, although she could feel people staring.

But nothing was happening in the mirror yet, either. In the oval, only her budgie looked back at her, one foot tucked up, content to be seen with penciled brows, green smudges above its eyes and red ones on its cheeks, a bright pink smile outlining its beak.

"Um, honey, what are you doing?" came a tentative voice, sounded like one of the other maids, from behind her.

"Nothing." She didn't even bother to turn and see who it was, just grabbed some more lipsticks: Pearl White, Wild Fuchsia, Raisin, Kiwi Kiss, Tropical Yellow. Confound it, if nothing was going to appear in her nice extemporaneous oval, she'd make something there. As Kleet beat his wings and chirped like a cheerleader, Sassy scrawled a pale oval face surrounding the smiling blue budgie in the mirror, then sketched in a mess of yellow-taupe hair, tilted green eyes, a full-lipped fuchsia mouth. Below the face she added a flow of green-gold gown, and for some subrational reason a pair of shining pearly wings—

"Sassy," said an all-too-familiar voice, "there you are. I'm *concerned* about you. You've been acting very oddly."

Sassy did not turn around. This was important, she couldn't let Frederick interrupt, she just couldn't, ignore him and maybe, *Oh Lord please, maybe he'll go away.*

"Saying I don't have any, you know," Frederick continued, sounding more peevish than concerned. "I *do so.*"

Feverishly Sassy continued with white lipstick, feathering the strange angel's wings.

"Sassy, are you listening to me? What—" Frederick's tone changed. "What the hell do you think you're doing?"

"Nothing!" Sassy could not withstand that bark of wrath. She jerked back from her artwork and whirled, flinching, to face Frederick.

Why his anger still frightened her she couldn't say, but it did. That sulky mouth, those narrow eyes—but when he caught sight of her face, his slitty eyes opened almost to normal wideness, and he spazzed into a fit of giggling.

The Wrath of Frederick would have been easier to bear. Or

if he had given forth a manly roar of laughter, like a real husband and not a twit, even that would have been more bearable
in front of all these people—quite a few people had gathered,
staring at Sassy and her artwork and now at Frederick making
an ass of himself. How very Frederick: he giggle-giggled,
burping out guinea-pig squeaks and squeals the way he had
always done whenever he thought he was bad-boy hot stuff,
whenever he and Sassy had run into a girl he was hitting on,
whenever he had told her that Binky-poo was just a friend.
Giggle, giggle, giggle, with his face turning rosy pink beneath
the freckles, with his pudgy belly shaking. Giggle SNORT
giggle giggle HICCUP giggle some more, and the spectacle of
his giggling froze Sassy, as it always had. You can accuse
someone of being mean or unfaithful, but how can you accuse
him of giggling? How can you tell someone not to giggle like
a jerk? Wasn't giggling in the Bill of Rights, like sneezing?
You can't tell people not to giggle or sneeze. So Sassy had
never known what to say. Even now she still didn't know
what to say.

"Why, Sassy," Frederick squealed out between giggles,
"you've got yourself all fixed up! For me?"

Sassy stood wooden, feeling Kleet perched as stiff as a dildo
on her shoulder but herself unable to react in any way.

"Fuck you with a donkey dick," said a voice that was hers
yet not hers. It came from the mirror.

Frederick stopped giggling with a grunt. Sassy gasped and
whirled to look into the lipstick oval, where—oh, thank Lydia
and all goodness, it was her, her, the one with shining wings
and laughing eyes and a Julia-Roberts grin, it was the one who
never touched the ground, the one Sassy did not yet know how
to name, the treetop shadow angel who would take her back to
the paradise of lost—

"*What* did you say?" roared Frederick's voice.

For once Sassy did not lose herself to his anger. She did not even turn around to see whether he was blustering at her or at the mirror. It didn't matter; she didn't care. She gave a glad, birdlike cry, and Kleet gave a joyous call that sounded almost human. He whirred off of Sassy's shoulder and flew for the mirror, and she flew at the same time, lunging toward paradise, hands outstretched. The vision in the mirror reached out to welcome her.

"I said fuck you, limpie," she heard that angel luscious Julia-Roberts voice retort to Frederick as the mirror embraced her and took her in, and Sassy found herself laughing, laughing rich and deep from the gut, from the bone.

Trying to stalk silently like the other outlaws amid towering trees—were they really redwoods?—Racquel turned his head, hearing a sound that was definitely not birdsong.

"Hark!" Robin heard it too. He paused, hearkening. So did the others.

"Hark unto a lamentation most sore!" cried Much.

" 'Tis the woeful plaint of a damsel in distress!" quoth Little John.

"Somebody's crying," Racquel said.

"Well and quaintly put, my Moorish friend," declared Robin. "To the rescue, my merry men!"

Half a dozen merry men and one Moor in jerkin and hose changed course and followed the sound of sobbing on the wind. Carrying the longbow Robin had given him, Racquel managed to catch the damn thing on every bush and vine. Robin's solution to Racquel's difficulties seemed to consist of adopting Racquel as an outlaw. In a mere half a day Racquel had learned to loathe the woods even more than before. Damn trees tripping him up with their roots all the time, poking twigs in his face. Damn rocks hurting his sore feet, damn condescending moss, damn smiling flowers, damn chirpy birds, and most of all, damn shabby jerkin and damn darned itchy woolen hose, making him look like Prince Bumpo or somebody. If the girl who was crying saw him she'd probably die laughing.

He tried to hurry his footsore, blundering pace; what was the matter, what had happened to her? The sound of her sobbing wrenched his heart.

Very near now—

At the edge of the woods above the waterfall, all of them except Racquel halted in mute astonishment. Racquel dropped his bow and lunged forward, crying, "Sassy!"

"She weeps green!" blurted one of the merry men.

Sassy turned toward them a face like a melting rainbow, dripping apple-green and cerulean eye shadow, peach foundation and pink blush. With her glasses in her hand, she sprawled like Wyeth's Christina in the soft grass at the edge of the falls, and on her shoulder perched a very concerned-looking parakeet.

An outlaw babbled, "Is that a damsel? But—but it wears trousers!"

"It bears feathers instead of hair!"

"The thing has an orange face under its azure tears! Is it human?"

Sassy gave them a glare worthy of an orangutan and wailed, "Damn it, she was just here! Where'd she *go*?"

"It cries out like a human," said Robin Hood.

One of the outlaws declared in lightbulb tones, "'Tis *tinc-*

ture on its face, forsooth. Woad and the like, such as the barbarians use."

"By my troth, 'tis verily so!"

"He speaks truth."

"Is it a barbarian, then?"

"Sassy." Boggled by the strength of his own emotions, Racquel reached her, folded to the grass beside her and put his
arms around her. She nestled against his chest, probably getting lipstick on his nice new Lincoln-green jerkin, and he tried
to stroke her hair. The parakeet fluttered to her head, gave a
screech and pecked at his hand. "Okay, okay!" he told it.
"Sassy," he begged, "what's the matter?"

She heaved her thin shoulders in a sigh with an air of finality
to it and stopped crying. "Oh, poop," she muttered to his
chest.

"No, thank you, I already pooped today." And it was no very
pleasant experience, not in the woods, not by his standards. He
hoped they didn't have poison ivy here. The stuff he had wiped
with had three shiny leaves. "What's wrong, woman?"

She sat up to look at him, rubbing her colorful face with
her sleeve, and gave him a small blurred smile, but did not
answer.

"You found your parakeet!" It finally registered with Racquel that the possessive budgie was a green parakeet with a yellow head. The parakeet for which she had been questing. The
parakeet they had rescued from the mist net in the hotel—
God, that seemed so long ago and far away.

"Yes, and I found you." Her smile widened slightly. "Or
you found me. Love your shoes, dahling."

"They're called pampooties," Racquel complained of his
soft buckskin footgear, "and Daniel Boone would have felt

right at home in them, but I do not. Would you please stop stalling? Tell me what's got you so bummed."

Sassy perceptibly clouded up to rain again. She looked away toward the treetops.

"Yes?" Racquel prompted.

"She brought me back," Sassy said in a voice barely above a whisper. "She took me in her arms, she called Frederick a limpie and she—she saved me. She pulled me into the mirror and there I was lying by the oval pool. And I got up and turned to thank her, I saw her for just one glimpse and she made a face at me and then she was gone. Just that quick she was gone. And I've been hunting all over creation for her but I can't find her."

 **TWELVE**

He looks good in tights, Sassy thought, as she crouched by the riverside above the waterfall and stole glances at Racquel. He was gathering mushrooms for a snack, and as he bent over, Sassy admired his butt, then averted her gaze, feeling a twinge of guilt. Since when did she look at young men that way? She was old enough to be his mother. Anyway, this was Racquel, minus his fancy female feathers, that was all. Sassy focused on serene water flowing at her knees—her blue budgie blinked back at her, its pink-lipstick smile blurred and sagging. Sassy sighed, shattered the reflection by dipping her hands in the river, and washed her face. The cold water quieted the stinging in her eyes and, she hoped, removed the runny remains of Lydia's makeover job.

Racquel limped back carrying two mushrooms like creamsicle-colored portabellas, one in each hand. The outlaws had discreetly taken themselves off somewhere—probably still babbling about her barbaric face paint, Sassy thought. Standing up, she asked Racquel, "Did I get it all off?"

"You look fine."

"That doesn't answer the question."

"Sassy, who cares? So you look like a watercolor rainbow, so what? You can use some color."

"Gee, *thanks*," she said with edge, turning back toward the water.

"Sassy, let it go! If I can go around in this getup, you can have some makeup on you." Racquel chose a level patch of sward and settled himself cross-legged. "Sit, for God's sake. You look about ready to fall over."

Sassy sighed and sat with him. "Do you think I've lost weight?"

"Who says you need to lose weight?"

God love him. Sassy found herself smiling.

He handed her a mushroom. "So give me a full report, woman."

She did. She told him about Frederick, about her own unsatisfactory responses to Frederick, about the cop (omitting her inquiry about Devon Shelton's family), about Lydia. Kleet sat on her knee, stiffly erect, keeping a hard, beady gaze fixed on Racquel as Sassy talked and ate. "He doesn't like you," Sassy said, bemused.

"Great. He's a bigot bird. Whites only."

"I don't think it's *that*," Sassy blurted, appalled. "I think he's jealous, that's all. According to Lydia, I'm his mate."

"You're confused," Racquel complained to Kleet. "You're supposed to give her back her reflection."

Sassy said, "It—it's not just that anymore." First she had thought that if she could only find the parakeet it would solve everything. Then, when she had stranded Racquel in the forest of lost dreams, she had thought if she could only find him again she wouldn't care about anything else. Now . . .

"So what is it now?" Racquel asked.

In stumbling words she tried to tell him about the lipstick epiphany at the hotel mirror, about—her. Lord, what was it about that sassy young thing in the mirror that brought tears to her eyes again just thinking of her? If she couldn't find her again, she might as well lie down and die. It was that simple and that desperate, this yearning. "She—hugged me . . ." Trying to speak of her strange shadow angel, Sassy choked up too much to say any more.

Racquel had stopped eating and was giving her a look that she could not quite read. Frightened? Exalted? Shy? "It's the bird-girl, right?" he said quite softly, as if this were a thing to be spoken of in a whisper. "The winged spirit who lives in the treetops? The one who never touches the ground?"

Sassy jolted bolt upright, crying, "You've met her?"

"Briefly."

"Racquel, I've got to find her again. I've *got* to!"

"That shouldn't be so hard." Racquel sat still giving her that same strange look. "You don't know who she is?"

"What do you mean?"

"You don't know, uh, her name?"

But this had to be the spirit no one dared to name. "How would I?"

"Huh," Racquel muttered, his gaze drifting down to the ground, his lowered eyes suddenly so grave that Sassy wrenched her attention away from her own wretchedness for a moment and wondered what was worrying him.

Everything, probably. Good grief, look at the fix he was in. She had told him that someone had filed a missing persons report on him, that his gender was no longer a secret, that his employees were keeping PLUMAGE open—but how long could they do that? She said, "We've got to get you back to your store. Your life."

"No rush," he said.

. . .

Racquel had never felt a more solemn responsibility. All his own problems paled by comparision. In the tawny glow of the outlaw campfire he studied Sassy.

"'Tis a hungry little barbarian!" Robin said to him with a belch, watching by his side as Sassy chowed down on hot venison and a trencher of bread.

Racquel nodded, smiling—but his smile quickly flickered away. Barbarian—all too apt. Sassy reminded him of something he had read about people in some primitive culture who had never seen themselves. Did not recognize photos of themselves. Did not own mirrors. Had no idea what they looked like. It had sounded idyllic at the time—wouldn't it be great not to know or care what you looked like? But the blind spot in Sassy was way more serious. How could she not recognize— her winged spirit, her soul, her self? She had lived with mirrors all her life; what had she seen in them before the budgie showed up?

Robin asked, "Is it the custom of barbarians to whiten their hair?"

Racquel gave him a surprised glance. "No."

With greater surprise Robin raised his fair brows. "But she is not old!"

"She's over forty."

"No! 'Tis not possible. Her back as straight as a girl's, every tooth entire, scarcely a line on her face—"

Racquel looked thoughtfully at his own half-eaten dinner and said nothing.

In a voice that sank to a whisper Robin asked, "In your world, are all folk immortals?"

The mood Racquel was in, remarks like that were enough to keep him awake at night.

Sassy slept, he saw. Nothing like roast meat and exhaustion

to make a person sleep like a baby. The parakeet perched on a limb just above her, drew one lavender foot up, tucked its head under its wing and slept. The outlaws slept—even the so-called sentries, Racquel noticed. He imagined sentries were just a formality anyway in this place. He thought about this and many other things as he sat staring, sometimes at the embers of the fire, sometimes at the gibbous moon, sometimes at Sassy, her face rapt and innocent in sleep. When had he become so very protective of her? Sitting guard over her, for God's sake, trying to think how to help her—what was he trying to be, some kind of hero? Hearing the owls softly talking, he gave himself a rueful smile, knowing that wearing a jerkin and tights—well, the wretched cross-gartered garment they called tights—had something to do with it. Leaving aside matters of personal hygiene for the moment, he did like being an outlaw. He liked the company of manly mead-drinking men who accepted him with no questions asked. This was the forest of lost things; had he found something he had lost?

Or was he himself a lost soul now?

Toward dawn he lay down and dozed. When Little John greeted him with "Breakfast, Moor!" and he awoke, he found that he had reached no answers regarding himself, but he had come up with a plan of sorts for Sassy.

"I need to find her," Sassy was telling the outlaws over lumpy porridge. "Where can I find her?"

"Anywhere," Robin answered after a silence. "Everywhere. Nowhere."

Racquel's plan required talk, not action. But he could see that he was not going to get Sassy to sit down and listen. He thought of his sore feet. He sighed and rolled his eyes when no one was paying attention to him. Then he told Sassy, "You and I can go have a look-see."

"Show me where you saw her!"

"Okay."

That was a damn devious thing to say. He did not know the way to the oval pool. He had a feeling that the geography in this place was fluid anyway, that the pool might not be where he had left it even if he remembered and could retrace his steps. But it didn't matter. He just wanted a chance to walk and talk.

Or limp and talk. Whatever.

He could feel the outlaws smiling at his back as he and Sassy left. Sweethearts, they were thinking.

Kleet rode on Sassy's shoulder, silent and still. Not even nibbling at Sassy's ear. Subdued, or maybe sulking. Hard to tell what a parakeet is thinking behind those little beady eyes. If *thinking* was the word for a parakeet's cerebral processes.

"What's the matter with your parakeet?" Racquel asked.

Sassy said, "Same thing that's the matter with me sometimes."

"Huh?"

"Everybody else seems to have a lovie."

Oh. Yeah, Racquel knew the feeling. And the damn sun was shining, making halos on the huge trees and even poking a few stray beams down into the shadows below, and every single bird in the damn forest—except Kleet—seemed to be caroling its fool feathered head off. The little birdies in this place didn't just go tweet, tweet, tweet either. Some of them weren't so little and they yawped, they squawked, they yodeled, they yelled, they barked and brayed and sang opera and whistled like hailing a taxi. Racquel saw flashes of tangerine cerise vermilion in the green canopy overhead, red orange yellow like every color of Sassy's rainbow face yesterday and then some. Sassy's face turned upward, wide-eyed, sweet and hushed, gazing at the birds, the forest.

God, she loved this place and its damn birds. Jeez. But her gaze gave Racquel a thought of how to begin.

"Sassy. If you were a bird, what kind would you be?"

She blinked, detached her gaze from the treetops a moment and gave him a glance askance. "I seem to be a budgie."

"Forget that. If you could choose. What would you be?"

"Huh. I don't know." She halted and turned to peer at him. "If you could have a tail, what kind would you have?"

"Huh?"

"You know. Like your cock tail."

"*What?*"

She puffed her lips at him in frustration. "Would you have a quetzel tail or a coatimundi tail or a jaguar tail or what?"

This was way more imagination than he had expected of Sassy. Maybe she wasn't as bad off as he thought. "Honey, I got a black tail as it is." Directing her back to his agenda, he said, "I asked first. What kind of bird would you be?"

"I—I don't know." She faltered to a halt and stood staring at two yellow orioles doing the kissy-beak thing. "Mating season," she murmured.

Racquel bet it was always mating season here. But he said nothing. He waited.

"I think I would be one that mates for life," Sassy said. "A swan, maybe. I don't know."

He knew it. He knew she was that kind of dreamer. He loved her for it. And hated it for what it had done to her.

"Uh-huh," he said. "One of the look-alikes. You don't want to be some drab little nest-sitting female."

The look she gave him was puzzled, almost shocked. She

started walking away from his words. She turned the subject away from herself. "What would you be?"

Racquel thought fast. "I wouldn't want to be a bird unless I was a duck," he declared.

"*Huh?* You want to waddle and quack?"

"No, but—" But only ducks had dicks. And he'd finally figured out why; because they did it in the water. Which sounded like fun. "Cloacas just don't cut it, you know?"

"Oh!" She blushed, but then she actually smiled. "Racquel, you keep surprising me."

"What I do best, honey."

But then he couldn't think of a way to steer Sassy back toward any topic that might help her put herself back together. They walked on in silence through mossy shadows, while Sassy gazed up into the trees again—this forest was just a huge mess of biggreen honeyleaf vine blossom moss birdsinging sun-shadow butterfly white yellow things flying all over the place, and in a cerebral sort of way he could see why she loved it, but it did nothing for him below the neck. It was all so damn—natural, that was the problem. Random. Ivy and stuff piled up every which way. You've seen one orchid, you've seen them all. Now Sassy stood spellbound, gazing at a pair of scarlet macaws, but Racquel found himself much less interested in the living birds than he would have been in their vivid feathers artfully arranged on, say, a red felt toque. Or a snakeskin belt. Or something earth-toned in batik. Or—

Out of nowhere Sassy said, "I guess maybe I wouldn't want to be a swan. I like bright colors too much."

Racquel took a deep breath before answering. "You do?"

"Yes."

He tried to sound very casual. "Hey, why don't you dye your hair, Sassy?"

She stopped staring at the birds, turning her head to stare at him instead. A stare with edge. "What for?"

"You like color—"

"So I should go around with magenta hair?"

"No, I didn't say that!" God, he'd hit a nerve. Kleet sensed it too, whirring off of Sassy's shoulder to a perch on a nearby tree fern, from which he watched with his head cocked. Racquel eyed Sassy similarly. "I just meant, you know, dye it auburn or whatever. Jeez, you're white, you've got all sorts of options. What's your natural color?"

Flat as roadkill Sassy said, "Gray."

"You were born with gray hair?"

"No, I was born with no hair. I guess maybe I should shave it all off."

God, she was pissed. He hadn't expected her to get so pissed. He'd never *seen* her so pissed, her face red and stretched like she wanted to cry. "Sassy—"

She snapped at him, "I guess you think I should get silicone in my boobs, too?"

Now he was getting pissed too. "They do it with saline these days." Just to be annoying, he added, "I thought of having implants myself. But breasts can be a pain in the ass." Or not in the ass, that would be a trip, but anyhow, they were a nuisance, they got in the way just reaching for something on a high shelf. "I decided to stick with detachables. How'd we get from hair to—"

"And have my lips plumped?" Sassy cried so fiercely he almost stepped back from her, so sharply that the macaws took fright, shrieked and flew away, their squawks as harsh as Sassy's voice. "I guess you'd like me to have my face lifted, right? And my eyebrows tattooed on, and a rhinestone surgically implanted in my belly button, and maybe some fat sucked out of my—"

"Sassy, for God's sake! All I said was—"

"All you said was I'm not good enough the way I am!"

"I didn't mean it that way!"

Tears started down her taut face but they seemed to just make her madder. She blundered away from him.

Now what was he going to do? Follow, like Kleet fluttering after her, poor parakeet, keeping a safe distance? Better make like the bird, Racquel thought; he could lose Sassy forever in this weird place if he didn't. But his pride kept him standing where he was. "Sassy, don't be such an idiot!" he yelled helpfully.

Turning her head to yell back at him, she tripped over a tree root and grabbed at a vine to keep from falling. "Go—go—" Instead of a shout, her voice came out a half whisper. She couldn't seem to get words out. "You—go—" Go what? Knowing Sassy, probably something pretty mild. Go back where he came from? Go to hell?

"Jesus jumpin' on the water!" yelled a wild soprano voice from somewhere out of sight in the treetops. "If you want to tell him to go fuck himself, just spit it out!"

Sassy felt like her heart was going to explode into jagged pieces flying all directions like her life falling apart. First there was Racquel in his macho outlaw getup, typical man, saying things just like Frederick—except Frederick had never said them, exactly, just looked at her with that pinched whiteness around his nostrils like she smelled bad before he turned away to ogle another chickie. And she had been such a good wife that she had never said anything to Frederick, exactly, just opted out of any cutie competitions, placing a silent curse forever on that shallow way of looking at things. She had hoped that he could learn to think differently, that he would see she was his wife partner helpmeet mate forever, not just some bimbo. *I am your wife*, she had said to him in every way she could, with her eyeglasses and her plain smiling face and her extra thirty pounds and her money-saving Wal-Mart clothes. *I am your wife, I have substance, my devotion runs more than skin deep.* With the lines around her eyes, with her gray hair. *I am your wife, you are my husband. We are supposed to grow old together.* She had grown old trying to show him what marriage meant. But he had not learned after all. So there was all that. And now—

Now there was that voice from the treetops shattering her heart with a force of emotion she did not understand. She barely heard the words; the voice alone almost knocked her over, snapping her head back as she peered up, straining to see—nothing. Nothing but greenleaf and sunspokes and butterflies.

"Where are you?" Sassy cried, her voice shattering like her heart, flying like the butterflies. "Come here!"

"Come here!" mimicked the voice from up there somewhere, hidden, never touching the ground. "Come here, she says."

"Please!"

"Why should I, pray tell?" drawled that voice Sassy felt to the marrow of her bones, knew somehow deep, deep yet could not recognize at all.

Another voice, whispering, barely registered in her mind. "Sassy," Racquel was breathing at her like he was trying to help her cheat on some awfully final exam, "think about yourself. How you used to be. How you used to look. Don't you have old photos? Pictures of yourself before—"

"Shut up, you!" the voice screamed, ricocheting nearer.

Branches rattled, butterflies scattered, Kleet cried out, wrens and ibises and little green honey birds cried out in what might have been alarm or ecstasy, Sassy heard a cry that she only afterward comprehended as her own, she saw great shimmering wings, a gown the color of moss in shadow, russet hair flying wild, a fierce fey elfin face, and—there, hawk-plummeting, there, hovering amid a startled breathless silence, there, almost within arm's reach, shimmering like a dream—there she was.

She. The one, the—

"You keep out of this!" the visitant flared at Racquel.

He did not answer. His face, Sassy saw, had gone taut, his brown skin tinged with blue.

She, the—what? Who? Sassy did not know.

With an effort she took a breath, got her mouth moving. "Thank you," she whispered. Just the sight of the winged spirit was—frightening, as she turned her face that seemed lit by an inner angry fire—but also somehow a blessing.

"No thanks to *you*," she snapped.

"I—you—please, who are you?" Sassy still did not understand why she so desperately needed to court this uncanny being.

"Who am I?" the bird-being mocked. "*Who am I?* I'm the one you blew off, idiot!"

Sassy heard a frightened chirp. Maybe Kleet. Maybe a choked sound from her own throat.

"It would be nice to have feet, you know," the hovering bird-girl said with a kind of ferocious nostalgia, "and someplace to go with them, and somebody to talk with besides cockatoos—"

"You're mad at me!" Sassy found her voice, and with it a strong sense of the unfairness of life in general and people in particular. She wailed, "Why is everybody mad at me?"

To her shock, the bird-girl made an absolutely gross gesture involving one dainty hand and her pert little nose.

Sassy faltered a step back. "What's the *matter* with you?" she gasped.

"Me? Nothing the matter with *me*! *You*'re the one who's been ignoring me for, what, twenty years?"

"But I don't even know you! What's your name?"

"It's up to you to name me, twit!" Her wings kicked even harder than her words, rocketing her upward and away. One hand lifted in a single-digit salute that made Sassy blink. With a fake-friendly wave of her upraised hand she yelled, "Nice talking with you, moron!" The words dopplered away into echoes as she dived upward and vanished into the green veil of canopy.

"Come back!" Sassy cried, tears starting—but why? Why should she feel such desperate emptiness in her heart over someone who abused her? And why did she want to cry when she was pissed off? She stamped her foot, furious at the bird-girl, herself, the world. She cried, "Did you see that? She flipped the bird at me!"

Sounding a bit as if he had been punched in the stomach and was just getting his breath back, Racquel said, "How very appropriate."

"It is not!"

"Because of all the birds, I mean. Lame attempt at a joke. Duh."

Looking at his worried face, Sassy heard in a kind of delayed reaction his whispered words still hanging on the air: *Think about yourself. How you used to be. Before—*

Before what? Before Frederick?

Before she had turned into a wife?

Her thoughts ran crazed. Wife, waif. Waif, self. And hazily

Sassy remembered a girl she hadn't thought about in a long time. An elfin-faced, pert-nosed girl who liked braids and silly hats and dreamed of wild horses and love forever and flying—

"Oh," Sassy whispered. "Oh!" Realization struck like lightning all in one deep-searing nonverbal instant. She could not have explained, but in that thunderbolt moment she knew to her bones how very much she had lost for so very long, and she could scarcely bear it. "Oh," she whimpered, and then the tears came.

Kleet perched disconsolate on a sprig of fern, not even interested in the seeds ripening in the gillyflower heads nearby. Nothing was going as he had hoped. His tree, his adored Deity, had not vouchsafed him a mate. Instead he was seeing her buffeted by trouble as if by stormy gales. Kleet did not understand the hu-hu-hu cry she was crying now as she leaned against the other one, the tall dark one, but he felt that it was not good. It made him feel very alone.

In the world on the other side of the hard air he had not felt so alone. Twee had been more with him there. But he had grown aware of many puzzlements, so many other trees like this tall dark one who was alive and twiggy and perchable yet not his tree, not Twee as his tree was Twee, not one whom he cared to skreek. When the other trees preened their plumage in front of the hard air, only similar trees looked back. But when Twee faced the hard air, a parakeet like Kleet yet not like Kleet, a blue parakeet, looked back. This made sense to him, for Bird is the spirit of Tree, Bird has been the spirit of Tree back to the Great Time, the beginning time of the One Tree—but, puzzlement, had those other trees no spirits?

Why was Twee so unhappy?

Did she want to preen her plumage like the other trees?

She was standing up now, away from the other one. Kleet chirped and felt his own fluttering heart make his wings beat; he whirred up from his perch and flew to her. He perched upon her warmlimb the way she seemed to like and nibbled at her foliage. For a moment she turned to him and stroked his feathers—but only for a moment. Then she seemed to forget him again. Hu-hu-hu she cried from deep in her trunk. Her crown turned away.

T H I R T E E N

Racquel watched the parakeet perched on Sassy's shoulder nibbling her hair and the edge of her ear. She barely seemed to notice. He could see that she was still fighting tears and trying to clear a stuffy nose, but he figured she could talk now. Really, what better time to talk about the crap of life than when you're already crying? It's not like you're going to lose it at that point when you've already lost it, so things are not going to get any worse.

Racquel sighed, selected a comfy-looking patch of moss to plop himself on, and said, "Sassy, sit down and tell me about it."

"Aboud whad?" Obediently she sat. Too tamely. Racquel liked her recent fury better than the despair she was showing right now.

"About how you came to forget, um, you know. Your real self."

"Frederig."

"Frederick is not your real self," Racquel said, trying once again mawkishly to joke; God, he wished he'd stop that.

"I thoughd he was."

"Huh?"

Sassy explained, nasals gradually clearing out of her speech

as she talked. Apparently she felt that she should have taken a
cue from the fact that she had seen Frederick's face instead of
her own when she looked in the oval pool. She told Racquel
about that and a great deal more. He listened and nodded and
said things at appropriate intervals. All the time he felt himself
tightening like a bowstring inside. Sassy was in worse shape
than he had thought.

"So it wasn't just that he didn't like you to try on hats," he
tried to sum up finally. "It was also that you took a stance. He
had this idea of what a wife was like, and so did you—"

"And I chucked away anything that didn't fit the role."
Sassy sounded dead calm now, but also dead tired, and she was
looking at bits of leaf and stick on the ground, not at him. The
parakeet stood motionless on her shoulder.

Racquel said, "God, Sassy, you are giving me the absolute
chilly willies of marriage."

She almost smiled. "Good. Hold that thought."

"Holding."

"What an idiot I was."

"Hey!" Racquel reached over and grabbed her under her little pointed chin; surprised, she focused on him. "Stop that,"
he told her. "Don't go putting my friend down."

Startled, she actually grinned.

"You did what you thought you had to do," Racquel added,
releasing her. "You gave the marriage everything you had. And
that's the way it's supposed to be, right?"

"I guess."

"So screw him. He did wrong, not you. And you're not
married anymore," Racquel added. "You're free now. You can
do whatever you want."

She shrugged and looked at the ground again. There were
periwinkle flowers growing amid the moss, and little mush-

rooms like pearls the color of peachskin, and snail shells as fancy as those Easter eggs they make in Ukraine, but Sassy did not seem to be seeing any of that. The parakeet chirped as if he were whispering in her ear, but she seemed not to hear. She was looking at dead sticks.

Racquel decided to try again. Very gently. Keeping his voice down, not to be obnoxious. Whimsy. Attempt whimsy. After extensive mental preparation, he blurted, "So, you never did tell me, what kind of bird would you be?"

Sassy did not look up. She mumbled, "Oh, who cares?"

"I care! Sassy, tell me about yourself. The real self. Not this wife person."

"What's there to tell?"

"I don't know. Anything." He knew what her natural hair color was now: a shimmer of tawny auburn. It had looked stunning over the winged Sassy's green gown. "Did you wear your hair in pigtails?"

"Yes."

"With ribbons?"

"Yes."

"Bright red ribbons?"

"No, I liked subtle colors."

"Such as?"

"Lavender. Dusty pink. My mom tried to make me wear white, with white-ruffled socks. I hated them." A hint of a smile now, Racquel saw.

"You didn't like ruffles?"

"I didn't like *white*. Actually, I had lace-ruffle lavender barrettes that I loved."

"Barrettes. That's adorable. Did your mom curl your pigtails?"

"Yeah. Banana curls."

Racquel let himself grin. "I bet you were cute. Freckles?"

"Right across the nose. I liked my freckles. I—"

Sassy stopped talking. Her mouth fell open. She looked as if she had been stepped on by something invisible but large.

"Sassy?"

"Oh," she gasped. "Oh, for God's sake." The strongest language he had ever heard her use.

"For God's sake, what?"

"Oh!" She leaped to her feet, startling the parakeet off her shoulder, hanging on to her head with both hands as if it might explode. "Oh, I don't believe it!"

"*What?*" Racquel struggled onto his sore feet, beginning to be alarmed, wondering whether something physical might have flown into her brain all of a sudden. With a person that sensitive to bird poop, it might happen.

But it wasn't that. "I don't believe it!" she yelled up at the forest canopy as she clutched her own squirrel-colored hair with both hands. "I'm still being a wife!"

"Waaal, smack my fanny and call me Suzie," Racquel drawled in owl-eyed down-home wonder. Luckily, Sassy seemed not to hear him.

"Hanging on!" she yelled. "Hanging on with my stupid gray hair and my stupid sacky pants! Still playing the same old sad song—"

"Waal, paint me green and call me Gumby."

"Paint me stupid! I wouldn't want him back if he came back, so what the—the—whatever am I trying to prove?"

"Waaal, dip mah balls in cream and throw me to the kittens," Racquel intoned. "I'll be licked."

"I can't believe I'm still acting like a—a—"

"Fricking-fracking," Racquel suggested.

"A ding-damn dopey mopey *wife!*"

"What the hell do you think I've been trying to tell you?"

"Good grief!" She looked at him for the first time since the beginning of this outburst. "I'm stuck in a rut, Racquel."

"No duh."

"No wonder I—she—"

Silence. Sassy stood gazing upward. Racquel lifted his head also to scan the green-lacework jigsaw puzzle overhead limned with cerulean blue. He saw that, and flits of gold like a dusting of glitter—maybe warblers, maybe butterflies—and dusky sunbeams filtering down into gray-green shadow. Nothing else. But he knew what Sassy was thinking. Or rather, of whom.

"No wonder," he agreed.

"I been looking at myself through foggy glasses."

"Yeppers."

Finally noticing his tone, she gave him a hard look. "Don't make fun of me," she said. "Twenty-seven years is a long time."

Oops. Yes, it was. Almost longer than he'd been alive. Abashed, he said nothing.

"Waaal paint me green," Sassy murmured.

Racquel smiled; okay, she wasn't really mad. He'd just shut up now for a while. Somehow the two of them had started walking again in no particular direction, not admitting at this point to looking for anything, just wandering through the wonderland under the trees with Kleet flying circles around them.

"You seem to be a lot more adaptable than I am," Sassy said after a while.

"I do?"

"Sure. You're a guy but you're a woman too."

"Most people don't call that adaptable," Racquel said. "Most people call it perverted."

"Well, phooey on them. You're awesome. One day you're in retail and the next day you're an outlaw in the biggest Sherwood Forest there ever was and it doesn't seem to faze you."

"I—I guess I've been through a lot of changes already." Rejection, though he didn't say so. His family. One develops certain tools.

Sassy asked, "Do you like the Robin Hood thing?"

"Sure."

"You like being a guy?"

He took his time answering. Had to think about it. Finally he said, "Here, yeah. I do like it." Made sense. In this world behind the mirror he was his own reflection—no, he was behind his reflection; he was his own secrets. "You asked once what's my real name," he said. "It's Devon. Devon Shelton."

"I know."

That startled him about as much as anything that had happened. "*What?*"

"I know. Cop told me." She hadn't smirked. She hadn't even blinked. She just looked at him and she must have seen emotion in his face because she added, "It doesn't matter, Racquel."

God. He wanted to hug her. But something, some shyness, kept him from doing it. They walked on.

"Do the outlaws call you Devon?" Sassy asked.

He shook his head. They called him Moor. "It would be okay here," he said, noticing that his voice came out a bit husky. "But back home—nah."

"Huh," Sassy said.

"Once I get back, I won't be able to wait to get into a really bitchin' dress."

"With a feather boa, probably."

"You bet. And a cockfeather bustle, and a ruff, and . . ." He let the thoughts trail away, because her nodding acceptance was squeezing his heart. "Sassy," he asked on impulse, "you still have some of those lipsticks on you?"

"Sure. Got 'em right here in my pocket."

"Pretty me up a little bit, could you? And braid my hair for me?"

"Hey. Sure."

She sat down, and Kleet perched to gaze down on both of them, and Racquel sat with his head resting between her cocked knees, cherishing the gentle touch of her hands working around his head.

Never in her life, Sassy mused, had she simply laid down on the ground under a tree to take an afternoon nap. And this was exactly what she and Racquel were doing. For some reason Racquel seemed very tired. He lay beside her sound asleep, his arms flung out as if he had been dropped from a height. She had dozed for a while but now she lay with her eyes open, gazing up into layers of leaflace and shadowlight, seeing the forest of lost dreams from a new angle. And in soft focus, like somebody had smeared Vaseline on the camera lens, since she had entrusted her glasses to a tree limb nearby. But she felt no urge to reach for them. Control didn't matter so much anymore. She lay listening to layers of silence and sound, birdcalls and midday peace and something else chirring and humming— tree frogs? Cicadas? Didn't matter. No urge to reach for an encyclopedia, either; it was sufficient just to be where she was. At peace. With Racquel close by. With sweet little Kleet perched close by. With—

At first a shining speck like a daytime star, then larger, spiraling lazily down, down, down like a maple wing, a white pinion floated toward her.

Sassy gasped and sat up.

The pearly shining feather halted in front of her face and hovered there.

"Racquel," Sassy murmured. The hum of peace in the forest was such that she could not seem to speak aloud.

Racquel did not awaken. The feather, however, darted at her face as if to shush her, shaking itself like an admonishing fingertip.

"Just me?" Sassy whispered.

The feather withdrew, nodded in the air, wheeled and pointed.

Sassy swallowed hard, taking a deep breath. "Okay," she breathed, getting up, a bit shaky. She put on her glasses and looked at Racquel sprawled there sleeping in his jerkin and hose and lipstick and Heidi braids, memorizing him in case she didn't see him again. In that moment she knew that there was only one thing in the world more important to her than Racquel, and this was it. She sensed in her bones, to the feathery marrow of her hollow bones, that this was it. "Coming," she whispered, and she followed the glimmering pinion.

It led her a long shadowy way between towering trees jeweled with efts, butterflies, finches, fungi, orchids, ribbon snakes, passionflowers; past mossy boulders studded with fiddleheads and toadstools; under the green-gold lacework canopy through a twilight of lost dreams to the oval pool.

Sassy knew where she was going when she saw the sunlight beyond the greenshadow and her feet stumbled. Her glasses fogged as her face heated and chilled as if with fever. No. She couldn't do it. She couldn't brave that place again.

But maybe she wouldn't actually have to look into the pool. Right?

Or maybe it wasn't really the same place—

It was. The feather led her into the shadowy dingle—she could not mistake that fullmoon circle like a green eye looking to the sky, the oval pool the winking pupil at its heart—Sassy had once looked into some animal's eye with an oval pupil of that same fathomless blue; what was it? A cat, a lizard, a horse, a goat? She could not think. It seemed to matter tremendously yet it didn't matter. She walked down the gentle slope and her feet faltered even on the smooth sward. She slowed, but trudged on down the hollow, right to the edge of the still water, to the verge rimmed in slate-green and gray-blue and rose-colored stone; around that verge calla lilies bloomed instead of narcissus. Sassy stopped a few feet short of the edge, blinking like a child in the presence of that mirroring surface.

The guiding pinion shot upward and disappeared into sunlight, dismissing her. Good-bye.

"No," Sassy whispered. She took off her glasses, wiped them on her sweatshirt, put them on again and looked around, anywhere except at the pool. Treetops looming as if they would fall in on her. Tiny blossoms in the grass, white, lavender, powder-blue. Something big and white flying over—her heart jumped. But it was only an egret, neck bestowed in an elegant S-curve, legs trailing like two sticks of spaghetti.

Nothing else.

"Hello?" Sassy whispered.

Only the distant chiming of tree frogs answered.

"Hello? Please? Where are you?" More loudly.

Nothing.

"Oh, come on. Please? Pretty please with peaches and cream? Come talk with me?"

Nope.

"Say something?"

Nope.

Sassy walked the rim of the oval pool, then turned and walked around it the other way, as if that might help. She called again. She looked around some more.

Nothing moving or shaking. Not even, seemingly, the sun in the distant sky.

"Oh, darn—darn—damn it all!"

She knew she had to do it. She knelt beside the pool. Please. *Please let it not be Frederick this time. Please let me be able to handle it*, whatever it was.

She looked.

The surface mirrored back to her only a blue budgie.

Blue. Like the sky. Like her mood most of the time.

"Huh!"

She stood up again and looked around. Nothing.

"Okay, you—"

You what? Okay, Sassy knew what she was, though she couldn't have explained it. But what was her name?

You must name me.

Sassy walked around the oval again, brushing her hand against calla lilies as she walked, tincturing her palm with saffron pollen. She reversed and walked back, brushing them with the other hand.

She looked up and said, "I name you Shadow."

Nothing.

"I name you Sassafras tree," she went on, for a being as important as Shadow could have more than one name. Many names. "I name you Perdita, because you were lost, and I name you Eureka, because I found you. I name you Freebird. I name you Rebel. I name you Deeproot, I name you Wonderwing, I name you Smart—Smart Alec. I name you Wise Child. I name you Sassy. I name you me."

Nothing happened, exactly, but deep in the hollow of the sky Sassy felt something holding its breath. The air seemed to hum. She felt a silent thrumming vibrating the lacunae of her bones.

She strolled around the pool again. Childlike, singsong, she chanted,

> *I name you Shadow,*
> *I name you Tree,*
> *I name you Rebel,*
> *I name you Free,*
> *I name you Birdsing,*
> *I name you Wonderwing,*
> *I name you Sassy—*

What else? Sassafras? Smart alec? Wise child? Nah.

> *I name you Sassy.*
> *I name you me.*

The echoes had not yet faded when, with wingbeats like distant thunder and singing pinions and flying hair and a glad cry and a thump as she landed on her bare feet on the grass, Shadow stood before her.

"Uh!" Racquel yawned, stretched, sat up and looked over at Sassy.

She wasn't there.

He felt a jolt in his gut. Waking up alone, all too much like too many sad songs—but he was being stupid. Probably she was just taking a pee somewhere close by.

He stood up, yawned and stretched some more, and addressed the forest, "Sassy?"

No answer.

Damn. If she'd gone to the corner store for a quart of milk or something, you'd think she could have left a note. In lipstick on a tortoise, maybe.

"Sassy?"

No answer. Just damn birds singing like nothing was the matter.

Now his brain had kicked in he was really starting to get worried, because where could she have gone? She didn't know the way back to the outlaw camp. For that matter, neither did he.

Damn. What would Robin Hood do? Look for clues, probably. No, that was Sherlock Holmes.

Look for—something. Tracks. Yeah, right. But something. Broken branches. A trail of bread crumbs. Stuff like that. Racquel started to circle the shady dell where he and Sassy had snoozed.

Sometime later, he realized that he had succeeded in losing his way back to that place as well.

Even though he had napped, he was still tired. And now he was hot. He was cross. And he was scared. Sweaty scared. He felt sweat trickling down his spine to creep under his rudimentary waistband and into his ass cleavage. He hated sweat. He hated it most of all when it ran down his back into his butt crack.

He stood still and yelled so hard that his eyes squeezed shut, "God damn it all to hell anyway. *Sassy!*" Where the fuck was she?

As the echoes of his shout wavered away he heard a familiar sound he could not place. He opened his eyes.

Sweeeet. Kleet!

Chirping, the parakeet whirred up to him and landed on his shoulder. It was the first time Sassy's pet had showed the least friendliness to him. And gee, that feather-light weight and those little warm feet did feel kind of good. Bird better not poop on him, though.

"Hi, Kleet, honey!" And where Kleet was, could Sassy be far behind? Racquel looked all around, expecting her to pop out from behind a bush or something, but she didn't. "Where is she?"

"Twee," said Kleet disconsolately.

"Has something happened to her?"

"Twee."

"Yeah, Twee. Lead me to her, Kleet! What's that you say, Lassie, Timmy's in the well again? Good fellah. Lead the way, boy!" He shrugged his shoulder to dislodge the parakeet, then yelled, "Wait for me!" and loped after it. Yeah, right, probably it was on its way to a birdie gang bang or something, not to Sassy. But what the hell else could he do?

Sassy stood—a feather could have knocked her down, but luckily none offered to do so. She stood literally breathless looking at her second self. In this mirror world, her reflection. Yet she felt a sense that Shadow stood there more vital and real than she was. The girl's hair glowed like silk fire in the sunshine. Color glowed in her tawny cheeks. Her eyes shone. She stood—

Stood. Sassy caught a breath and gasped, "You have feet!"

"About time," Shadow agreed, her tone more wry than harsh. "Why the devil did you name me Shadow?"

"You don't like it?"

"Not really."

"But it's pretty! I mean, the shadowland under the trees. All kind of muted and gray-green." Subtle colors, the kind Sassy liked. Moreover, a mirror reflection was kind of a shadow, and there was the whole me-and-my-shadow thing, and all the Jung stuff she had read when she was young. Get it? Young. Ha. Probably Shadow wouldn't get it. "Actually," Sassy added humbly, "I feel more like your shadow than vice versa."

"Well, no wonder."

Shadow said this with decision but no visible spleen. Sassy asked, "You're not mad at me anymore?"

"Not right now." Shadow did a funky little shuffling dance with her bare feet to illustrate why. "Sometimes." In a judicious tone she added, "You *have* been trying very hard lately."

They looked at each other.

She is so beautiful, Sassy thought, not even seeing the wings anymore, not even caring about them anymore—Shadow liked feet on the ground better. Just seeing the girl. *She is so beautiful. How could I not have known I was beautiful?*

She blurted to Shadow, "Do you like hats?"

"Yes!" Shadow's whole face lighted up with her Julia-Roberts grin. "We'll get lots of hats. Big floppy flowery ones and little goofy ones."

"Okay. Sounds like a plan to me. You like long hair?"

"Yes."

"Braids?"

"Yes! And barrettes—"

"They have stuff that's better than barrettes now," Sassy informed her. "Scrunchies and plastic gripper things with lots of feet, like big bugs. And butterfly wings. All colors."

"Super!"

"And we can get hair ribbons, and feathers, and scads of lace—"

"Not white lace."

"No," Sassy agreed, "not white." She stood gazing at the young wonder before her. She gazed so long that Shadow actually asked, "What is it?"

Sassy requested, "Teach me to really, really cuss?"

FOURTEEN

The damn parakeet really did seem to be leading him somewhere, Racquel decided. Kleet flew from one tree to the next, perching on low branches and peering at Racquel over his feathered green shoulder as if to say Come on, hurry up. As Racquel ran after him, limping and panting, all too aware that he had never in his life been what you would call athletic. Not that he was fat, but not no jock either. He was not liking this, but he persevered. And every time he puffed up to Kleet, the damn bird would take off with a busy buzz of his pointed wings, fluttering onward.

"Give—me—a—breather, dammit!" Racquel gasped.

Necessity gave him one in the form of a stitch in his side—why the hell they called it that, who knew, but it sure did feel like somebody had just inserted a giant needle between his ribs. Through clenched teeth he whispered, "Shit." He couldn't run another step. For the moment he couldn't even walk, and standing upright was not an option, either. Hunched and gasping, he focused on not moaning more than was necessary. An outlaw had to preserve some semblance of dignity.

After a minute, as his pounding heart and his breathing quieted, he grew aware of two voices conversing at no great distance.

"Okay," said a clear, sweet, girlish voice, "repeat after me: prick, dickhead, asshole, cocksucker."

The second voice obeyed in wispy tones. A mumble.

The girlish voice said, "Louder."

"I can't."

"You can't? How you going to cuss Frederick out like that? Repeat after me: you dickheaded cocksucker—"

"I can't say that!" It was Sassy. Racquel felt sure now. He breathed out.

"Do you want to learn to swear or not?" The other one—and Racquel hoped he had guessed right who it was—sounded more amused than pissed.

"Yes, I do!" Sassy sounded as sincere as a tract pusher about this. "But not like that! You'll have me saying the f-word next!"

"What are you going to do? Grade-school insults? Tell him he thinks he's hot snot on a silver platter but really he's a cold booger on a paper plate?"

"He's *what*?"

"When he was born, his mama looked at his head and his butt and said oh boy, twins?"

"Shadow, you're going too fast!" Sassy wailed. "How am I going to remember all this?"

"You're not supposed to remember! You have to learn to extemporize. Cock, prick—"

"I can't!"

"Okay, okay, for you we'll bend the rules." The girl sounded downright mirthful. "Look, if you need to vent but you don't want to really offend anybody, the thing to do is take a bad word but just combine it with a stinky food. Like this: Onion balls. Baloney dick. Salami ass."

"Onion balls," Sassy repeated obediently. "Baloney dick.

Salami—" She started to giggle. "Salami—" She giggled harder, then burst into a laugh such as Racquel had not yet heard from her, a happy laugh that came from somewhere deep under her belly button. "Salami dick!" she howled.

"Or ass. Whatever." The girl was laughing too.

Still hurting, Racquel managed to turn and look. A breath of light over there beyond the trees. Clearing.

Hoo boy. He bet he knew which one, too.

Uh-huh.

Standing in the shadows of the giant hemlocks looming over the dingle, with Kleet perched silently nearby, Racquel looked down a gentle green slope to the glassy oval pool in its frame of glossy stones and white flowers. Sitting cross-legged in the grass, face-to-face and giggling like long-lost friends, he saw Sassy and her strange angel.

Hmm.

"Banana cock," Sassy suggested.

"Good!" The Sassy girl bounced Tiggerishly on her bony little bottom. Her auburn hair bounced, and her glossy wings.

"Burger butt."

"*Burger* butt?"

They both became incoherent with giggling again.

Racquel looked over at Kleet with some degree of understanding. "Jealous, dahling?" he inquired. He intuited that Kleet might be feeling a bit cut out of Sassy's affections. He assumed that jealousy might be the motivation that had made the parakeet fetch him. Or might he be projecting onto an innocent bird? In a subrational way he was feeling a wee tad jealous himself.

And in a far more rational way he was wondering: what was Sassy going to do now?

How would she get herself together? Would she just stay

here, where all a person had to do to eat was lean over and pick a mushroom?

Would she ever want to go home again?

"Okay, then there are the intensifiers," the Sassy-girl was lecturing again. "You know: damn, goddamn, hell, bloody, freaking, like that. You use them mostly to fill in and put together a nice cuss string."

Racquel realized that he couldn't just stand there under a tree forever. He had to get moving one direction or another.

Stay with Sassy?

Or go away?

Go home?

He didn't know. He stood there.

"Son of a goddamn banana pickle," Sassy said.

"Good!"

In that moment Racquel realized that she didn't need a whole lot of help from him any longer.

He swallowed and reached out a hand toward Kleet. The parakeet stepped tamely onto his finger. With the bird on his hand he walked down the gentle slope toward the oval pool and the two Sassies sitting in the grass.

For just a moment Sassy saw a falconer approaching, perhaps a hero, a tall man in medieval garb striding out of the sunset with his raptor riding on his hand. Then she blinked, and it was Racquel, and her heart started pounding as it had not before.

Racquel walked up to her and Shadow, and Kleet flew from his hand to her shoulder, where he perched without speaking.

Racquel did not speak either. He was not smiling. It was not that he was being moody, Sassy intuited. It was just that he did not know what to say. And he was restraining himself from the sort of babbling he usually did in that case, trying not to put on a clown face.

She told him, "I'm sorry." She stood up to face him more levelly, although Shadow remained seated on the grass. "I'm sorry, I didn't like to leave you like that, but I had to."

Racquel nodded.

"The feather came for me, and—"

"It's okay." It was not, really, she could tell by his voice, but what was he supposed to say? What could either of them say?

He said it first. "What now?"

She did not know. She looked at Shadow.

Shadow returned the look, peering up at her with a pixie grin, but did not speak. Shadow's eyes shone with a fey gleam. Mischief? Fun? Prescience?

Racquel stood silent, waiting.

Sassy turned back to him. "For me, I don't know," she said, her voice wavering a little. "For you—I think we ought to get you home."

"That's not your problem," he said.

"Yes, it is. You could lose your shop."

"I'll worry about that."

"Racquel, it's because of me that you're here. I worry about you too. I love you."

The l-word stopped everything for a moment. The sunset, the slow dancing of clouds in the sky, the tree frogs singing, the winging of birds, earth, air, Racquel's breathing, Sassy's heart, all seemed to stop. He gazed at her.

Sassy's heart jump-started itself and pounded. "I do. I love you." She strode to him and hugged him. Warm, it was so warm and solid and good to press against his chest and shoulder, his arms around her. She felt him swallow hard. Felt him bow his head to lay his face against her hair.

Heard him say, low, "I love you too. More than you know."

True. It was hard for her to understand how he loved her, even though she knew how much he had done for her.

But she understood what she had to do for him.

She nodded against his shoulder, then pulled away to face him, her hands on his shoulders. She looked straight into his eyes, seeing hope and pain there, the hope and pain of a lost child found. "I will always love you," she told him. Then, gentle yet hard, she ordered, "Now you get your salami butt out of here."

"*Salami* butt?"

"Whatever. Racquel, you've got to go home." She released her grip on his shoulders and stepped back.

He took a deep breath, his chest heaving.

"Try the pool," she said.

He nodded.

Sassy sat next to Shadow again and watched, wordless, as Racquel walked to the tip of the oval and knelt there, placed his hands on the smooth blue-green stones and looked into the water.

Nothing happened.

Sassy listened to birds chittering, tree frogs chirring.

Nothing more.

After a moment Racquel called to her over his shoulder, "I'm just seeing me, that's all. I mean me the way I am right now. Braids and lipstick and a dirty jerkin."

"Keep trying." Sassy heard the strain in her own voice.

For the first time in his presence Shadow spoke, her voice clear and mirthful. "Let Sassy try for you."

Racquel stood up, turned around and took a good look at

Shadow. Sassy peered at her as well. Shadow sat there with her lips closed in a smile like a new pink moon, her eyes glinting with fun, not saying a word.

"She's up to something," Racquel said.

No kidding. There were several trenchant things Sassy could have said, mostly to Shadow, but she pressed her lips together. She clenched her teeth. She got up, her back hard; she had been dared, and she knew it. She walked over to stand beside Racquel at the edge of the oval pool.

Without a word she crouched and looked—at the pool, not into it, for it was inscrutable. She scanned its shadowshining face, its thin skin dimpled by Jesus bugs walking. Not knowing what to expect, she took care to expect nothing.

Too late, she realized that her attitude was all too much that of a wife. She gasped. From the water, Frederick peered back at her.

She froze. Time seemed to slow down, glacial, giving her opportunity to experience all over again his plastic smile, his cinnamon hair and freckled watermelon-pink skin, his pallid eyes. There was time to fear all over again his power to make her miserable. His power to make lifeless wood of her as she stood there, petrified.

He smirked and reached for her.

And she couldn't move, and time sped all too fast now, no time to get away, frozen where she stood—

From right inside her head a fierce, almost forgotten voice said, *To hell with this.*

Sassy unfroze.

"No!" she shouted, struggling against Frederick as he grabbed her by the forearm. She tried to brace her feet, but damn, it was too late, the stone edge of the pool sloped all too smooth, she was slipping—

"Hey!" she heard Racquel yell as he leapt to help her. He bent over her and grabbed her around the shoulders to keep her from being pulled in. His tall shadow fell on the water. Frederick looked past Sassy to see who was interfering, and he lost his smirk. He seemed to recognize Racquel, but not pleasantly. His face curled as if he were about to make like a vulture and try projectile vomiting. His mouth gaped. "You!" he belched, froglike, from the water. He let go of Sassy and seized Racquel.

"Aaaaa!" Caught off-balance, Racquel toppled forward and splashed at the edge of the water. Sassy snatched at his jerkin to hold on to him.

"No!" she screamed at Frederick. "Don't! Let him alone! Let go of him, you—"

You what? You coward, you womanizer, you liar who took the best years of my life and left without even a thank-you-ma'am, you—you toad-prince who destroyed my dream—

Frederick's pink-and-orange head protruded snakily from the water as he tried to wrestle Racquel away from her. What the hell he wanted with Racquel, Sassy had no idea, but judging by the glare shirring his pink face, something about Racquel bothered him enough to make him forget all about her. Of course, when hadn't he forgotten about her? Frederick, what a snarf. The way his wet head stuck out of the water almost froze Sassy again. She could see Frederick's once-beloved lumpy ears, his piggy little eyes, his nose hair—he had more of that than he did eyelashes.

You—betrayer—

She felt fire run through her veins. She felt herself blaze into incandescent fury.

"Let go of him, you banana turd!" she screeched. "You goddamn consummate dick-challenged jackass! Traitor! Go ahead,

take everything I've got! You did it before, try it again, you
jellobutt, you donkey breath, you—you pretzel stick! I hope
you get pinkeye all over. I hope you get crabs. I hope you get
foot fungus and jock itch and terminal acne and—and pickle
dicks grow from your ears. Salami face! Onion balls! Stinking
tomato fart, go—"

She wasn't nearly finished telling Frederick all the things she
had never said to him, she had raised her voice to a banshee
howl to be sure he could hear above the splashings and thrash-
ings, what a mess, dripping sopping wet with her feet in the
water at the edge of the pool she hung on to Racquel while
Frederick kept trying to pull him in and Racquel yelped like a
scared puppy and Sassy cussed and blurrily amid too much
slosh Sassy heard somebody laughing, laughing like music, a
clear sheer soprano laugh of delight while Sassy yelled at Frederick, "Go eat boogers! Go stick yourself in a weed whacker!
You cheese prick! Garlic tits! Son of a slime mold! You—" and
she still had more to say but she heard Shadow's laughter right
in her ear, felt Shadow's breath warm on her cheek, felt warm
slender arms go around her from behind, hugging her, oh
heaven, oh help, thank Shadow, Shadow would help pull Racquel away from Frederick—

Wrong. Shadow gave a gentle shove.

Aaaaak!

But after that first shriek, Sassy did not scream. She did not
cry out in fear. Instead, she yowled a yawp of pure joy as they
all toppled into the oval together.

Flat on his back on the carpeted floor and soaking, streaming
wet, Racquel blinked up at plumage swaying over him like the
feathery fronds of lost-forest trees, at marabou and oriental

pheasant and peacock, ostrich, bird of paradise—was that real bird of paradise? It decked barbaric capes and masks, chalky masks displayed bizarrely upside down—no, those were the faces of his employees. And a very startled cop. And that turd-ball Frederick.

Still lying on PLUMAGE's deep-pile moss-soft carpet, Racquel yelped, "Sassy?"

"Right here," she said, her voice a sunny soprano, from somewhere off to his side.

The cop bawled, "Youse two cut that out! Wasting my time, trying to be smart with your fancy tricks. I ought to run youse in!"

Paying no attention, Racquel sat up, his head momentarily spinning. Sitting nearby, Sassy grinned back at him.

"Hey!" he whispered.

Her smile shone in her shadow-green eyes. Funny that he had never noticed the wonderful color of her eyes before; they were to die for. Hard to tell for sure the color of her dripping-wet hair, but Racquel thought he saw a tawny auburn glow to it, and for sure he saw not a trace of gray. Her face looked ten years younger—or maybe it was just the smile, but—no, something more. The light in her golden-green eyes. A glow about her more than just watergleam. She was paying utterly no attention to Frederick. Maybe she hadn't even noticed him.

She said—she said she loves me.

Racquel could not think what to say, so naturally he blurted the stupidest thing he could. "Hey," he babbled. "Hey, Sassy, you're okay. Where's your glasses?"

She raised her brows, lifted one hand from the floor to feel at her face, and smiled even wider. "I must have lost them in the fracas." She scanned him like a sunbeam. "Hey! I don't need them anymore!"

"Have you looked at yourself?" Racquel asked.

But the cop wasn't standing for any further debriefing. "Okay, youse two, on your feet!"

Racquel thought it best to obey the police ossifer. He stood up, feeling a bit unsteady, and very conscious of the way his wet tights clung; should he try to maneuver something in front of him? Sassy looked better than he did all wet.

As she stood, Frederick complained, "Sassy, *what* are you trying to prove? I've been looking all over for you."

Sassy peered around for the noise, then focused on Frederick as if she barely knew him. "What for?"

"You said something very disturbing to me and then you disappeared!"

"So what's the problem?" Tired of him, she turned to the mirror, and her eyes widened. "Whoa!" She gazed at her own reflection.

Whoa, indeed. "No more blue budgie?"

She shook her head, her gaze fixated on the mirror. She seemed to lack breath for the moment to say anything.

The police ossifer seemed to be getting more exercised rather than less. He roared, "I want some answers here!"

Three PLUMAGE employees, Racquel noticed, stood looking at his jerkin and tights and yes, his codpiece, and grinning like jackals. Didn't seem too surprised.

Frederick said imperiously to Sassy, "I am going to take you to a doctor."

"Not until I'm done with her!" the cop snapped at him.

Sassy seemed to hear none of this. She gazed at the mirror. "Shadow," she whispered, her eyes alight like candles. "I got my shadow back."

Racquel felt his eyes misting. She was really something. She really was. "Yeah," he told her softly.

"Wings and all. You can't see them, but they're there. Wings. In me."

"Yeah."

For a moment he felt like he heard the heartbeat rhythm of wings.

He did. He heard a fluttering that was not his own heart, and there was Kleet winging down. Whir of wings, and the cop startled as if somebody had pulled a gun. Goofy little parakeet must have been hiding on top of the belt rack or something.

Kleet landed on Sassy's shoulder. "Sweetie!" Turning away from the mirror, Sassy put up a surprised finger to stroke his breast feathers.

"Twee," the parakeet said sadly.

Frederick barked, "What is that animal doing in here? You know I'm allergic! Get it away from me!"

For the first time Sassy seemed really to see Frederick. Her eyes narrowed. "Oh, stuff yourself with a cucumber," she said.

"*What?*"

"You heard me." Sassy sounded irritated and bored with him, nothing more. "Go away. Get out of my face."

"You need psychiatric help!"

"I did when I married you. Not anymore."

"You—"

The parakeet perched on her finger now. She lifted it to her face and puckered her lips, making kissy noises. Kleet nibbled at the corner of her mouth.

"Ewww!" Frederick flapped his arms and strode out.

That left the cop and the grinning employees to deal with. Racquel looked at the cop. The cop looked at him.

Racquel shrugged, arching his brows in mute inquiry.

The cop's square, flat face flushed, looking more uncomfortable now than irate. He turned and said gruffly to the employees, "Youse people go back to what youse were doing."

They did, grinning. The cop waited until they were out of earshot before he asked, "Where you been?"

"Behind the mirror."

"Thought you were going to say that."

"It's true."

"Her too?" He glanced at Sassy, who was whispering to Kleet.

"Yes. All two of her."

"Don't talk no riddles at me. Give me something I can put in the report, dammit."

Racquel asked, "What's the complaint?"

"None anymore. Youse were missing. Now you're not."

"Tell them we went to Saskatchewan."

"Look," the cop told him, "no more. I don't want no more people jumping at me out of mirrors and I don't ever want to see your he-she face again. You understand?"

Racquel nodded. Understandable sentiment on the ossifer's part. "I think we're done," he said. "Really."

"Youse stay put," the cop growled. "You hear? You better say yes, sir, you hear me."

"Yes, sir. We hear you."

"Good." The cop stomped out.

"Welcome home," called one of the "associates" from across the store.

Home. What a concept.

Racquel went and hugged Sassy, laying his head for a moment on her hair. Despite sogginess, a kind of psychic warmth emanated from her. He felt—he felt very much at home.

"Twee?" asked the parakeet.

Sassy hugged Racquel back, and leaned against him. Probably feeling his warmth. "I think you're right," she told him with only a little sadness tinging her tone. Mostly, she sounded bemused. Whimsical. And happy. "I think we are back for good."

"Twee?" Kleet whimpered.

Sassy told him, "Sweetie, I'm not your tree. You couldn't have made me your tree if I'd been whole to start with."

"Twee?"

"Oh, poor baby." She stroked his green wingfeathers, as green as Eden. "What am I going to do with you?"

 **FIFTEEN**

Wearing lip gloss, lavender eye shadow, and a glossy-feathered periwinkle-and-canary baseball cap, Sassy knocked on Lydia's door. Same old sign, LOOK DOWN, with eyeballs in the OO and a Magic-Marker arrow pointing to the floor. It had been, what, a week since her last visit? Seemed like it had happened in a different life.

Lydia opened the door and said, "Sassy!" Sounding at first glad to see her, and then totally surprised. "Sassy?"

"Hi!" Sassy stepped in, watching the floor so as not to step on a cockatoo or anything. "I brought Kleet to visit." She opened her coat to unswaddle the parakeet riding on her chest.

"That's—that's great." Lydia's broad, homely face appeared dazed. She wore a different T-shirt, this one advertising safe sex, but the same spangles of poop. "You look good."

"I feel fantabulous. A lot has happened."

"I can see that! You've dyed your hair, got contacts, what's next, pierced ears?"

"Probably." Sassy smiled and let Lydia's misconceptions pass. "I've been thinking about it. I'd like wearing pretty ear-bobs. Feathered ones." She felt her smile dimming, though, as Kleet flew across the room. She had hoped being with Lydia's birds would put some life back into him, but he hadn't made a sound.

"That's good." Lydia took Sassy's coat and hat, parked them on the coffee table, then sat down on the sofa to study Sassy some more. "How's your job?"

"Haven't got one right now. I'm looking." Ambling around Lydia's apartment with the other bipeds, Sassy watched Kleet land on the mirror perch with the other parakeets. "I'm living with my friend Racquel," she added.

"Good! It's good you're not living alone no more. Is she nice?"

"Yes. She's a he, and he's very nice." Sassy felt a smile spring warm from her heart to flower on her face.

"She's a he!"

"Yep. He has the most fabulous clothes. Runs a boutique at the hotel." And neither his employees nor the hotel management had said a word about his gender. At least not to his face. They grinned a lot, that was all, and not even nasty grins. Sometimes people do okay.

The denizens of Racquel's apartment building grinned a lot too. "His neighbors think we're a pair of lesbians," Sassy added.

Lydia's soft mouth had stretched wide open in an O. Eventually she got it closed enough to gasp, "Well, are you?"

"Lesbians?" Sassy said just to tease.

"Lovers."

Sassy gave her a Mona Lisa smile. "We're two people who love each other."

"You can do that now?"

"Sure."

A dayspring light shimmered in Lydia's eyes, like dawn on quiet water. "Well, color me stupid," she murmured.

"Huh?"

"I see now. I was thinking it was just changes. But it's a lot more, ain't it? You found what you lost."

"Yes."

"That's way special, Sassy."

It had been a while since Sassy had actually blushed, but she did now, like a preview of the hot flashes she could look forward to in a few years. She felt the warmth rise clear to her eyes, which kind of boiled over. She stood still, facing Lydia, but she could not speak.

In that moment she realized that more than one person loved her.

And she had more than one person to love.

Life could be good.

Scanning her some more, Lydia nodded and said, "You ain't worried about anything now except Kleet."

"Yes!" Surprise helped Sassy recover. How did Lydia know she was worried about Kleet? But then, why not? Lydia knew things. Obviously.

Sassy turned to study Kleet . . . dammit. On the perch with the other parakeets, he sat. That was all. Sat. They gathered around to gabble at him, but he did not reply.

Lydia asked, "How long's he been like this?"

"Since I got back."

"Back?"

Sassy sat on the sofa next to Lydia, shooed a parrot away from her ear, and explained as best she could. If she closed her eyes and listened to the conures and cockatiels and finches whistling and singing all around her, she could almost imagine she was in the forest of lost dreams. She felt bad for Kleet, yes, but also for herself when she remembered that unicorn place; the sorrow in her life right now was that she would never visit there again. That world where lovely lost souls wandered was closed to her now.

How could she feel so happy in this world yet so aching, so yearning?

When Sassy had talked herself out, Lydia said, "That's really something. Let me look at you in the mirror."

"Sure." Sassy bounced up with the energy of a teenager. At the mirror, she offered her hand to Kleet. He stepped onto her finger. She ruffled his feathers with her other hand, and he leaned into the caress, but he did not look at her. His sadness was unmistakable.

"It's too bad, sweetie," Sassy murmured to him, feeling the tug of a similar longing, a similar sorrow.

"You're you," Lydia said from beside her.

"I know." Sassy's reflection showed Sassy just as Lydia's reflection showed Lydia. Of course, Sassy did not see other people as birds anymore, either, not even Racquel as a hornbill. She told Lydia, "I'm kind of betwixt and between. I feel so good just to be alive, you know? But I—sometimes I wish I'd never been there if I can't go back. And I wish I could think what to do for him." She tilted her head toward Kleet.

"He's in love with you," Lydia said.

"He *thinks* he's in love with me. I'm not what he thinks I am."

"He thinks you're still a blue parakeet, huh?"

"Not exactly . . ." But once again Sassy did not bother to correct Lydia's misconception. Sometimes a single inspired mistake is worth barrels of truth. Sassy turned to Lydia with wide eyes but did not dare to say what she was thinking: *that's it!* "Lipstick," she whispered.

" 'Scuse me, honey?"

"You got any more of those lipstick samples?"

"Sure. I got a truckload." Lydia waddled off toward the kitchen.

"Kleet, sweetheart," Sassy murmured to the parakeet, "I hope this works. Oh, I hope this works, poor baby."

Lydia returned with a shoe box of even more dynamic proportions than the previous ones. Red Wing Work Boots, this one said. Sassy deposited Kleet back on the shelf in front of the mirror and opened the box.

"Oh, good," she told Lydia or herself as she fingered ranks of tiny lipstick samples in almost as many colors as the birds of the glory forest. Thank goodness for punk fashion. "Okay. Here we go."

She faced the mirror. Kleet's eye level as he perched on the shelf was about the same as hers as she stood looking past him. Sassy said, "Lookee here, Kleet," and with a flare-red lipstick— Primary Red, the label said—she traced the oval of her own face. Not a perfect oval, more egg-shaped, but she had been through this before; perfection didn't matter. The size of the oval mattered more, and this one was about the right size for Kleet, she hoped. She took a Tropical Sunshine lipstick, basically a slick yellow crayon, and drew some filigree frills around her oval by way of an ornate frame. Fine so far. With the same lipstick, she began to draw a budgie where her face was.

Doing this was easy. For weeks on end she had seen a blue budgie in the mirror instead of her face; she just drew it there. Only she was no longer blue, so her budgie wasn't either. She drew it with a yellow head and a vivid green body, Jungle Green the lipstick said. And a touch of Danube Blue on the wings. And yellow uppers on the legs. And a coral patch around where the eye would be. With its Tropical Sunshine head cocked.

Just like Kleet.

Sweet Kleet. He had shown no interest while Sassy drew the oval frame, but as the parakeet in the mirror began to take shape his head came up and Sassy thought she heard a chirp.

"Do you like her, sweetie?" Sassy hoped it was a her. Most budgies, the genders looked just alike except for the cere color. Sassy did not know for sure what a female Carolina parakeet looked like, but she gave her lipstick parakeet a cute pink cere and hoped for the best. If only this worked . . .

Kleet craned his neck, ruffled his feathers, and cried "Kek!"

"Just let me finish her, honey." Carefully Sassy gave her parakeet a sweet beady-eyed stare, then stepped back.

"Kek! Kek! Kek!" Kleet fluttered his wings, ducked his head, and sidled forward, twittering to the mirror budgie.

Watching him, Sassy felt a huge responsibility squeeze her heart in its fist-of-a-giant grip. "Oh, God," she whispered to Lydia, who stood beside her, "I hope I'm not just teasing him."

"It'll be okay," Lydia whispered back.

Yeah, right, she'd say that. Sassy bit her lip, watching Kleet. All the other budgies had gone quiet at the far end of the perch, looking on as if they knew something important was happening. Even the roomful of parrots and lovebirds and mynahs seemed quieter. Courting the mirror parakeet, Kleet did not yet dare to touch; he turned aside before he reached her and strutted along the shelf, showing her his handsome pointed tail feathers. He turned, fluttered his wings and stood on tiptoe.

Someone knocked at the apartment door.

"I'll get it." Lydia turned and padded away, her weight creaking the floorboards. Sassy swore under her breath. Goddammit, whoever it was had better not bother Kleet—

"Hi. Sassy told me she was bringing Kleet here," said Racquel's voice.

Sassy felt her heart warm even in the fist of fear; Racquel never left the shop in the middle of the day. She took a quick look over her shoulder—couldn't quite believe it was really him. But there he stood, teetering in four-inch turquoise-blue heels, his silver-lamé gown dripping with bugle-beaded turquoise plumage, a stole of midnight-blue-and-turquoise faux emu thrown around his neck and shoulders. With his replacement boobs in place and his makeup on—a few sequins glued just under the eyebrow—and his hair done up in a silver-plated cock-hackle crest, he was stunning.

"Shh!" Finger to her lips, Sassy shushed across the room to him. "I'm over here."

"Kleet's courting himself a missus," Lydia explained.

Racquel tiptoed over as quietly as he could in his heels, explaining in a whisper, "Thought you might leave the little twit here, and I never said good-bye . . ." He stood by Sassy's side. "Bogus!" he breathed when he saw what the "missus" was.

Sassy hoped it wasn't too bogus.

And oh, God, she hoped Carolina parakeets mated for life.

Kleet turned and sashayed back along the shelf like a teenager doing the stroll. He dipped his wings then lifted them. He cocked his head and said, "Kek?" He faced her at a distance of three or four inches.

"Kek?"

Racquel advised under his breath, "Just do it, dude!"

Sassy whimpered, "What if it doesn't *work*?"

Standing lumpen on the other side of Sassy, Lydia said placidly, "It'll be okay."

Sassy gritted her teeth.

"Kek! Kek! Kek!" Kleet bowed, sidled, hesitated, then approached. In the mirror his image superimposed upon the lipstick budgie so that it almost seemed like a living bird—

Sassy gasped.

Kleet kissed his mate gently, ever so gently, with his beak, and she tilted her head to kiss back. Kleet trilled to her and nibbled her cheek. Coyly she retreated. Kleet lifted his wings, gave a glad cry, and flew into the mirror after her.

Sassy breathed out.

Racquel turned and hugged Sassy. She leaned against him for a moment, then flung back her head and yelled, "Yee hah!"

She heard a similar screech from Lydia and a chorus of caws and cackling and squawks and whistles from the other onlookers, the ones with wings. Sassy was laughing, Racquel was laughing; he grabbed her by the hands and danced her around. "You are something else *entirely*!" he yelled. "Grab your hat, girlfriend. We're going shopping."

She hugged him, then turned to grab her hat as instructed, but something, a thought, a breath, green-scented air from another world, halted her. In abeyance, a kind of psychic limbo, she looked to Racquel. "Is it real?" she asked.

"Say what, Sassy?"

"It—I—I don't know. For a minute there—some kind of déjà vu. Something about a rain forest, a parakeet—like I was some kind of a bird or something in another life."

He gave her his tender cerise smile. "Were you? I didn't know you then."

"What were you? In a past life, I mean? A Hollywood goddess?"

"Huh." He blinked, stared at her with a puzzled frown and said slowly, "You're not gonna believe this, but I think—I think I was some kind of black Robin Hood."

Sassy laughed, delighted, letting the distant, teasing dream-memory of an enchanted forest slip away; it didn't matter. She felt as lighthearted as a child. "Racquel, you're full of surprises!"

"That's one way to put it." He stood there in the glory of all his plumage, feather boa and lovingkindness and turquoise-dyed turkey fringe and quail earbobs and friendship and emu fluff and wise brown eyes and cock-hackle froufrou and fidelity like a rock. He looked around. "You want to buy a budgie or something? Hey, Lydia, what's that lipstick on the mirror for?"

Lydia gave them both a slow, ineffable smile before replying. "Not a thing." There was a whole world of secrets in her smile. A universe of hidden dreams. This was a woman who could do things she was not about to reveal. All she said was, "Just playing with the parakeets, that's all."

"You want to buy a pair of lovebirds?" Racquel asked Sassy.

"What for? We don't need them." Sassy scowled, scanning the small room alive with wings and singing, trying to remember something she'd forgotten, something about parakeets, then gave it up and grinned. She knew what she wanted to buy Racquel—a pair of stiletto-heeled marabou mules, if she could find any large enough to fit him. "Let's go."

They closed the door gently, leaving behind them a simple lipstick oval the size of a human face on Lydia's mirror.

Kleet and Kek perched shoulder to warm green shoulder, hidden by sunny treeplume. By the foot of their tree gleamed still-water, its shape a big egg, nest of sky. Whiteplume plants all around. Seeing these things, Kleet and Kek pressed together but did not speak because of humans down below, like walking trees in their browngreen plumage yet not quite like—her, someone or something Kleet could not quite remember, something of Deity, One Tree—the thought wafted like a dream, passed and did not matter. Down below, the humans made sounds he almost felt as if he should understand.

"Whence came that tree?"

" 'Twas not there a fortnight ago, I'd swear it!"

"Any sign of the Moor and his little barbarian?"

"None."

"They've gone back to their own world, methinks."

"Of what kind is that tree?"

"I've never seen the like of it!"

"Not so tall—"

"Its leaves, like hands."

"Like mittens."

"But not all alike. Look. Some with two thumbs—"

"Some with one."

"Some right hands, some left."

" 'Tis a three-handed monster tree."

"Not so monstrous."

"Perhaps 'tis a barbarian tree."

They wandered off, still gabbling.

Kleet shrugged, fluffing his feathers. He turned to his mate, kissing her beak with his. He liked this tree because of water shining below and because it caught the sun and because— because of some call he did not understand. But with Kek by his side it was not important to understand. Softly he chirped to her, *Hometree?*

Hometree, she agreed.